NEW MUSIC FOR OLD RITUALS

New Music for Old Rituals

Tracy Fahey

BLACK
SHUCK
BOOKS

Black Shuck Books
www.blackshuckbooks.co.uk

First published in Great Britain in 2018 by
Black Shuck Books
Kent, UK

Versions of the following stories have previously appeared in print:
Under the Whitethorn (*Faed*, A Murder of Storytellers, 2015)
The Crow War (*Tales from the Lake*, Crystal Lake Publishing, 2016)
The Changeling (*Drag Noir*, Fox Spirit Press, 2014)
Playing In Their Own Time (*Cold Iron*, Cold Iron Press, 2017)
The Green Road (*Into The Woods*, Hic Dragones Press, 2017)
Scarecrow, Scarecrow (*Dystopian Express*, Hydra Publications, 2016)
The World's More Full Of Weeping (originally published as **Come Away**, *The Spooky Isles Book of Horror*, 2018)
The Black Dog (*The Spooky Isles Book of Horror*, 2018)
The Cillini (*Piercing the Vale*, Fox Spirit Press, 2016)
What Lies Beneath (originally published as **All Our Rooms Are Ensuite**, *Women in Horror Annual II*, 2017)

978-1-913038-20-5

The past is always present.

Across the world, folk tales survive. They linger in language, in prayers, and in rituals. Tributes are left, words of protection are uttered and rites are observed. This is true of contemporary Ireland; on the one hand, self-consciously cosmopolitan, on the other hand, observant of superstitions. Without asking ourselves *why*, we skirt fairy forts, avoid causing harm to whitethorns and leave Great Houses and Famine villages alike to fall, unhindered, into ruin.

New Music for Old Rituals is born from folk horror, a style of horror that uses traditional folk mores to induce fear in the audience. The terrain it walks is that of folklore and the Gothic; a blend of legends, rituals and superstitions. These stories are concerned with the constant interplay between modern Ireland, its inhabitants and their folkloric past. They explore how contemporary anxieties – financial uncertainty, fear of contagion, the creation of ghost estates – act to trigger older, darker memories and rituals.

For in this strange country, the past is always present.

Listen. Can't you hear it?

Stay perfectly still.

If you try, really try, you'll catch the faint melody.

New Music for Old Rituals.

I'd like to acknowledge the consistent support and love I've received as a writer from my extended UK horror family. I'm hugely indebted to my editor and publisher, Steve J. Shaw, who worked with me on this project. It found a perfect home with Black Shuck Books.

Thanks also to the editors I've worked with previously who offered me feedback on earlier versions of these stories: Adrean Messmer, Andrew Garvey, Adele Wearing, K.A. Laity, Hannah Kate, Frank Hall, C. Rachel Katz, Eileen Jones and Peter Mortimer. I'd like to acknowledge their time, patience and generosity.

Finally, special thanks to those who made the writing and editing of this so much easier through a combination of beta-reading, advice, coffee, soothing noises, and general balm administered during dark hours of the soul; Darren Maher, Maura McHugh, Priya Sharma, Justin Park, Kate O'Shea, Kathleen Bartlett, De Henderson, Tara Fahey, Brona Nilsson and my wolf, Freya.

UNDER THE
WHITETHORN

e're careful to keep the twins from any whisper of trauma. We try to fill their lives with happy memories. We bring them on trips to the beach, sandy expeditions that leave seashells rotting with the sweet-stink of seaweed in the back of the car. We tell them carefully expurgated stories about brave children with happy endings. We monitor everyone who comes into their lives. We buy them pink dresses and glassy-eyed dolls. We take them to the counsellor, like clockwork, twice a week, where they draw pictures of huge people and tiny houses. We're The Aunts, a benign power, a determined, encompassing force-field that surrounds them with anxious care. Their lives are cellophane-packaged, bright, shiny, and resolutely ordinary. *How do you think they are doing*, we ask each other, constantly, worriedly. We don't talk about Jessica in case they hear us. We swallow down our own, private grief and when we talk about her, we do so late at night, in whispers.

For a while it seems that everything is receding, returning to a bright, artificial version of normalcy. I work from home anyhow, writing for several magazines, so I can be there with them as much as possible. Laura and Kate are quiet and well-behaved in a dry, listless sort of way. Even on the forced expeditions of strained jollity – to the circus, the fair, the zoo – they are polite and disengaged. Kate is sucking her thumb again. She rarely speaks, but she cries at night. We hear her mewing, distressed calls, but when we wake her, she just keeps sobbing. Laura draws endless circles, over and over, on the bits of spare computer paper that we feed her.

The endless winter slowly greys out to reveal a cold, bright spring. We encourage the girls to spend time outside. We try to get them to abandon their toys and books, to play and run around instead, drawing in deep breaths of damp, earthy air. Instead they protest. 'Auntie Jenny, Auntie May. We want to stay in.' So they do. We give in. Laura draws more, larger, circles and starts to colour them in black. Kate lies on her tummy on the hearthrug, reading her books, fairy-tales mostly. In an effort to get them interacting (the therapist says talking is good) we start playing with them. At first we play simple games. We dress the dolls up. We play school. We have a wedding for one of the dolls and a dusty old action man belonging to our brother. We're enjoying ourselves more than we should as we re-enact all those old rituals from our childhood. Jenny leads the games. She is bossier than me, as she was then. And slowly the girls begin to join in. At first they watch us, solemnly. Jenny and I pretend not to notice. We brush the dolls' hair and discuss their outfits with each other in a serious manner. Finally Laura, the bolder one, reaches out to touch the doll with long, black hair and gauzy angel-wings. She fingers the doll's dress tentatively and whispers something.

'What's that, love?'

'I like her hair. She's pretty, like a fairy.' Laura shows the doll to Kate, who finally removes her thumb from her mouth to nod in approval. Kate picks her up and examines her carefully. We don't have to even exchange a look. We start to move quietly away, like soldiers on a minefield, careful not to make a sound. When we get to the door, Jenny risks a look back. She sighs, happily. 'Time for a congratulatory cup of tea. Or something stronger.' I take a quick look. Laura's blonde head is bent over the pile of dolls, exchanging clothes, small fingers unbuttoning and fastening with precision. Kate is still cradling her dark-haired doll, winding its hair around its neck with slow deliberation. No-one is crying. We nod at each other. This is a victory for the Aunts.

We tell them stories. We like to see their eyes go round and excited, transported by dreams of castles and ponies. We reject most fairy-tales as too dark. We excise mentions of tragedy, of death, and especially of dead mothers. They listen keenly to the stories, little voices asking insistent questions afterwards in the darkness of their bedroom – 'What did she do then?', 'Are they all dead now?' and most perplexing of all 'What happened *after* the happy ever after?' And when we run out of stories, our elderly neighbour, Bridget, volunteers to take over. We trust Bridget. She knew our parents. She knew Jessica. She knows us.

'Poor little things.' Bridget, as well as the whole neighbourhood, knows their backstory; there is a whispered underground network for any misfortunes in the locality. The twins love her. She never tires of their ceaseless questions and she tells endless tales that Kate informs me are 'really, really true fairy stories.'

The twins are back at school. We didn't want to send them back too soon, although the therapist advised it. 'The sooner they start to socialise again with their peers the better. Try to normalise their circumstances.' She looks at us over her thick-rimmed glasses. I know we must look doubtful, so she gets more emphatic. 'They have had such a remarkable change in their lives that it's good to reinstate as many helpful patterns as possible, to make them feel more secure.' I shrug. It's worth trying, after all. Laura still wets her bed from time to time. Kate still cries at night, sometimes, in her sleep. I watch them from the doorway, heavy and helpless with love.

When we ask them about school, about homework, friends, teacher, they are non-committal. 'It's OK' says Laura dismissively, then, evidently seeing we are going to persevere with the questions until they are answered, she adds 'It's *all* OK'. We have to be content with that. They gather their dolls and retreat to the garden, their new playground. They like to play best in the laneway. This is perfectly safe, as the top of the lane is secured by high electric gates – something we installed when the journalists started to come around after Jessica. Laura and Kate like to play under the whitethorn tree, which stands apart from the bushes that run in a ragged line up the lane on top of the old stone wall. The whitethorn is bare and spiky, outlined black against the sky. The girls play grave, silent games with the dolls in the tree and in the crevices left by missing rocks in the old stone wall. There are gaps like broken teeth in the stone walls which they use as caves. Sometimes when I come home I am surprised by rows of blank-faced doll heads staring at me from the fissures in the wall, from among the branches of the bushes. 'We're playing that they are fairies,' they tell me solemnly. 'Bridget told us about them.'

Bridget calls in that evening as usual, at bedtime. When I ask her about the inspiration for the girls' games she sucks her fissured cheeks inward. 'I told them about the fairies, alright. But you shouldn't let them play under the whitethorn. You know that it's used by the Little People?' I shake my head. 'Well it is. Sure isn't the *sceach*,' – she pauses to wave a hand at the tree – 'sure, isn't it famous for that. The fairies do use it for gathering under, they make merry under it and they plan their wars there. It's not just me saying it, mind you, any of the old folk will tell you this. And PJ from down the road, well he swears he saw lights under it one night going home.' I nod, pretending to believe her. PJ is a notorious drunk, liable to see anything on his way home from the pub. Bridget senses my disbelief. She frowns, and her thick eyebrows waggle at me like untidy brushes. 'You need to respect the fairies,' she says, obstinately. 'Otherwise you'll anger them.'

I ignore her. The girls seem happier; their faces rosier, rounder. Once I hear them laughing, high and bell-like in the thin spring air. It is too good to be true, too good to last. And it doesn't.

One evening the girls come home. Jenny is still at work. I hear their voices outside and I peer through the steamed-up kitchen window (I am cooking macaroni cheese, which is proving more difficult than anticipated.) I see them, heads bent together, talking quietly and earnestly outside. I return to stirring the macaroni methodically, wiping away the warm sweat of my forehead with the back of my hand. The lack of footsteps alerts me something is wrong. I open the door.

'What's happened?' Kate is openly crying, Laura's face is red and furious.

'Nothing'. It's such a blatant lie I don't even bother to acknowledge it. 'Who made you cry, Kate?' I ask. 'Was it Laura?'

'No way.' Laura is indignant. 'It was her. The mean one.'

I abandon any attempt to coax words out of Kate. She is snuffling wetly into her jumper sleeve. 'Laura, what *happened?*'

Neither of them says anything. Kate's sobs falter into a choked quietness. I look from one to the other. My voice is low, dangerous. 'What *happened?*'

Laura tilts her chin. She pours out her bag on the table. The books topple out, followed by disembodied doll parts, their heads wrenched off, their limbs a flesh-coloured tangle. One doll face has been scribbled on, another – Kate's favourite, the doll with the long dark hair and wings – has a string knotted maliciously tight around its neck. 'They did this!' She is red with rage. Kate looks at me, face blotched and tight with crying.

'And they were saying stuff about Mommy.' Her eyes are glassy with tears. I feel my heart break. A still, cold anger runs through me and I want to punish those children with a savagery that frightens me.

Kate is still crying. 'They hung my doll... hung her from the tree at school.'

'Never mind, darlings.' I try to hush them 'They didn't really hurt her. It wasn't real.'

Kate's face is angry and upset. 'It was' she insists. 'We saw it.' I stop trying to explain, and instead hug her close, hoping my warm body against hers will say all the reassuring things I want to – *I have you, you are safe, I love you.* It's too hard to explain to children. Their belief systems are unshakeable.

Kate cries endlessly that night for the fate of her dolls, even after I've taken them away – 'to the doll's hospital' – I lie. She doesn't listen. Though I love her, sometimes to an upsetting degree, I feel a rash of anger at her incessant sobbing. Jenny has given up trying to sleep and is smoking a cigarette outside. The acrid smoke curls in the open window. Laura starts whimpering too. 'Make Kate stop.' 'Hush, Katie' I say weakly. I am so tired I want to cry with her. I feel her forehead gently. It is fever-hot and almost spongy to touch. She opens her eyes. 'Why did they do that to her?' she asks, eyes wide and reddened. 'Why did they do it?' I can't answer her. Instead I stroke her face, over and over, until she finally quietens and sleeps.

Jenny hovers in the doorway. 'All OK?'

'No,' I say softly. 'But we'll fix it. We always do.'

The summer is coming. I can smell the warm breeze on the air, the greeny-sap smell of growth. The whitethorn tree is budding, hard green buds tipped with white. The girls seem more settled now. There are no more reports of disruptions at school. Jenny and I start to relax. The twins flit around the garden, playing games, playing house, conducting adventures with their dolls. Their favourite place is still under the whitethorn tree. Even Bridget accepts that their playground is centred around it. She gives up her warnings and joins in. I see her worn grey head bowed over the two little blonde ones, as she talks to them quietly. They listen, rapt. They decide to decorate the whitethorn bush 'because the fairies like it when you do'. They demand flowers from the garden.

'There are no flowers in the garden,' says Jenny exasperated. 'They're just weeds.' The girls' faces fall. She relents and smiles. 'You'll have the best the petrol station has to offer, though.' And she goes off to buy them.

I take one small hand in each of mine and walk with them to the whitethorn. Almost overnight it has burst into flower, its branches a lacy white froth.

'Is Bridget still telling you fairy stories?' I ask. They nod.

'She tells us about being good to the fairies,' says Kate solemnly. 'We have to be nice to the tree, always. The nicer we are to it, the more the fairies will like us. And maybe then our wishes will come true.'

'One wish,' corrects Laura. I am intrigued.

'What's that, darling?'

They look at me as if I'm insane. 'No-one's wishes come true if they TELL!' says Laura scornfully.

'In the olden days,' I say, 'people tied rags to the May bush to help their wishes come true.' They are struck by this.

'Can we do that?' asks Kate, shyly.

'Of course!' I lead them inside to ferret through my sewing box and steal away the scraps of fabric there.

'Oh. My. Sweet. Lord.' Jenny is back. I can tell that she has seen the bush. She drops the cheap orange and yellow flowers on the table. 'It looks like a tinker wedding out there!' 'Traveller' I say automatically, frowning slightly at her. She is oblivious. 'It looks hilario— I mean, lovely' she corrects loudly, smiling warmly at the girls. 'How lovely and colourful!'

'It makes our dreams come true,' pipes up Kate, smiling, as she ties another careful bow in a pink ribbon. 'Look, I made another one!'

Jenny looks around the garden, the ribbon-bedecked bush and the dolls in various stages of fairy-undress scattered all over the grass. 'Who would have thought it?' she says softly. 'I just wish Jessica could see them.' I nod, throat tight with emotion. 'Me too.' 'Though, mind you, she would have *hated* this kind of crazy fairy-mania,' adds Jenny, her mouth curving in a bittersweet almost-smile.

Bridget approves of the decorated tree. 'They're good girls, nice girls,' she says, almost to herself, running a gnarled finger over a red bow, tied on crookedly.

I glow. 'They are sweet little things, aren't they? All because they want to make a wish.'

'Aye.' Bridget looks at me sideways. 'I'm keeping an eye on them too,' she says. 'The fairies protect their own. It's never a good idea to get too caught up in wishes. They might grant a wish, alright, but they grant things, and then they want things back. But don't worry. I have an eye on them.' The twins don't give up on their craze for the whitethorn tree. As the month goes by, they redecorate it faithfully, replacing faded flowers, retying ribbons. Bridget even shows the girls how to stew the whitethorn blossom into a kind of herbal tea. 'Great for anxiety,' she says, offering it to Jenny and myself. I take a sip, so as not to be rude. It has a faint, green taste, with a slightly dank undertone. And so it goes on, day after day, till the last night in May.

~

The girls have been restless all morning. They talk among themselves, in low voices, urgently, but won't tell me what it's about. 'Can we go over to Bridget's?' they ask after breakfast. 'I'll ask her,' I tell them. I am wary about inflicting too much juvenile company on Bridget. But Bridget doesn't mind. She just nods and opens the gate to let them in. I see them point at the whitethorn tree but I don't catch what they say, as I close the kitchen door behind me, glad to get back to some uninterrupted writing.

~

That evening, I hear them talking late into the night. Every time I go in to their room to remind them to go to sleep, they quieten and look at me with their big brown eyes, solemn and good, until I leave and the whispering starts again. It is, they tell me, the last day of May, so they have to wish extra hard. 'Honestly' I say to Jenny, 'It's like they're *trying* to drive me mad.' 'Leave them be' says Jenny. She's kicked off her shoes and is curled up on the sofa, reading a book. 'They only do it to get a reaction out of you. The little terrors.' But she says it fondly. I flick the remote control, and we're just becoming enmeshed in a detective drama when we hear the scream.

We both run in to the bedroom. Laura is still screaming, a thin, high screech that pierces our ears. Kate is out of bed, standing with hands flat against the wall behind her, eyes huge, completely silent with terror. 'What IS it?' shouts Jenny. I pick up Laura and cradle her, ignoring the scream that has turned into sustained squealing. 'Ah Laura. It's OK. Come on baby. It's OK.' I say it over and over again, a soothing, ritual murmur. She stops squealing, her body heaving with sobs. 'What is it?' asks Jenny again, in a gentler voice, as she pries Kate's hands from the wall. Laura is too agitated to answer but Kate whispers something in Jenny's ear. I see my sister bend down and listen intently. 'Really? Well it was a dream, you know... Yes, of course it was. She's not real.'

I look up from Laura's bed. 'What's not real?'

Kate looks at me. 'A woman,' she whispers. 'She came in our room. She was horrible. All dead and horrible.' She sits upright.

'I want to go outside now.' Jenny and I look at each other.

'Out to the garden now,' she insists.

'OK.' Jenny pats her on the head. 'For five minutes. Get a bit of fresh air.'

Laura is still hiccupy; I feel her wet snuffles on my arms. She is still crying. 'The fairies brought her back. But I didn't want her back. She smelled bad.'

Jenny switches off the main lamp, after making sure that the bedside light is still on. I gently lower Laura back into her bed and kiss her damp little forehead goodnight.

'Aunty May,' she hisses.

'Yes?'

'Come closer,' she says. I lean over her. 'Closer,' she insists. I bend further till my face is practically touching hers. I can feel her warm breath on my face as she whispers in my ear.

'It wasn't just a woman, Aunty May.'

'Who was it?'

She looks at me steadily. 'I wished for mommy to come back. We both did. And she came back. The fairies brought her back. Her face was all gone but I knew it was her. It was mommy, and she was *horrible*.'

There is no reply I can make. She curls her hand into mine. I just sit there, looking at her blotched little face, weak and helpless under the weight of her terror.

Jenny gets up. 'I'll bring Kate back in.' She leaves. The minutes tick by as I hold Laura's damp hand. I look at the clock and I'm startled to see that ten minutes have passed. Listening keenly I can hear voices in the garden. I carefully untwine my fingers from Laura's and follow the sound.

Outside, I can hear more crying, loud voices. Kate stands between Jenny and – is it? – Bridget. Her body is small and defiant, hands clenched by her side. The whitethorn tree has been hacked in a systematic frenzy. Broken branches lie on the ground, which is spattered with white blossom. The tree bleeds dark, thick sap that glistens in the moonlight. *It looks like blood*, I think automatically, but my mind shies away from the thought.

'Ah now, Kate, what did you do?' I ask. She says nothing, her fierce little face dark and closed. Bridget blesses herself with shaking hands. 'The bush...to harm it...to cut down the bush. It will bring great misfortune on us all.' She is crying openly now, tears running down her lined face. I put an arm around her. 'The fae will have their way,' she says, almost to herself, as she wraps her cardigan tightly around her bony body.

—

In the morning I am making breakfast when I hear a crash outside. Jenny's face appears at the window, pale and terrified. My heart jolts. 'The girls?' I feel the panic rise in my voice.

'Yes. They're alright. But it's bad. Really...' Her face is working like she's trying not to be sick. It is a beautiful early summer morning. The sky is already dazzlingly blue, the lapping breeze smells of flowers and warm grass. I round the corner of the house and gasp.

'Is...?' I can't say it. I try again, my voice deep and strange in my mouth. 'Is it one of...'

'No.' Jenny's voice is thick, as if she's still trying not to be sick.

And now I see the hair, the tell-tale hair, is grey, not blonde. My treacherous stomach rolls in relief, my breath sucks in in a shuddering gasp. It's not one of the twins. My mind repeats it over and over, a charm against the horrid reality. It's not one of the twins, but it is Bridget. Her body hangs limp and solid, hair falling over her face, neck bound tightly in an ugly, dirty twist of baling twine. Red, ragged ribbons from the bush loop and wave slowly as we stand and stare, silent with shock.

We hear a piercing scream. I don't even remember turning, but what I will never forget are the girls' faces, mouths splayed open in terror, the horror in their eyes, that dreadful, piercing scream. Kate clings to Laura, burying her head in her red pyjama jacket, while Laura screams on and on, a shrieking train whistle as she stares before her. Jenny's arms go out to the twins, she grabs them and holds their faces firm against her body. She looks at me. Her face is bone-white in the bright sunlight.

'A tragic accident,' she says resolutely. 'It was a tragic accident. Poor Bridget wandered into the garden and fell. She caught herself on the tree.' We look at each other, steady and strong. I feel our bond, our care, our love for the twins like a solid form between us. We know what lies before us: the endless meetings, the fuss, the journalists, the therapists, a series of endless policemen in infinite cells. We have done it before. We can do it again.

'We're the Aunts' I say to the twins. 'We're here to protect you. We'll take care of this'.

And we do.

This is a story of the Irish fairies, the Good Folk, the Other Crowd, na Sidhe. Na Sidhe are not your average Shakespearean or Victorian conceptions of tiny, artless creatures that grant wishes. In Irish folklore they are reputed to be the original settlers of Ireland, the Tuatha de Danann. Na Sidhe exist as oddities within the global fairy pantheon; they are pale, almost full-sized creatures who can pass as human. They are to be crossed at your peril; many legends tell of the dangers of situating a home on a fairy path or warn of the repercussions of accidentally straying into a fairy funeral. Na Sidhe are warriors, dangerous and cunning folk who may grant wishes, but there is nearly always a terrible price to pay. They are associated with the sceach, the lone whitethorn, which is thought to be a tree of great folkloric power. Whitethorns are thought to act as meeting points for the fairies, and harming or interfering with them in any way is believed to bring bad luck.

THE CROW WAR

ave you ever driven through Ireland on the back roads? I don't mean on the antiseptic motorways that cut an indifferent grey swathe through fields, rivers and forests alike, but the strange little B-roads, the C-roads and the unmarked, pitted, little *boreens* with their stone walls and cratered surfaces. If you do – if you make this long, bumpy and sometimes perplexing drive in the summertime, you will see the truth of the small towns laid bare. Ireland has always been a land of a hundred kingdoms, in spirit, if not in geography. Each parish or village or town has its own behaviours, dialects, traditions, and of course, its festivals. In the summertime you can't miss the festivals.

As you drive down these roads, lurching slightly through the potholes and stopping for the odd sheep, there are many reasons to stop off in the little towns that dot your route. You might pause to fill up with petrol or to buy limp, pre-packaged sandwiches, sweating under their plastic containers, or simply to check the success of your navigation of the last few unmarked crossroads. And when you do, you'll see the tell-tale signs – a dirty string of bunting over the main street, the trailer of a lorry abandoned in a public square, a forlorn tootle of music played across a crackly PA system, an excess of children running around, high and angry on sugar. Look a little closer and you'll always find a banner. Some will be intelligible and self-explanatory – 'Annual Summer Charity Fete', 'The Horse Fair', 'Vintage Steam Threshing'. Others will be infinitely more arcane – 'The Long Ropes Weekend', 'The Black Cave Festival' or 'The Glass Boy Championship'. They've been going for years, since anyone remembers, although in some villages the natives would be hard pressed to remember their origin. But when the summer is on the cusp of shifting and becoming something darker, when the nights begin to encroach on the day, you'll find the strangest festival of them all on a little boreen in County Clare. You'll follow a tiny road with savagely buckled tarmac, a bright, mossy stripe of grass sprouting up the middle. It's the road to Bive, and what lies down it is odd beyond imagining...

What do I know about it, you might ask? Ah, I know all the celebratory rites in the little towns. I've travelled criss-cross across Ireland for years as a salesman, with my bright smile, my bulky suitcase and my battered car. I'm the last of a dying breed, as I visit and talk and sell my way around the country. I know all the dips and turns of the roads. I know the local stories that are only whispered around family fireplaces. I can smell where I am by what's cooking, the packet and tripe of Limerick, the coddle of Dublin. I can tell the seasons as they turn by the festivals that straggle over the midlands.

So.

Bive.

Bive's festival. I want to tell you about that one.

Well, I could tell you all about it, but it would be a lot more fun to show you. So let's leave the motorway on this sleeping Sunday. The sun is climbing high and weak in the sky, and the late summer chill has started to melt into a bright but windy day. Come down the road now. Feel yourself relax, free from the competitive snarl of the motorway, that eye-aching glare from the never-ending ribbon of pale grey. Drive slowly. Look around. And as you drive, you start to notice things again. On either side are fields of corn, their surface a smooth surge of yellow in the breeze; other fields are dark green velvet with grass, cows lying flat in the deep, luscious shadow of the hedgerows. Then the light dims, turns a cool and grassy green as trees start to meet above you, above the road. Their branches sway together, a glossy yellow-green dappling the road underneath. This is the plantation that grows thick and fertile around Bive. You turn a corner and there it is – a dusty sign that says: 'Welcome to Bive', with a little symbol of a black bird in the corner.

It's not a big town, but it's got a lovely market square with a diamond, a central monument like a Gothic church spire, and a comfortable cluster of colourful houses and shops on the main street. All around the town huddle the big coniferous trees of the plantation, their branches now waving slightly in the breeze. It's a real, old-fashioned country town. I like to read the names over the shop doors – there's 'O'Malley Butchers', with a glassy-looking plaster pig's head in the window, beside it is 'Flynn's Cobblers (and Key Cutters)' with its smell of hot metal, and 'Reilly's Grocery Store'— no...wait, it's gone. In its place there's an antiseptic mini-version of a bland, white-lit supermarket chain-store. I pause and sigh. This happens more and more every year, another little family business gets eaten up, the shop owners die and their children put out their hands for money.

Sure, the last time I was in Kilkenny, I didn't recognise the place. The familiar, family shops were gone and in their stead a range of expensively-plain restaurants, all lower-case fonts and no visible menus.

I'm rambling.

The point I'm making is that although the rate of corporate invasion is a lot slower in the country towns, it still happens, steady and relentless as the tide coming in. Even in Bive.

But let's not get melancholy over the inevitable. We're here for the festival, after all.

And what a festival it is! As you drive towards the main square, you see figures start to move around it, and the set-up for the festival begin to blossom among the trestle tables and the parked cars, their cluttered boots spilling out a muddle of boxes and tablecloths. Bunting is being strung up by two large men on twin stepladders. There's a PA system being set up in the corner, with an unhappy-looking teenage boy whispering 'one-two' softly into the microphone, face flaring with self-consciousness. That staple of the festival, the tea-marquee, is rising majestically into the air, as figures strain against the ropes. So far, so normal.

But I promised I'd show you something odd, didn't I? The surprise is that everything is black. The marquee, the bunting, the tablecloths. Even the people's clothes. Draw closer. There's a reason for it. Look at the details – the shape of the napkins, the pennant that flaps from the top of the marquee. Everything has the crow emblazoned on it. This is Bive's annual 'Battle of the Crows' festival.

Bive means 'crow', in Irish – it's spelled '*Badhbh*'.

Back in the olden days, Badhbh was a fearsome war goddess who most commonly appeared as a large black crow. You might know her better as the Morrigan from the *Táin* saga, and that famous illustration by Louis Le Brocquy – the giant, brooding, hunched figure of the crow goddess. Sometimes Badhbh would appear before a battle, wailing like a banshee, as a premonition of death. Once the battle started, she would circle around, causing confusion, swaying soldiers to her side. But round here she's Bive, the Anglicised version, the crow, the emblem of the town.

Even as I'm explaining this to you, a small child runs round the square with the buzzing energy of an escapee. He is wearing a crude crow mask behind which his eyes swivel, fast and excited, as he watches the Hallowe'en pageantry of the square unfold around him.

"Hello stranger!" I turn and smile. It's Joe O'Malley, the butcher, instantly recognisable by the purple birthmark that streaks a jagged path down the left side of his face. We shake hands. He is still strong and stout, but his body seems somehow lighter, more depleted. 'Good man, good man,' he says, still pumping my hand up and down. 'Great to see you. Your usual spot is free over there.' He drops my hand to point over beside the tea-tent. I smile over at the ladies carrying jugs and kettles. They're the ones you want to make sure remember you when it gets warmer and thirstier in the afternoon.

Ramble round now, take it all in.

The doors to the chapel have opened, and the crowd come spilling out in a raggedy line from the doors to the square, their voices gradually gaining volume as they leave their subdued church-tones behind. The band, who have assembled behind us, strike up a downhearted folk air. An instantly-remembered call rings out behind me, the fair-cry of the vendor on the refreshment stand – "Apples, pears, lemonade and chawk-late."

She slurs the words together as she calls again, automatically dragging out the last word in a plaintive two-tone descant. "Apples, pears, lemonade and chawk-late".

She used to walk around with a kind of wheelbarrow stall, I remember. Now she sits heavily at a table, her body thickened and her face more sunken, almost indefinably older. I've set up my own stall, selling crow masks and black plastic rods with feathers to the children. These were put together by a group of women in Cork who make batches of them for me every August.

Here, look at this one. Prime quality, that. Look at those feathers – *real* ones, you know, they gather them up and sew them on to the masks.

At this point I put one on and chime in my call perfectly between the pauses of the old lady's refrain. "Crow masks here!" I shout. I waggle my head so that the feathers glint in the sun. 'Get your crow masks here!'

It's now late afternoon. Everyone has turned out for the festival. The square looks like a strange and gigantic funeral has camped down on it. The black pennants wave overheard. I am chatting, selling, happy. My trestle table is nearly empty, and I am satisfied to notice a black, sticky ring round the mouths of everyone under ten – my liquorice stock has sold well. There is a candy-floss machine that whips sugar and black food colouring to create an endless stream of edible storm clouds. A solid ring surrounds the trailer in the square, where the local, black-clad band of musicians keeps churning out relentlessly mournful folk ballads. I recognise the elderly man who plays the melodeon. He sees me too; his salutation is an upward jerk of the head and a wink. I nod back. If events follow their usual pattern, I'll be seeing him later. My right hand slips down to touch that other bag by my feet. There is a thin, high, squeal. I look up, distracted. The children have started to run in a complicated circling motion around the square. They scream and squawk their way through the crowd, frantic for sweets, for fun, for games. And there's no shortage of games. The most popular one is a version of Hallowe'en apple-bobbing, where the children with their crow beaks try to peck liquorice sweets out of a hillock of fairy-dust. The air is punctured with their squeals of victory. I smile and watch them flock around, happy and excited.

Of course in the old days everyone would be playing – small children, large children, teenagers, even some adults. I am saddened to see some of the older children sitting on the grass verge of the square, faces twisted into deliberately bored scowls. They are flipping through small electronic devices. Their thumbs move rhythmically – tap-tap, slide, tap-tap. They sit side by side and never interact. Occasionally one of the tiny children will run out of the crowd to brandish a prize or a sweet at an older sibling, but the only response they get is an irritated twitch as earphones are removed, a sneer, and a quick, plunging motion as the earphones are replaced. The sun is starting to sink in the sky, basking in the reflected glow of the late afternoon warmth. The air itself is heavy and golden. It glitters palpably on the corn fields behind and infuses the scene with a rich, pastoral glow. I draw in a breath of warm bodies, sweet candyfloss and flattened grass and wait, contented and expectant for the Battle of the Crows.

And yes, here it comes. The six o'clock bell chimes, low and deep behind me. In the air is the faintest stir and crackle of noise, like a saucepan being scraped. The big golden sun is resting almost on the skyline now, streaking the fields with streams of yellow light. Now there is a rustling, a staccato burst of rough noise. In the square the children divide in two and line up on either side, pulled into place by adult hands. Joe O'Malley stands in the centre keeping the lines apart, his birthmark glowing purple in the sun. The children's oversized crow masks and their small bodies with sticking-out tummies make them look like giant, confused birds. Heads bend over them, whispering caution. The bell strikes again, and again. On the third toll we start to see them; first a few, then more and more until a mass of dark shapes start to cloud the air, trailing black lines of birds strung out across the sky from the horizon. The children run to each other across the green, tapping one another on the head with the plastic, feathered rods.

Fourth toll.

Their shrill screams are drowned out by the flickering blanket of crows overhead blocking out the sunlight with their beating wings, filling the air with their relentless, discordant cawing. In the shadow, I give a sudden quick shiver, a goose walking over my grave. The crows are flying home to the plantation, to roost and caw and circle over it. They are right overhead now.

Fifth toll.

The sky is thick and dark with movement. We stand, together but separate, on the green, heads tipped back, eyes and ears full of the spectacle.

The sixth bell tolls.

As the bell-stroke dies in the shattered air, some old people cross themselves, the rest simply roar. Everyone on the green shouts out together, a wordless yell at the sky. I shout too, feeling the noise fill me, something primal, deep, thrilling. The sound is almost unbearable as it fills the world, the dying tones of the bell, and the sound of open throats calling together, the dense cawing of the crows.

And then, abruptly, it is over.

The crows have passed overhead, settling like a whirling cloud on the silhouetted trees on the skyline. The children, already bored, are pulling off their masks. Two of them continue to fight, trying and failing to land blows with the light, bendable rods. Parents start to tug them towards the nearby cars, calling to the bored teenagers. The Battle of the Crows has been fought again; a timeless ritual, its origins unclear, but still enacted year after year.

"Another one down," says the old woman behind me. She sniffs and rubs her hands together.

"Aye," I agree, repacking the few remaining masks for a Hallowe'en market. Smooth, fold, wrap and stack. I am clearing the last few from the table when I hear a long, low whistle. I look up. It is the old man from the stage, his melodeon now in its case, resting on his knee. He nods at me, and jerks his head towards the hills behind. I hesitate and then nod abruptly. I'm going, of course. I always do.

My bags are packed up in the car. The sunset is a tie-dyed burst of yellows and oranges at the bottom of the sky, and the dusk is falling, I accept a Styrofoam cup of tea gratefully and sip its scalding contents. It's grown colder now. I close my eyes and sense the tingling warmth of the tea sending hot fingers into my stomach. I sit on the bonnet with the old lady from the stall. A group of young boys – possibly her grandchildren – are packing up her wares. She offers me a bar of chocolate. The taste is rich and milky on my tongue, almost too rich for someone who hasn't eaten all day. I swallow hard to quell a sudden surge of saliva, a feeling of nausea or anticipation. The sun, exhausted, is sinking fast now, into pillows of dark cloud. It's time to go. I push myself off the bonnet and pick up the last bag of merchandise.

The old lady grunts. "Are you off then, so?" Her eyes are shrewd in their pocketed wrinkles.

"Aye." I am non-committal.

"Good luck to you then," she says quietly.

I feel her gaze on me as I walk out of the market square.

Time to go. It's also time for me to leave you now. You've seen the festival, eaten the black sweets, watched the children play-fight. It's been lovely. But the sun is down, and it's time for all visitors to leave Bive. Wait! Don't protest. I'm a visitor too, I know, but I've something they need now. I get to stay. There's no need to be angry with me. I don't make the rules. I wish you a safe journey home, back onto the motorway and beyond.

—

My feet find the remembered path. The crunch of pebbles beneath me is crisp and reassuring. Between steps I strain to listen, but I can't hear any other movements. They're probably all there ahead of me. It's dark now, that pressing dark you only get when you're walking among trees, when darkness brushes against you from a black void. I keep one hand up beside my face. The wispy, damp strokes of the leaves feel clammy, like wet feathers on my skin.

It can't be much further ahead I think, and then almost instantly, I see the yellow light of windows ahead. I step into the clearing. The huge shape of the barn looms overhead, its roof blurred and deformed by the huddle of crows roosting on top, drawn by the warmth within. I step inside, and instantly there is a low crackle of conversation, interlaced with the melancholy sound of the melodeon. I look around. There aren't many people there – about fifteen, all drinking beer or homemade cider, the air heavy with the scent of it. Their faces are animated by the flickering glow from the old hearth in the corner. One corner has a curtain over it, its heavy folds absorbing the light within the dense fabric. I see faces I recognise – O'Malley the butcher, the man with the melodeon, and even the old lady I shared a cup of tea with an hour ago, a lifetime ago.

She moves towards me. "Do you have them?"

"I do." I hand over the bag.

She opens it and smiles. "Lovely work, as usual."

I turn to the old man with the melodeon. "Grand evening," I say.

He nods. "Good to have you here." He runs a twisted arthritic finger over the shining surface of his instrument, and then looks up. "We need to get cracking now. Do you have them?"

I jerk my thumb over to where the vendor is carefully unpacking my bag. She slowly draws out two crow masks, and gives a sharp, admiring intake of breath. If the children's masks were well-made, these are splendid, beautiful objects. One woman in Cork has spent months on these; they're made completely from crow feathers, stitched with gold thread, with jet beads of decoration encircling the eye holes. Someone stamps the ground loudly with a heavy boot, one, two, three. Immediately the old man with the melodeon begins to saw out a searing, plaintive air, a song of longing and complaint. Heads nod in rhythm. A man stands up – he's the farmer who owns the land, as far as I remember. Everyone stops speaking. The music softens, quietens.

He opens his mouth and shouts: *"Bive! Bive! Bive!"*

The small crowd echoes him. There were other words, before, but no-one remembers them now.

The curtain parts and there are two men, both stocky, both middle-aged, both wearing the special crow masks. A cracked bell rings, a sharp *ting-ting* of sound.

The figures turn to each other and start to fight. One launches himself at the other; there's a solid thud of body hitting body. Both fall to the dirty floor. A roar goes up, a mass of shrill and deep voices, shouting. Some are chanting. Others are shouting encouragement, or just plain shouting, thick, wordless yells. The air is heavy with the spoiled-fruit smell of cheap drink. The masked figures sweat and grapple on the floor.

I stand with the others, watching the fight, but what is happening is like a film projected onto a more compelling image. Instead of the small crowd, the thin shouts, I can see clear as light the earlier years, those wonderful, terrifying years of mass fighting. Then, the barn seethed with young men, stripped to the waist, their crow heads dangerous and sharp as they struggled. I remember the dark patches of blood on the floor and the screams of the women. I am seized by nostalgia so powerful it brings tears that blur my vision at the edges.

It's an ugly, low fight. They pull at each other, and claw at each other's bodies. Blood is already running down their chests from scratches and slashes. They stumble to their feet, collide, fall again. Their wrestling is weaker now. I can hear their exhausted pants as breath tears from their throats. They grab each other, locked together as their razor sharp beaks slash wickedly at each other's arms and heads. One mask starts to slip, and the opponent sees his chance. His beak rips a cruel red V in the hollow of the other man's neck, and red blood pulses and spurts from it like a hose. The injured man flops to the ground, no sound, just a thick throaty gurgle of blood as he twists below me, head coming to rest beside my feet. Underneath the glossy black feathers with their sleek oil-gleam is a shock of grey hair, a sightless red eye turned upwards and a livid purple birthmark that drips down, from eye to mouth. A thin cry goes up from the crowd, a small shout of victory that dies almost as soon as it begins.

The door is opened with a squeal of rusted hinges, and the crows fly in, thick, fast and hard. They flock around the limp figure on the floor, and their sleek heads dissolve into a blur of pecking and pulling. The faces of the others are blank as they stand, enthralled. I wind my coat around me and walk outside.

I stand outside on the edge of darkness, and stare at the flicking lights of the town at the bottom of the hill. Down there, people are talking, going to the pub, watching television; it is another place, another time, centuries away.

I am still holding a soft mass of feathers in my hand. I think of the lined face of the old vendor, the arthritic hands on the melodeon, the lurid purple birthmark under the crow mask.

In another year this will all be gone.

I shrug and release the feathers into the cold breeze. They spiral and flicker in the wind, dipping and swirling, a dark benediction raining down on the town below. In a few hours the sun will be up and it will be time to go.

I breathe in deeply, and inhale the cold fetid air that smells like autumn, like all our autumns coming, dark and inevitable as time itself.

The crow in prevalent in Irish mythology. There are three war goddesses who manifest as crows in Irish legend, the Badhbh, Macha and the Morrígan. They are associated with battles, and with the pre-shadowing of death. The story is also influenced by two pivotal childhood memories. As a child, I lived beside a large plantation, and every evening, the skies would turn black as thousands of crows would fly home, cawing loudly, to roost in the nearby trees.

It was also influenced by my experience of being driven across the Irish countryside, from east to west, for our annual holidays. Before the existence of motorways, navigation on this journey was tricky, taking the car through a series of towns and villages, big and small. And on this journey we'd encounter many different, tiny festivals, each one born out of old traditions and ancient custom.

And so I began to wonder, what if one of those festivals centred around crows? And so this story was born.

BURIED

e've always lived here, on the bog. It can be beautiful on a sunny day. Like today, as I'm watching the shimmer of pale willow leaves in the breeze. A fragile, chalk-white butterfly flutters in the air. I can see the puffs of heather blooming, the bulrushes lined up smartly with their beefeater hats, the sun glinting on the pools of water between the tussocks. It's so quiet now, just the *wish-wish-wish* of the rushes rustling and the low, constant hum of tiny insects living, flying and dying among the long grasses over the wet ground.

It's not a working bog, just a few useless, pretty acres that are just...there. There's a little turf, only a small part of its acreage suitable for cutting. It's just a bog. It's been there for millennia. In comparison, we're blow-ins; we've only been here for the last two hundred and fifty years. Our house stands on its own in the landscape, white and defiant in the green lumpy expanse of marsh. There's no one else around and that's the way we like it. Nice and peaceful, my father says.

—

Once evening I found a lump of bone when poking round aimlessly with a stick. It was too small to be a cow, too large to be a fox. I turned it round in my hand; a lumpy, discoloured fragment, a nodule on one side, and a circular groove on the other.

'What is it?' I asked my father. He turned it round in a large, dirty hand.

'Ah, a goat, I'd say. Medium sized bone.' My father was a man of few words.

'How did it turn up here?'

'Lots of poor beasts end up in the bog,' he said. 'That's bad old ground out there, it'll suck you down before you can bless yourself.' We stood quietly for a moment, looking out over the trees, moving in the wind. He slipped the bone in his pocket.

'Come on, now,' he said, jerking his head towards the house.

—

We're not big talkers in the family. We say what needs to be said and not a lot more. My mother's father, my grandad, was a talker. He used to tell me stories, ignoring my granny's sulky silence and her lined face, puckered sour as a crab apple. Mind you, he wasn't from around here. The rest of us are quiet. We leave school when we can and work on the farm. It's hard labour, with the cows and the milking, but it keeps us busy. At night we watch TV – soaps and news and late night chat shows. I like the detective dramas best, but I'm the youngest so I don't get much of a say-so. We live too far from the town to be on the water scheme, so we have our own well and sewage system. No bin service either, so what the animals don't eat, we burn at the corner of the lane. Not legal, I know, but it's what we've always done. It's a hardworking life, but a good one. That's what we agree on.

And it's beautiful here, in the early spring and summer.

It's just that sometimes, only sometimes, when the moon is out and the birds are crying out over the bog, long and lonesome, I feel an odd sort of yearning. And the next day, the yard looks sadder and muddier, with the black plastic of the silage bales weeping puddles of rain. On those days the dirtiness and endlessness of the work pulls me down. It gives me a queer ache in my chest that makes it hard to catch a proper breath.

And then, just like that, it fades, and I'm back to normal again.

Coming in to winter it's different here. Then the winds pull and tug the trees like washing on the line. The rain falls on the roof, heavy as stones. And the bog creeps. In the wet, dark months of January and February, that dreary time when the clock ticks slower through the long nights, there's the underlying, slithering feel of water that's slowly, ever so slowly, creeping up towards the house. The ground underfoot is wet and treacherous, the little pools of brown water bleeding together into one amorphous marsh. The dampness sinks into our bones; we come home from the fields and sit, rubbing numbed feet briskly by the fire. Our wellingtons turn cold in the swampy water, the chill held deep in the rubber, penetrating layers of socks.

I like the bog though. Unlike my brothers, who ignore it as a piece of useless farmland, a wet nuisance, I spend a lot of my free time there. In summer especially, when the days are long and there's plenty of light in the evenings, I like to explore it, winding my careful way from tussock to humpy tussock. When I was younger I used to draw maps of the bog in my notebook, careful, badly-drawn zig zag paths, with all the trees and clumps of rushes marked in, as well as the 'islands' as I called them, those isolated hillocks in the swamp water further out, further than I was supposed to go. My mother used to worry about us out there when we were children. I'll never forget one day when I lost track of time, reading a book, curled up on hard marsh grass dried brittle in the sun.

From a distance I could hear her calling, but by the time I got back she was all fired up, face red and angry. She hit me on the legs, over and over until they were blotched red and painful to touch.

'You had me so worried!' She was almost crying, her breath heaving.

I was bawling by then, big, broken sobs. I knew she was just frightened but I was too, scared of her red rage and the violence. Later I wrote 'I HATE HER' in my notebook, still raw from the slaps and the injustice of it.

It's one of my most vivid memories of her, and I'm sorry about that.

It's been a few years now since she left, and the house has never been the same. The flower garden she tended has died off, overpowered by thick, crawling weeds. It's coarse and manly, full of old boots and coats that smell like wet dog and fields. No matter what we do, the house always looks a bit grimy, the windows cobwebbed, the skirting-boards mouse-grey with furred dust, the press shelves ringed with stains under the pots. Sometimes I try. Once I spent ages polishing up the kitchen. I even broke off branches of white heather from the bog and put them in a jam-jar. The rich, heady scent of the heather filled the room like an exotic perfume, and for a second I almost believed she was back. But then everyone came back in and the floor was tracked with mud, the smell of wet tweed overpowering everything. My father threw out the white heather. He said it was because it shed, but I know he thought it was somehow unmanly to care about flowers.

The only time I don't like exploring the bog is in late autumn. Then the nights get longer, the waters rise, and the light fails so quickly you can be left out there as it greys out, the ground dissolving underfoot, and the firm green earth of the field suddenly a long way away. At this time of year you get the marsh gas rising. The wetlands, baked in the summer sun and cooled in the autumn winds, start to ferment. Sometimes during the day you can see bubbles rising, brown and slow, to pop audibly on the surface. *Bog farts* we used to call them as kids because they smelled dankly of rot and buried things. And then there's the marsh lights. You can see them at night, if you know where to look – out deep in the bog, beyond the willow trees. Like little fairy lights, they flare up, only to flicker and sputter out into the still dark. My grandad used to tell me they were Willy-the-Wisps, and that they'd lead you astray at night if you went wandering. The old boys down in the village say the same. Sometimes I'll sit out on the roof on clear nights and watch them. It's a fine, lonesome feeling on a dark night to see them spark off and drift into darkness.

It was a night like that, in dark October, that it happened. The night they found it.

—

It's dark when I wake, and for one confused moment I'm not sure what time it is – I think it's morning, but there's no light outside. And then suddenly there is; the long, unsteady light of a torch. I lie in bed, confused. There's a flurry of heavy boots under my window, and huddled shadows flit by the curtains. If I strain my ears I can hear low voices, hushed against the night. The luminous dial of my clock shows three a.m. I pull the old floral curtains to one side and then I see it. Out in the bog, I can see lights darting round. For a second I think it's the marsh lights, then I blink strongly and realise it's just more torches, dipping and wavering out in the bog.

This is too strange. I need to go and look.

I'm outside, jumper pulled on over my old pyjamas, feet shoved into shoes, no time to find wellingtons. Only the chill in the night air convinces me this is not a dream. I follow the sound of voices, hands extended in front of me to grope my way. Now is not the time to end up in a boghole. The ground sucks loudly at my shoes, making me stumble, but my knowledge of the bog carries me, sure-footed, over tussock after tussock, through the willows and beyond. Now that I'm nearer I can see they're grouped in a circle. My father and my brothers stand, silhouetted against the yellow light of their torches. There's a spade and a tarpaulin at their feet.

With one last suck and stumble, I'm with them.

'What's going on?'

My father clears his throat. 'Dan came across this,' he says. 'Burying the calf that died.' That's the sad little mound under the tarpaulin. He plays the light of the torch down into a rough pit dug in the dark brown earth. At the bottom of it I can see something big, curled up in a lopsided S-curve. I step closer, mesmerised. It is tea-brown leather like my shoes, but you can see the bones and sinews, and even the hair, thick and perfect, springing coarse and orangey-brown from the shrunken head.

'I know what it is,' I say. 'It's a bog body.'

I've seen bog bodies before, up in Dublin, in the museum. Before I left school we went on a trip. A long trip to the city with a busful of kids, fizzing over with sweets, fighting and shouting all the way. We did the educational stuff first, that was the deal, before we could go to the amusements in Skerries. And that's how we ended up in the National Museum that morning. There was lots of stuff there, interesting stuff, like a big boat made out of a tree-trunk, and the girls liked all the gold collars, but there was only one thing that held me; the bog body, a small, stringy mummy of a man preserved in the cold waters of a Midlands bog. While the crowd boiled over the shop and poked at the cases with the guns and swords, I just stood there looking at it. It was a dusty looking brown, with stringy muscles like dried banana-skin peeling from the dry bones. It wasn't the prettiest thing in the exhibition, but it was the *realest*; a real person who'd just lain in the bog for all that time.

Later at home I drew it in my notebook, a brown, twisted, broken mass.

I climb down awkwardly into the pit. There's a rich, overpowering smell of turf. It's lying below in a little pool of water, still partly covered with soggy earth. Close up it's even more amazing. There's nothing scary about it; it's too perfect to look like a corpse. I can even see the little teeth. The droplets of water on its face and skin make it look lushly alive, nothing like that dried-up, sinewy body I remember from the museum. Its hands are clasped in front of it; I can see the tiny creases of the fingers, even the fingernails. One is badly cracked. I squat on my hunkers and look for a long time at that small imperfection, wondering if it was broken before or after death. The face is lovely, peaceful, eyes closed against the water that puddles around it. It looks like a man, but I'm not sure. I have the eeriest feeling he's just sleeping there, resting in the bog like some marshy Rip Van Winkle. A light plays down, and for a second, as it glitters on his face, I imagine I see the eyelids flutter. I jump up.

'I'm coming out.' I scramble out, filthy and wet.

'Your good shoes!' says Sean, scandalised. He sounds so like our mother everyone laughs, weak, shaky laughs.

'It's a bog body alright,' I say, shivering. 'Been there thousands of years. We need to call the museum in Dublin. They'll know what to do with it.'

There's a long beat of silence that tells me this is an unpopular idea. Dan cups his hands and lights a cigarette. The flame flares bright-hard for a moment, and then it's gone.

'Thousands of years, you say?' My father's voice is meditative. 'Sure then we don't need to call the guards or anything.'

'Definitely not.' I know this from reading about archaeology.

'Sure why can't we just...?' My father gestures towards the spade. Dan is murmuring in Sean's ear.

'We could, right enough,' says Sean. 'But, you know, maybe people would want to see it.'

Dan can't wait for him to come to the point. 'Maybe people'd pay to see it!'

My father straightens up. His face is still in shadow but his voice is strong and steady. 'I'll not have people traipsing all over my land. Looking and digging and interfering with us. That's not the way we live.' He moves to go. 'Cover it up.'

'We can't cover it up,' I say, stunned. 'This is important.'

'There could be money in it.' Dan's eyes are hard, glittering in the light of his cigarette end.

'You'll get small good from that money,' says my father. 'Do as I say.'

Dan doesn't move, but Sean puts down his torch on the ground and picks up the spade with a shrug.

'Is anyone listening to me? We need to let people know about this!'

But everyone continues to ignore me. My father and Dan walk off, still arguing, while Sean stolidly heaves the tarp into the hole with a thump and splatter, and then starts to shovel the dark earth back in. I stand watching him. The earth spatters down in a series of thuds. For a second I'm reminded of my grandfather's funeral, the smack of dirt on coffin. I look down but it's already disappeared from view. That beautiful, intricate body is hidden again.

I go back to the house but I don't sleep. Before dawn I get up and go to the open window. The breeze ruffles my hair as I stand and look over the bog. There are tears in my eyes, but I don't know exactly why. From time to time a bird cries out forlornly, a low, keening wail that cuts through the still night air. I think about him, that strange man, lying out there, eyes closed, sleeping silent in the dark bog.

'Buried' is a quiet little story about something that's always fascinated me – bog bodies. Like the protagonist in the story, the first time I saw one in the (amazingly preserved) flesh was in the National History Museum in Dublin. I was fascinated by how the unimaginable sprawl of time since he was buried seemed to diminish as I looked at this body, with its hair and fingernails and knotted tendons. The actual setting is my own family home in County Louth which stands on a couple of acres of scenic bogland; a pretty place of weeping willows, pheasants, otters and moorhens.

THE
CHANGELING

ell, we all know how the story ended. Even if you wanted, you couldn't escape it. Wherever you went, there it was. Newscasters murmured it over background photos of the woods, eyes cast down, their voices low and grave. It whispered out of the radio. It was in the bold print of the newspaper headlines in the rack outside McNally's shop. The only place you didn't hear about it was in the village. To be sure, there were slow conversations that would stop when you walked outside the church, or opened the door to the pub or the bookies. But we didn't discuss it. Not publicly. The closer you got to the woods, the quieter the story got, until under the trees, all voices fell silent.

So much for the ending. How it began was a different matter.

It was what people always did in Killnapouca, and always had done, time out of mind. For as long as anyone could remember back, infant boys were traditionally dressed as girls. It started originally as an old *piseog*, or superstition. The name of the village, Killnapouca – *Coill Na Puca* in Irish – meant the Forest of the Fairies. Old stories recited around the hearth at night would tell of children who had been taken or 'swept' by the fairy folk. Even my parents, who were enlightened people, would put out a glass of milk at night for them. Angering them was considered a senseless thing, attracting them was just as bad. 'Stay away from the fairies,' my granddad pronounced, as he planed wood in his shed in long, swooping movements. I was fascinated. 'Oho,' he said darkly, pausing to squint down the length of wood to test its smoothness, 'they're the boys would sweep you, alright.' He ran the plane down again, blowing softly at the sweet-smelling curls of fresh wood that peeled silently off. 'When I was a lad like yourself, the young MacDonald boy from my class went off one day and was never seen again, though an oul' fella once claimed to hear him crying, deep in the woods. That's why you never go into the forest by yourself.' I held a curl of warm wood delicately in my hand as I nodded, large-eyed.

Last night I couldn't sleep and went through one of my old boxes in the attic, and there, finally, I found it: an old, faded sepia-toned photograph of my round, smiling face, crowned by a floral bonnet, and stout, dimpled legs jutting out from under a foamy mass of lace. I stroked it slowly, my wrinkled thumb feeling the gritty dust on the surface of the glossy print. Pretty as a picture, I was. Pretty as a girl. My eyes glazed over as I stared at my smiling infant face which seemed to shrink, smaller and smaller, until I felt a strange vertiginous dizziness that this tiny image had contained the seeds of the rheumatic old man I am today.

No one could explain why the tradition of dressing boys as girls became so popular, but it was. One slow news day there was even a segment about it on television. Everyone was delighted, even though it was clearly one of those afterthought items, the hicks of the village ranked with dancing squirrels or dogs that could count. Sub-text wasn't big in Killnapouca. Each year, local newspapers would run stories on it; there was even a special annual bonny baby competition, where all the be-frilled infants, boys and girls alike, competed for a beauty prize. Some mothers liked it more than others. Patricia McAllister from the dairy would boast about her boys being 'born boys'; they would cry and tear at their finery, even when dressed in their best for Sunday mass. Dawn Reilly, the freckled, grinning girl who had four rowdy boys used to say that at least she got to play at having girls for the first few years. The one who enjoyed it the most was the curate's wife, Mary Shannon. The curate's *widow*, I should say, a quiet Protestant woman who lived in the rectory. Her Jamie was the prettiest baby in the village, and not only did she dress him in expensive pink dresses, but she grew his hair long and blonde and tied it up in matching ribbons.

I'm getting on a bit now, so it might seem surprising that I remember them all so well, but I was the local primary school teacher for many years, and the school was small, so they stood out, all of them, family resemblances, battered schoolbags, every cheeky face, every cowlick.

~

I remember the first time I saw her, clear as clear. It was a day in early spring, one of those fine, cold days with a white, bright sun that mercilessly lit up every cobweb and dust particle on my window pane. Some boys were playing football in the street, all dirt and swearing and swagger as they shouted and jostled each other over the ball. I was sitting at the bay window, enjoying the warm, near-forgotten tingle of sunshine on bare forearms, when she stepped off the bus. If I live to be a hundred I won't forget that moment. She was like something from a film, high black heels, her scarlet dress tugged by the wind around her, her long black hair blowing around her face. She smoothed it back, and her face was vivid, sharp as a photograph. The ball bounced off down the road, forgotten, as the boys stood to watch her. I saw her smile at them as they helped pull her matching tan suitcases over the street. She turned then and deliberately waved at me, her red lips curved in a wicked smile. I realised suddenly I was standing, staring at her. Her chin was pointed, elfin, her face at once familiar and unfamiliar.

The next day I was at Kelly's, the butchers, waiting patiently for my half-pound of mince, when I heard about her. The woman next to me pushing a pram to and fro, rocking her child (red hair, peculiar light grey eyes, definitely a Fitzpatrick) raised her voice in conversation with the butcher. 'A Jane Shannon, a cousin of some sort. Fancy looking piece, isn't she?' Jim Kelly nodded, absorbed in slicing her bacon rashers on the antiquated metal slicer. The Fitzpatrick girl looked out the doorway. 'Here she is now!' I felt my heart stutter and jump, and then beat rather faster than my doctor would have liked. The door tinged. She was even more breath-taking close up – her eyes large and dark, eyelashes fluttering like soft moths above them.

'Hello.' Her voice was low and soft, even a little nervous. Silence.

'Hello,' I returned, my voice a little gruff. 'Welcome to Killnapouca'. She smiled at me, a slight dimple appearing in her pale cheek. 'Thank you. It's good to be here.' Sunlight touched her head like a spun-gold nimbus, stray hairs delicately picked out in filigree. In a daze, I noticed that her ears were shell-small and ever-so-slightly pointed.

'What a lovely baby. And her dress is so pretty.' She turned her smile to the Fitzpatrick girl (*Mary? Marian?*). A red-nailed finger stroked the child's smooth cheek. The mother smiled back, slowly, almost grudgingly. 'Ah, he's a pet,' she said proudly. 'His wee frock, well that's the custom here.'

She nodded gravely. 'A lovely tradition.'

I was still smiling idiotically when Jim hefted the damp bag of mince into my waiting hand. She had that kind of effect on you.

—

Jane was the talk of the village. The women murmured about her dramatic dresses, all warm colours, a rainbow of reds, oranges, pinks. They whispered about her elegance, her heels clacking neatly on the rough pavements as she wandered arm-in arm with her cousin, Mary Shannon, their heads together, giggling softly like young girls. There were a host of rumours that circled her. She was an actress. She was a model. She was, in some indefinable way, *famous*. Mind you, the talk wasn't all positive. There were also pursed faces at her undeniable glamour. 'Who does she think she is?' breathed a customer in McNally's as Jane lined up her purchases at the counter – a fine bottle of red wine, some Belgian chocolates, red nail varnish. Even her shopping seemed perfumed with her inherent allure. Who *did* she think she was? I didn't know. She was fascinating, that was enough.

The men were even more straightforward in their interest. Wherever Jane went there was a kind of masculine vapour trail that followed her. Never had so many grocery bags been carried in the village. The pavement outside the Shannon house became a popular gathering point. Teenage boys languished in her wake, even schoolboys shouted louder in her vicinity, their faces twisted in a mixture of delight at her presence and fear of being noticed by her.

We were all a little in love with her, you see.

—

Even the McAllister boy was taken with her, and he was a real tearaway. Most of the lads that stayed in the village were fine boys. You could see that in ten, twenty years' time they'd have the greying hair and sloping bellies of their fathers and uncles, and most of them would follow the same trades. Kelly's son would be the new butcher. McNally's would be the new grocer. Few stuck out, but Sean McAllister did. Even at school he was a tough kid, his face often bumpy with bruises, eyes truculent with an endless desire to fight and conquer the tiny nation of the classroom. I didn't mind a fighter, that spark could be interesting. What I minded was a bully, and Sean McAllister was that. Like Georgie Porgy, he pinched the girls and made them cry. He had a genius for picking on weaker kids, an ugly knack for knowing what would hurt the most. The Kelly girl stopped coming to school for a while, and when she did, her mother marched in with her, pale and furious, pulling up her daughter's sleeve to show me still-visible scratches. Poor little Jamie Shannon got it worst; he had his long hair pulled, paint poured on it, even once knotted round the goalpost in the yard, till his mother cut it. I leathered McAllister for that one, I'm not ashamed to say, it being the days when you could do such a thing – a few straps across the back of the legs, and oh, the satisfaction of seeing the bully in pain! Ah, I'm sorry, I'm wandering off the point a bit here. It's hard to tell stories straight when you're my age; when you've lived in a place all your life there's too much detail in the picture to see it clearly.

If the other lads were keen on Jane, McAllister was – if it's not too fey a word – *enchanted*. He stopped his favourite pursuits of drinking in the pub till closing time and spitting on the footpath outside McNally's. I'd see him staring after her on the street, scraping whatever acknowledgement he could from her; a hello here or a nod there. He told a crowd in the bookies that he was going to have her as his girlfriend if it killed him. Actually, that's a polite translation of the story I heard, but this public pronouncement showed a determination he had previously reserved for avoiding work in the family dairy. His crew, with nothing better to do, followed him obediently. They were all solid low-achievers, doomed to the back of the class from their earliest days in school, just smart enough to work out who the leader was, who their protector could be.

Mary Shannon looked better than she had in years. I could see that Jane's presence made her happier than she had been since before her husband died and her son left home for university. Their two heads, black and grey, were often bowed over catalogues in McNally's or whispering close together over a teapot in the café. I could see Mary enjoying the glances that Jane got in an almost proprietorial fashion, her face proud and lively with admiration for her glamorous cousin. Me, I felt I was walking lighter than I had in years, and I won't deny Jane's smiles had a lot to do with it. We talked regularly, and I found out the information that the village was so hungry for. Jane was not an actress, or a model, or someone famous. She has a degree in early childhood education, but was resting up after a tough final year of study before finding a job. She had taken a fancy to me from our first meeting, and would often come and sit with me and listen to my stories of the local children, the folklore and the traditions of the village. There's no fool like an old fool, they say, and I was foolish and happy in the hazy golden light of those long summer afternoons, with the flies buzzing sleepily against the window-pane, the best china tea-cups out, and Jane's long, elegant hands shuffling through my old photographs.

~

Summer slipped by and it was late August. Blackberries were starting to bloom red and hard on the brambles, and the fields were coloured with the rich ochre of haystacks. Jane had been in the village for a few months. Her presence was a little less spectacular, but her glamour was as intense as ever. I'd never seen a woman so chic. Her hair was always beautifully arranged, her heels light, her dresses long but figure-hugging. And the sway of her hips! – but I'll stop now. I sound like one of those vulgar fellows in the pub late at night – I sound like McAllister.

    His courtship of Jane, if it could be called that, continued, rough and awkward as it had always been. He followed her about, there's no softer way to put it, and I could feel her irritation at his constant presence. I didn't say anything to her about it as it worked in my favour. As McAllister would never come into my home, her visits to me became more frequent to avoid him. Sometimes I'd see his red face looking vainly in my window for a glimpse of her. But he never dared come to the front door. I still like to think that the strapping might have haunted him, phantom marks still smarting on the back of his legs.

~

I wish now I'd said something. Of course I do. I considered talking to Mrs Shannon, but I have to admit that at the back of my mind I was afraid that Jane would leave the village if her cousin became worried. One day, having tea with Jane, I jokingly referred to him as her stalker. She just rolled her dark eyes.

'He's vile,' she said softly, and then shrugged her shoulders in quick dismissal, settling back in her chair. 'Tell me the story of your grandfather and the fairies.'

⁓

It all came to a head in September. The first day of school had ended and the village was flooded with new maroon uniforms and swinging bags as school children stood about in lazy, careless groups on the pavements. It was a warm day, and I was in my usual place at the window, enjoying the September bustle, recalling past autumns and the chatter and excitement of a new term. I saw Jane tip-tapping along in her high-heeled shoes as she carefully wove her way through the crowds, smiling at the children. That's when I saw him – McAllister – pushing an unsteady route towards her. His face was redder than usual; he was staggering, his eyes glazed. I got to my feet. Even from across the road I could see he was swaying in a drunken stupor, that he'd lost all sense of caring what he was doing. In slow-motion I saw him reach her, just outside McNally's shop. His large hands grabbed her, bent her backwards. I saw her foot slip out of her shoe, she stumbled, and then his face was on hers, his red, fleshy lips pressing against her. My hand went to my mouth in shock, like a Victorian woman. 'Oh God,' I said faintly. Jane's hands were on his face, pushing him away. The schoolchildren surrounded them in a laughing ring, cheering and clapping. I flung open the door and shouted 'Stop!' Their faces swung round to me, their instinctive reaction to my shout was to scatter. Even McAllister raised his bullish face in shock. It was enough for Jane, who grabbed her shoe and ran off, hopping and scrambling to get away. I think she was crying.

'Leave her alone.' My voice was low and steady. I could barely look at his flushed, porcine face.

'Whadda you know, ol' dried up teacher?' he muttered thickly. 'Get back to your books. She's mine.'

He raised a hand to me. 'If you dare,' I said quietly, looking him in the eye. He dropped his hand, belched and roared to his cronies behind him. 'Did ya see that? Did ya?'

'We all saw that.'

It was Jane, both shoes on now, standing a little way up the street. She was white-faced and furious. 'Everyone saw that!' she shouted again. Then she started laughing, loudly and wildly. 'Everyone saw your filthy self grabbing me!'

'So what?' he roared back.

'So what?' she repeated mockingly. 'I'll show you what!'

Then it all seemed to happen in slow motion. I could see Mary Shannon running down the street, alarmed by the noise, her eyes frantically searching the crowd for Jane. The school-children, interested, had turned back again.

'I'll show you what,' said Jane again, almost mechanically. Her eyes were wide and blank, her breath was coming in short, sharp pants. She raised a hand to her head.

'No!' screamed Mary – 'Don't do it,' – but Jane had grabbed her own long black hair and pulled it defiantly. For one horrible, long moment, I thought she had pulled it out, then realised that underneath was cropped golden hair.

'No – Jamie, my Jamie – don't!' wept Mary. An '*ahhhhhhhh*' went up from the crowd, a mass sound of excitement, revulsion, incredulity.

Jane tossed her wig on the ground, and turned proudly on her heel, one glorious moment of scorn as she walked away with exaggerated care, one precise foot in front of the other, then faster and faster as she reached the edge of the village. I saw her red dress flicker and disappear among the trees as a giant roar went up from McAllister. His large face was stupid with realisation.

'That...thing,' he spat 'I'll kill it!' His voice was shaking and thick with rage. The children started laughing, which made him even crazier. He grabbed the arms of the McNally boy. 'Who's with me? Come on!' He started staggering towards the woods. 'Come on!'

I still can't believe it, but they went with him. Not just his gang, but others. Good kids. Women. They went, one by one, till it was just me standing with Mary, arms around her, smothering her terrified sobs in my shirt.

We could still hear him roar, distantly. 'I'll fucking find you.'

I waited up. The papers will tell you that it was me who raised the alarm. I saw them coming back, you see. When I saw their faces under the streetlamps and the dark blood on their arms, I knew. Everything inside me turned to water. I held the arm of the chair as stars bloomed in front of my eyes.

They say every bone in her body was broken when they finally found her in the woods.

It's a cold day now, one of those clear, bright days that come at the dawn of spring. I don't sit in my bay window anymore. There is nothing I care to see out there, nor anyone, not any more. My doctor thinks I am ailing. I know I am; heart-sick, heart-sore. In fact, I don't know how many more springs I'll see. Every day that passes, I feel my engine running down, my body beginning the long, slow fall into forever.

All I know is I would give anything for it to be that same cold day in early spring with the weak sun coming through the windows, the shouts of the boys playing ball carrying in the clear air, and me knowing at any moment that the bus would crunch to a stop, the door would open, and I'd see her again, for the first, the last time.

One of the most famous tales about na Sidhe is their propensity to steal human children and human women; women for breeding (one of the legends in relation to Irish fairies is that they are angels who have lost their souls and who seek to interbreed with human women to have children who possess souls) and children, who they often substitute with their own. As with all stories, the writing of this started as a result of several unaligned thoughts coming together – the persistence of supernatural rituals in rural Ireland, a gruesome murder in Northern Ireland, and the old belief that you needed to disguise the sex of a baby to save it from been 'swept' or 'fetched' by the fairies. The fairies, it was said, would steal away an unprotected baby and replace it with a sickly fairy child who would dwindle and wither away, despite all human efforts. I became fascinated with the idea of 'infant drag', where clothing, hair and adornment function as a protective, gender-masking disguise. The idea of drag in this story is a double-edged sword. It is a catalyst for concealment, transformation, but also for revenge. I began wondering how this experience might translate into later life...and so this story came to life.

The story has an unhappy ending, but then, all fairy stories do. They end in tears, in partings, in kidnappings, desolation and death. Our poor changeling fares no differently.

PLAYING IN THEIR
OWN TIME

I t's two in the morning when we hear the voices; a crackle of static, a faint burst of sound that dies away almost at once. I start and catch Matt's arm.

'Did you hear that?' I mouth at him. He nods, eyes distant, head to one side, carefully listening. I swallow, my heart beating light and fast in my chest, and wait to hear if there's more. I inhale a long suck of air that smells of cold stone and damp floors. Seconds tick by. I strain my ears into the aching, waiting silence. Matt lifts one finger to alert me, and then presses it to his lips. There is nothing but the drumming in my ears…and then I hear it. A small voice says '*play*', so quietly and faintly that I am frozen. I see a zig-zag of green dance up and down on the computer screen. Our tech guy replays the burst of sound on his headphones, I see the blip dance again. He gives me the thumbs up.

We got it! I am torn between fear and glee.

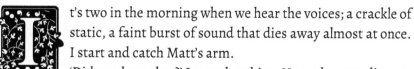

John Farrell puts on the headphones and listens intently. I watch his thick eyebrows knit together as the first sound traces its seismic thread across the screen. He makes to take off the headphones. I circle my hand urgently in the air to signal that there's more to come, and he relaxes back in the chair, only to sit forward sharply again.

'That's her!' The headphones are on the table, his face ablaze with eagerness. 'That's the same girl I hear!'

I signal to Matt, a barely perceptible flicker of my fingers to signify that he should start to film. 'Tell us more, John. Tell us about her.'

He puts his palms flat on the table. 'Not much to tell. We've always heard things. Like the sound of doors closing where there were no doors. Like voices talking together, but like an old BBC broadcast, old-fashioned voices, and only for a few seconds each time. And the little girl. Just a little thing in a white dress, you'd see the material flutter out of the corner of your eye. But if you looked at her full on, you'd lose her, she'd just go indistinct and fade out, like a bad TV signal.' He smiles. 'When Deirdre, my daughter, was little she was always plaguing me, wanting to play with her. Now she's turned seven, she doesn't do it so much anymore. But back then she'd cry and chase around the gallery after the girl, and I had to explain to her that the castle was full of people, but all locked in their own time. We can see and hear them, sometimes, like an echo, but they're lost in the past, they can't see further than their own time-span.'

'Are you afraid of them?' I ask, curious.

He shakes his head. 'We're very comfortable with them. Them in their time, us in ours.'

—

We're upstairs in the gallery, coiling up cables, dismantling the installation, packing up the gear in the cold wintry light of the afternoon. I pack my notebook into my satchel, then stick my hands under my warm armpits and wiggle the numb fingers around in an attempt to recover some feeling.

'God, it's cold.'

'Imagine living here.' It's Matt, blowing on his hands.

'It's fine,' says a little voice beside us. We both start, and then laugh. Standing beside us is a small girl. It's Deirdre, John Farrell's daughter. I recognise her from the photographs in the Great Hall. She scowls at us, obviously insulted by our casual denigration of her home. Matt smiles at her apologetically and moves off to pack up the sound equipment.

'It's not so cold,' she insists. Deirdre has a cute, cross little face, sprinkled with freckles.

'You've seen the girl in here?' I ask. Strictly speaking I shouldn't talk to her, John was quite adamant he would be the spokesperson for his family, but my curiosity is too great. Her face is scornful.

'Yes, of course,' she says. 'I see her all the time. And I hear her.'

'What does she say?'

She stares at me with her clear blue eyes for a moment. 'She wants to play. She always wants to play. But she can't see me.'

'What does she look like?'

Deirdre's blue gaze doesn't falter. 'Look behind you. She's there.'

I whip around, rattled, and see...nothing. At least I *think* it's nothing. My heart is beating too quickly. Deirdre turns and her footsteps clatter lightly down the stone steps. There's a sudden wriggle of shadows in the corner under the mezzanine. The merest breath of a giggle that hangs in the air. I don't hesitate. I turn and run after her, my steps huge and blundering, all the way back down to the Great Hall.

―

Years later, I've almost forgotten Ballinagh Castle. We're at the dreaded Monday staff meeting, the slowest hour of the week, when we get together and 'throw ideas around' as Peter calls it. Peter is a good decade younger than me, with a luxuriant, lumberjack beard and hair that's greased and parted carefully on his narrow head. He's a terrible human being. He's also our boss.

'Didn't you film the original episode at Ballinagh Castle?' Peter points at me, pistol fashion. I nod.

'Right, so, for the new series we're revisiting the most popular locations over the last six series – Ballinagh always tops the polls – we cover what's happened since our visit, any further manifestations, blah, blah.' He clicks his fingers. 'And of course we'll intersperse the new recording with the original footage. Only half the filming needed!' He smiles broadly around the table.

Idiot, I think automatically, as I do every Monday morning. But this is a special kind of stupid, even for Peter. The real expense of any shoot is transporting equipment, crew, the elaborate set-up, the time-consuming take down. None of these equate to the exact minutes of edited film produced. I say nothing and suppress the strong desire to eye-roll at Matt, who is now our senior technical officer.

―

After the staff meeting, it's a tradition that Matt and I have our own staff meeting in the local coffee shop, allegedly to draw up new plans, but where we *actually* compete to parody Peter's latest bright idea.

'Back to Ballinagh, then,' says Matt, forking a strip of bacon into his mouth. 'That was the spookiest place we went to – definitely the oddest place in that series, if not in all the series we've filmed.' He chews solemnly. 'Even you had a weird moment there, and you're a hard-core sceptic.'

I draw in a breath, remembering that moving shadow, that giggle, as if it were yesterday. 'Yeah, there was something there alright. So should I ring ahead and book a slot?'

Matt nods, absorbed in cutting his sausages into neat, bite-sized chunks. Then he looks up.

'Hang on, before you do, I've just remembered. I heard something, something that happened there.' There is a note of urgency in his voice. 'It happened a few years after we were there.'

I look at him, puzzled. 'Like what?'

'Like some kind of tragedy.' His face is knotted in near-recollection, and then he waves a dismissive hand, and instead thumbs out a Google search on his phone.

'Ah,' he says. 'Oh no.'

'What is it?'

'That poor wee girl.' Matt's Belfast accent is stronger when he's upset. 'Deirdre. She died.'

I catch my breath, her freckled, grumpy face clear and vivid in my memory. 'Jesus, that's awful. What happened? Are the family still there?'

'She fell, it seems.' Matt's face is soft with pity as he reads off his phone screen. 'And yes, they're still there. His name is still on the contact page of the castle website. God love him.'

The feelings this evokes are dark, overwhelming. I am caught between an intense pang of sadness and an almost simultaneous guilty throb of relief that it wasn't me, that it wasn't Amy.

—

'Ah the luxury of TV travel in Ireland,' says Matt, stretching out in the limited space of our van cab.

'A little more cramped than usual,' I say apologetically. 'I have to go by Joanne's house to collect Amy.'

'Bringing a kid to a haunted house?' Matt looks perplexed.

'Look, you know Joanne. It's her weekend away, so she's being totally adamant about it. If I don't stick to the arrangement, she'll do that passive-aggressive thing of 'forgetting' arrangements or booking Amy in for activities on my time...' my voice trails off as I remember the succession of complicated peace treaties negotiated after Amy's birth.

Matt nods. 'Ah, I know,' he says easily. 'It's fine by me. As long as you don't expect me to babysit.'

—

John is there to welcome us, just like the last time. I'm shocked at how much he's aged; his thick hair and wiry moustache are now white. Strong lines have dug themselves into the thick flesh of his forehead and carved deep runnels either side of his mouth. He smiles when he sees us, but it's a quick, fleeting grimace.

'Welcome back,' he says, stepping back from the door. I follow him inside as Matt and the crew start to back up the vans.

'I'm so sorry,' I say, quick and embarrassed, moving in to shake his hand. He returns my grip, but weakly. I persevere. 'I would have been in touch earlier, but I just heard.'

He looks up. 'You met her, didn't you? Little Deirdre.'

'Yes.' I can barely look at him. The glint of tears in his eyes makes me feel like bawling. I think of Amy in the car, and again I feel that same, sick, churning mixture of grief and relief.

He shakes his head, as if to clear his thoughts, and silently motions to me to follow him inside.

Inside the door, in the former Great Hall, everything is more cluttered than I remember. Classical music plays from an ancient record player in the corner. Thick, furred dust covers the heap of newspapers piled up behind the door. The bookcases are even fuller, the books lining them now two and three deep, but they too are white with wood-smoke dust. The cut wood seems to be the only recent addition to the room, and the crackle and spit from the fireplace is the only cheerful sound in it.

'Daddy?'

It's Amy, standing just inside the door. Matt must have let her out of the van. She shrinks back a little from the strange house, and the strange man inside it.

John's head shoots up, and he smiles. A real smile this time, pure with pleasure. He cocks his head at me.

'Is this your own little one?'

'Amy.' I supply.

'Come here to me, Amy, and say hello!' John opens his arms and, to my surprise, Amy, bashful little Amy, whose phrase of the moment is a piteous 'I'm SHY', simply runs forward. She opens her chubby arms wide, her full weight falling against him with the happy, heart-breaking confidence of a child.

'Well aren't you just fabulous?' says John, giving her a tight hug. 'Have you come to see me?'

'Yes,' says Amy, smiling up at him. 'Do you have any toys? And sweets?'

John grins. 'I have apples out the back on the trees. Is that OK with your Daddy?'

I nod, relieved. Amy stands with her tummy stuck out, considering the offer.

'FOUR apples,' she pronounces.

'One,' I correct her, with mock severity, and watch her skip off with John.

—

It's later, much later. Amy is asleep on a pull-out bed that John has made up by the side of the fire. She sleeps on her front, one arm thrown above her head. From time to time she makes a small, muttering sound that lapses back into wavelets of serene breathing. Matt and the crew are manning the rooms upstairs, as John and I talk by the crackling fire.

'So you stayed here?' I ask. I don't add the word 'afterwards', though it hangs in the air like an unspoken thought.

He dips his head, watching a glowing coal roll slowly down the stack of burning wood beneath. 'A place like this, it's hard to leave. My wife Grainne did, though. She couldn't take it, you know, the perpetual reminder. It's hard. It's all hard. Having a family, loving them, losing them.'

'It is.' I feel compelled to share my own story, if only to dilute the awfulness of John's. 'Amy's mother, Joanne, we were never really together. It just happened, and she wanted nothing to do with me. I had to argue my way into being part of Amy's life. I see her every weekend, but I'm always afraid that Joanne will go for sole custody. And I live in dread of being sent on weekend shoots.'

'Like this one?'

'This one's fine. You were very good to make her so welcome. Other shoots would be more difficult, in among ruins or inaccessible spaces.' My voice trails off. I hear the self-pitying tone in my voice and am miserably conscious of my own relative good fortune. There is a silence as we both stare into the fire, hypnotised by the soft hissing of the frail wood as it burns down to dust and smoke. There's only a lamp pooling soft light beside the stairs, for the crew to get up and down.

'Calling Seb Jonas.' Matt's voice crackles through my earpiece.

'Here' I say, automatically moving away from the fire, voice dropped so as not to wake Amy.

'It's cold as hell up here. Not a peep out of anything. I guess we're still listening out for the little girl, right? We can use the old recording but it'd be great to get some fresh activity. It's the logical hook to connect with the last episode and with the recent tragedy.'

I steal a glance at John, hunched over in his tattered velvet chair. 'Yes,' I say quietly, feeling wretched. 'That'd be good.'

—

It's an hour later, and I'm just on the verge of sleep, in a cycle of small motions where my eyelids continuously droop, fall, then start open again.

'Listen.' John whispers the word. I open my eyes fully and sit up straight in my chair. The fire is dying down in the glowing grate and his face is cast in deep shadow. I see him raise a finger to his lips.

'Hush,' he breathes. 'She's back.'

'The little Victorian girl?' I whisper. *I hope Matt's catching this.* John leans towards me. His eyes close in a blink to signify *yes*, and then he settles back. His eyes travel over and back around the open door to the stairs. I feel a crawling sense of cold travel downwards, like a giant stone breath exhaling down the dark passageway. Amy is still sleeping. I watch John's gaze play around the corner of the room, and I'm suddenly afraid, feeling the kind of crawling, out-of-body horror that I've only experienced once or twice in my life. Then John sits forward abruptly.

'There she is.'

I strain my eyes, but all I can see is a flicker, a jump, a squiggle of shadow, so fast it's almost invisible. The best way to describe it is like a flaw in an old VHS tape – an abrupt burst of static that disrupts the screen. I watch intently for a few seconds, then look away – and there it is! A wave of movement, right at the edge of my vision, a flicker from another space, superimposed onto ours.

'She's there, all right, in her long white frock.' John is speaking softly, almost to himself. 'There she is, playing away. Don't be scared, she can't see you.' I feel cold dots of gooseflesh stipple themselves on my arms; I see them raised on my wrists. Then I hear a long, slow exhale beside me.

'And here she is. My own little girl.'

His eyes glint with heavy, trembling tears, and all at once there is such a look of love and grief on his face I have to turn away. Tears roll down his craggy face, falling into the lines either side of his moustache. I move closer, and put an arm around his shoulders. I can feel my own treacherous tears rise, as his eyes travel back and forward across the floor.

'It brings me such comfort,' he whispers, rough breath catching in his throat. 'Such comfort.'

A coal falls in the fire with a thump. We both start; it breaks the spell. I act on instinct and pick up the sleeping Amy, holding her tight, so tight, her body folded into mine, her shallow breath warm on my neck. I glance across. John's head is buried in his hands, gnarled fingers ruffling through his thick white hair.

'That's why I don't leave,' he says quietly. 'Not while she's still here. Grainne didn't understand it. In the end she hated me for it. But I can't leave. As long as she's here, so am I...'

I feel the moth-soft flutter of Amy's eyelashes against my neck.

'They're still parted, you know.' His voice is gentle, almost hypnotic. 'They're playing in their own time. But now that they're both in that space...sometimes they can see each other. Sometimes I see them wave.'

My arms are trembling. I hold Amy, feeling her sleep-heavy body slip slightly against me. She murmurs, and I bend to catch her words.

'Play.' Her breath is milk-sweet and soft against my face.

As Amy lies, warm and heavy against my chest, I know absolutely what real terror is; that precise moment when you feel everything sure and certain and warm in your life start to slip away.

This story was completely born from a trip to Leap Castle, allegedly one of the most haunted places in Ireland. There are many colourful stories told about it; its bloody history has generated tales of battles, murders, and horrid imprisonments in the oubliette. However, I was most fascinated by meeting the owner of the castle, Sean Ryan, recounting his own encounters with paranormal elements in the castle. One of his stories was about a little girl that he and his family had seen many times, dressed in archaic clothes. She was a benign spirit, and he described the experience of seeing her as being like catching a remote radio frequency; she was in her time, he in his.

And so I had it – the gift of a story title.

DARK IT
WAS INSIDE

O how frightened I was, how dark it was inside the wolf!

tories take seed, root and spread. They bud into flower, generation after generation. Some stories exist before you, and you transmit them. Some you originate and tell, to have them retold, years on, as faint echoes of the original.

This is a story I wandered into by mistake, but now the roots intertwine around me. I am it, and it is me.

2

I first hear the news from my mother, when I call over to see her.

'Your grandmother is dead. Heart attack when out walking.' She says it quickly, the words tumbling out.

'German Granny?' I'm startled. 'I forgot she was still alive." I tot up the years on my fingers. 'She must have been nearly a hundred.'

My mother is tight-lipped. I know that she never liked German Granny. Even the family photos of her wedding are carefully excised, my father's family disappearing from the dusty white album so completely that their memory, like smoke, has drifted away.

'I suppose she was,' she says dismissively. 'But the real news is that she left a will, and everything is left to you. You were her only grandchild.'

I sit down heavily. 'Everything?'

'Well I was talking to the solicitor. There's a small cottage and some effects in Freiberg. The catch is that you have to go over to complete all the formalities.'

I nod my head. I have some faint memories of German Granny, from when she travelled over to Ireland to see me. I remember a heavy accent, her thick blonde hair, the marzipan-sweet cake she brought and her thick glasses that flashed in the sunlight. I am like her in that I am also severely short-sighted. 'Blind as your grandmother,' as my mother would say, exasperated, as I cannoned into walls or accidentally knocked a cup.

3

And when you go into her room, remember to say good morning and not to stare all round the room first

The house is from another world. From the outside it is like a fairy-tale cottage – old, sturdy and squat with peaked windows like eyebrows. It's right on the edge of the forest; just a few yards away is a path that twists into the darkness of the tall trees. Only two other cabins are near – a green hut that seems to sink into the undergrowth, and a vivid orange house with a complex interlacing of wooden timbers on the walls. My grandmother's house is a cosy cabin; there is the smell of old, warm wood both inside and outside. Someone has lit a fire in the hearth. The flames crackle and spit, orange, violet, white. Herr Hartmann, my grandmother's lawyer, sniffs approvingly. 'Very good. Her neighbours have lighted the fire for us.' He lays his stack of papers down on the wooden table. I touch the table-top, my hand running along its pitted surface, the faint rings telling a story of long-ago drinks, until a low growl from the corner startles me. It is a dog, half-hidden in the shadows.

She is silent, staring at me, head lowered. Her pointed face is elegant, the hair on her head rising to an absurd coxcomb. Every muscle in her body is still, watchful. I move forward, she steps back into the shadows. Her eyes regard me, cataract-milky, studded with black pupils. It is only those pale blue eyes that differentiate her from a wolf.

Beside me, Herr Hartmann clears his throat. I look up, confused momentarily by the unfamiliar sight of carved wooden shelves, the checked table-cloth, and the polished flags of the floor. 'Her name is Lupe,' he says. 'She belonged to your grandmother.'

I cannot take my eyes from her. 'She's beautiful,' I say simply. And she is. I extend a slow hand. She creeps forward, one silent paw-pad after another, and licks my palm with a hot, silky tongue.

4

But Little Redcape didn't know what a wicked beast he was, and wasn't afraid of him

Now I'm living in my grandmother's house. Sometimes I feel I have slipped out of my own life and into hers. It's cold here in the forest, autumn has turned the trees to rustling brown, and the air is crisp and chill. I light the fire, using the stack of wood in the lean-to shed. I use logs every day, but the pile never seems to reduce. One day I see one of my neighbours, a slim man with a woollen cap, disappear into my shed with an armful of chopped wood, and the mystery is solved. I wave at him through the window; he waves back stiffly, face averted.

Once a week I carefully walk the winding road down from the edge of the forest into Freiburg. I wander around the town, buy groceries, have a coffee and a cream-filled pastry, and get a taxi home. Lupe stays behind, and greets me with joy when I return, my glasses misting up with her hot breath as she wiggles and wags her plumy tail. She never barks, just jumps up in excitement, whining, pale eyes ablaze with joy.

One day I'm strolling through the Altstadt, admiring the towering red edifice of the cathedral, when I hear someone shout.

'Hallo!' I don't look around. Then I hear it again, insistent, close.

'Hallo!' I turn around to see two men beside me. I squint at them through my glasses. I realise one is the wiry man I saw replenish my woodpile. He stands back awkwardly, twisting his woollen cap in his hand; the hair revealed is long and blonde and messy. The other man is tall and dark; he is smiling directly at me.

'Hallo,' I respond, then, shyly add, 'Kein Deutsch. Englisch?'

The dark-haired man keeps smiling. *How handsome he is*, I think, distracted. I slip off my glasses and put them in my pocket. 'It is no matter,' he says. 'We know you are Birgit's grand-daughter, yes? You are here to live?'

'For the moment. There are many legal documents to go through.'

He frowns. 'Many papers?'

I nod. 'We welcome you to Freiburg. I am Johann. I teach in the school at the bottom of the mountain. This is Walter.' The blonde man inclines his head brusquely. They invite me for coffee, and I agree. It turns out that both are my neighbours. Dark-haired Johann, who talks a lot, and waves his hands energetically, lives in the orange house, Walter, in the green cabin. They both knew my grandmother well. Johann tells me she often mentioned a granddaughter in Ireland. I bite my lip.

'We are so sorry she is gone,' says Walter gruffly. He seems agitated by my presence; he keeps pulling his black woollen cap on and off.

'Thanks,' I say, touched. 'And thanks for the wood. It's been so kind of you.' He doesn't respond, just nods.

We walk back together, and when I open the door to Lupe's rapturous welcome I feel a glow of belonging. *This is my place now*, I think. I've never thought that before.

5

Watch your step like a good girl and don't stray from the path

The clothes I've brought aren't warm enough for autumn. I've taken to wearing my grandmother's thick wool sweaters, her shabby red coat that I found hanging by the door. My days have a new purpose. I get up early and walk Lupe. I've never had a dog before. She watches me with a quiet desperate adoration in her white eyes. I am constantly torn between love and anger as I walk her. She pulls hard on the lead, straining to smell, pee, investigate, so much so that my wrist is stiff and aching when I return home. She loves long walks, so I start to walk a little further every day. Gradually my legs grow stronger, my knees stop aching so much. The forest is magnificent, silent, golden, immense. Moss is thick on the ground, creating a soft cushion underfoot. We walk by streams, up hills, down winding paths. Sometimes we're joined by Johann, who points out different plants. I learn the German names for the fading wildflowers; *Gänseblümchen, Löewenzahn, Rittersporne*. He cautions me against picking unfamiliar berries, pointing at a cluster of shiny, dark berries. *'Teufelskirsche,'* he says darkly. I am intrigued.

'Devil-berry?' I ask. I am learning new words every day, and using them to puzzle out composites.

'Or *Wolfsbeere*, or *Schlafkirsche*. You would say belladonna. And poison! So be careful.'

One day I pass by a cluster of houses, an inn, a small white church. The door hangs open, and I pause to read the sign outside: 'The Pilgrimage Church of St. Ottilien.' It is a tiny, cold building; the walls smell of chilly mould and dampness. There is a crypt in the church with a huge cairn of stones that surrounds an underground spring. I hug my old red coat tight around me. Upstairs the colours of the wall resolve themselves into mottled flakes of paint, plaster frescoes. Lupe sniffs curiously at a nearby pew. I wander closer to the simple altar. A large, gold-clad saint stands to the left, eyes rolled piously to one side. Her head inclines towards the book she carries aloft on a chalice. With a jolt of disbelief I see a large pair of lidded eyes protrude from the book. My rash of gooseflesh has nothing to do with the chill of the empty church.

As I wander through the forest, I see other signs of the presence of St. Ottilien. There are Stations of the Cross dotted around the steep path that leads from the church, small stone depictions of torture and crucifixion. Sometimes I see old women cluster around the church. They leave tightly bound bunches of wildflowers beside the strange statue.

Autumn flowers in the forest, great swathes of leaves burn yellow and orange, then fall to lie crisp, brown and brittle beneath my feet. The ground smells damp and fecund, a cold, rich smell that rises from the leaves as we walk, Lupe and I. Sometimes we find neat piles of sticks. One day, Lupe unearths a tiny jacket from under a heap of slimy leaves and dark, devil-berry plants. It is a beautifully made jacket, embroidered with gold threads, too small even for a baby. *Some child is probably crying at home for this*, I think, and lay it carefully on a nearby log, within full view of the path. The next day it is gone. Lupe and I wander like explorers, unearthing a strange mass of contorted fungi, a sea of twisted brown lumps erupting under an old, fallen tree. '*Pilze*,' confirms Johann, waving his hand at it.

'Pilze,' I repeat.

'So where are you going today?' He leans against a tree, breath smoking in the morning air.

I shrug. 'Through the forest. Maybe as far as the St. Ottilien church? I meant to ask you, what's the story with that weird statue?'

He frowns. I rephrase it – 'I mean, who is the saint Ottilien – with the eyes on the book?' I open my own eyes widely in mime.

His face clears. 'Oh yes. She is an old German saint. They say she is even older, like a sun god. She was blind, then the priests put the water on her...'

'Baptised her?'

'Yes, and then she could see again. That is why the blessed water is in the church'

'The spring underground?' He nods. We walk on in easy silence.

6

She was surprised to find the door open, and when she went into the room everything seemed so strange that she thought: Oh my goodness, how nervous I feel today

It's an October evening. I'm walking back from the town, dry leaves crunching underfoot. I'm idly reflecting on how fit I am, compared with a few months earlier, when I notice it. My front door is hanging ajar on its frame.

My hands go to my face. 'Oh no,' I say in a small, frightened voice. Then I panic. 'Lupe!' I shout, running inside, smashing my palm against the sockets. Lights flash on. The big open space of the kitchen-living room is a mess of paper, broken plates, and up-ended furniture. 'Lupe,' I pant, distraught, my voice tiny and airless. I can't see her anywhere. I am afraid to look in case there is blood, or worse. My glasses fall off as I blunder about, and I stand on them with a crunch. I turn over a chair and sit down, weak with shock. My arms curl over my head, pulling my face down to my chest. Finally, I begin to cry, sitting amidst the wreckage of my house, great choked, hiccupping sobs.

The rest of the night is a blur. The room is a kaleidoscope of colours and noise, made all the more unreal by the loss of my glasses. Somehow Walter arrives. Then Johann. Then a policeman. Someone makes me a hot cup of tea that I cradle in my hands until it goes cold. There is no sign of Lupe, apart from the deep parallel scratches of her paws on one of the chairs, and the drift of white hair that carpets the floor. Johann talks to the policeman, giving him all the information he needs, helps him to photograph the room. Walter, stolid and quiet, starts to put the furniture back in its original position. He piles the papers and books methodically on the large dining room table.

The kind policeman politely waits for the men to leave, then interviews me in halting English.

'So, how long you know the neighbours?'

I consider it. 'A month, maybe more?'

He writes it down. I can see him press hard with his pencil; he is thorough, precise, even down to his handwriting.

'They have no reason to do this?'

I stare at him, head heavy stupid with crying. 'Them? Johann? Walter?' My voice squeaks with surprise. 'Why, do you think they had something to do with this?'

He shrugs his broad shoulders. 'Probably not. But we need to look at all the things.'

His words have made me uneasy. I close the door behind him, and bolt it. Then I pull the large dresser across to partly block the door. A drawer comes unstuck and falls to the floor, behind it a small snowfall of paper drifts down. One of the pages lands by my foot. I pick it up. It is a photocopy of a photograph of me – I recognise it instantly, it is a duplicate of one framed at home in my mother's house. I turn it over. On the back, inscribed with a shaky hand, are the words 'Meine Enkelin'. *My granddaughter.* I feel more tears prick hot behind my aching eyes. *Meine Oma*, I think, *my grandmother*. I pass my hand over my eyes, and this time the wetness is for memories never made.

7

This delicate young thing, she'll make a plump morsel, she'll taste even better than the old woman

I wake up the next morning, and in the silence I miss all Lupe's annoying mannerisms, her whine, and the scrabble of her claws scratching at the bedroom door. In the kitchen the sight of her bowl and rumpled, hairy dog-bed bring a fresh trickle of tears down my face. My eyes hurt, sore with tears and inflamed with the constant squinting.

Johann calls over at lunchtime. 'The dog?' he asks. Dumbly, I shake my head. Johann's dark eyes are soft with pity. We are sitting side by side. Gently he takes my hand and holds it in his. I snuffle, feeling wretchedly unattractive, all scruffy hair and inflamed eyes. He strokes my arm. My breathing sounds loud in my ears. I bury my head in the warm down of his jacket, feeling his shoulder, bony against my cheek. Time stands still.

He finally stirs. 'I have to go now,' he says apologetically. 'The school is starting'

'Of course.' I sit up hastily. 'Thank you.'

'Shall I call later?'

'Please.' I don't want to be on my own.

When Johann leaves, I wander around, aimlessly. I've tidied up the worst of the mess from yesterday. I'm restless. I decide to go for a walk and try to find Lupe. For the rest of the afternoon I wander about, calling, my voice a long series of mocking echoes among the hazy trees. The sky is dark blue when I admit defeat and start the long walk back, the light from my torch bobbing and weaving in front of me. Though I can't see anything but an impressionistic blur, my feet know the path now; they step carefully to avoid the gnarled knots of roots, the loose stones.

Nearly home. In the distance I squint and see the golden glimmer of porch-light. I have left the light on since the break-in. I start walking faster, thinking of Johann, of Lupe, wondering, hoping. A hand touches my arm and I scream, loud and shrill, dropping the torch. I blunder and wail and squeal in the darkness.

'Oh please, I am so sorry'. The voice is soft with distress...and familiar.

'Walter!' I shout furiously, bright anger coursing through me. I march on, torch abandoned, scrambling onward, ignoring his shouts. I stand at the front door, and slowly the rage turns to a dreary sadness as I turn around and I realise there is no dog, no Johann, just awkward Walter standing outside the pool of light, his shoulders hunched in apology. I

~

open my mouth to invite him in, but then hesitate. Like a movie I see the policeman's concerned face, and hear his question, '*So, how long you know the neighbours?*' I slide my hand into my pocket to locate the heavy metal key.

'What are you doing here?'

'I was worried,' he answers bluntly. 'I wanted to make sure no-one comes back.'

I frown. 'Have you been here all day?'

'Some of it.' The thought of him standing silent guard disturbs me.

'You must go home now,' I say, my voice artificially bright. 'It's cold out there, and I'm going to bed now.' *There, I can't be any more direct.*

He bows his head. 'Good night,' he says and walks off. I feel guilty, and then cross, as I unlock the door. *A bath*, I think, *a bath, then bed.* I lock the door behind me and test the handle.

Minutes later I'm running a hot bath. The air is milky with clouds of steam, and the smell of warm roses rises from the bath salts. I think of Walter as I last saw him, disappearing around the bend in the path that curves into the trees. As I slip into the bath, I think of him standing in the darkness – alone, silent – and I shiver, despite the heat.

I'm almost dozing off, all reddened languor and damp hair, when I think of Lupe and sit up. Flesh hot and damp, my nightdress sticking to my skin under my old red coat, I take her bowl outside and empty food into it to coax her back. I wander back in. I put my face close to the clock to read it. Nearly ten o'clock. I shrug, realising that Johann is not coming back. Instead I busy myself with clearing up the remnants of the mess in the kitchen. Slowly, methodically, I restore order, arranging books back on the shelves, spines grouped by dominant colour, shading from white to black. I feel my soul soothed with the repetitive work. I pick up an old German book with lovely botanical drawings and a folded slip of newspaper falls out. It is a page from a newspaper, the local *Badische Zeitung*. The newsprint is a haze, but the headlines scream '*Die Bestie von Scharzwald!*' – Black Forest – beast – murderer? I unfurl the paper, and then freeze. Below the story is a boldly-executed drawing, clearly a police sketch.

'It looks like...' My voice falters and dies in the sudden silence of the house, a silence only broken by the heavy tick of the kitchen clock. I don't trust my eyes. I crumple the paper, and then unroll it again.

I try again. 'It looks like—'

Then I look up and see his dark shape in the doorway.

I jump and grab the edge of the table for support. *He knows*, I think, crazy with fear, *he knows*. The paper lies on the floor, the image revealed. For one long moment we both look at it. He shrugs.

'I knew the old woman had that. She knew.' He steps forward. 'Come here.'

I move behind the table, heart hammering. He reaches into his coat, never taking his eyes off me. 'Come here.' His eyes glitter queerly.

His hand flings outward. There's a sudden crash of wetness all over my face. My eyes are on fire. I splutter, gasp, and scrub frantically at them with the sleeve of my coat.

'Come here.' I dodge clumsily round the table, my hip cannoning into a chair.

'Come to me.' I run to the door, half-tripping, and into the night. My eyes are smarting unbearably, but my bare feet find the path instantly, that spongy softness of leaves and pine needles.

'You can't run!' he calls. 'You can't see!'

8

'Why Grandmama, what big eyes you have!'
'All the better to see you with'

I can see a little, but I'm burning with pain. My vision is doubled, blurred over in hot fire; the trees seem far away and horribly near, all at once. I shut my swelling eyes and trust to my feet, my memory of the path, and keep moving.

'Lupe,' I whimper, over and over as I stumble on, rubbing my face. 'Lupe.' The pain grows now, tremendous, and my heart drums louder and louder. I keep tripping, half-falling over, as the path seems to buckle and twist under my feet. Dimly in the background I can hear the thump of his feet behind me; through the streams of hot tears I see a wavering torch-light. *He can't see me* I think, as I blunder on. My bare feet are hurt, bruised, cut, but leave no footprints on the soft leaves.

'Come to me!' I open my eyes in shock as he calls. The forest loops in front of me, gigantic and swooping, branches dancing and dipping, hideously magnified. I whine sharply, burying my streaming, blazing eyes into the crook of my elbow

'Come to me!' He calls again. His voice sounds nearer this time.

9

O how frightened I was, how dark it was inside the wolf!

It seems like I've been running for hours, but my feet tell me I am at the top of the hill leading down to St. Ottilien. As I stumble on I count the landmarks, *the old log, the sharp turn, the big flat stones on the path*. My heart thuds and booms. It takes every tiny last reserve of my strength just to keep moving. Dry sobs bubble up, tearing my dry throat. My eyes are an inferno, crusting and swelling over. The world blurs around me, tipping and wheeling, as I run through the leaf drifts, falling, stumbling, and sliding down the hill towards the church.

'Come to me!' I must keep going. As I run, I see a woman beside me; she grabs my arm to pull me onwards. Her blonde hair falls around her face. My eyes squint in a haze of tears at the shining light of her hair as it bobs before me like a beacon. Down, down, down the hill, my drained legs stutter and skip as I run. I'm holding hands with her now; my heart beating a crazy rhythm, my vision swooping up and down, in and out of focus. Her hand in mine is hot as fever. We're running faster and faster, the path strangely soft and pliable under my feet. I dash savagely at my eyes, wiping at the mess of tears. As my vision clears, I see the path is a path no longer, but a swirling mass of limbs, arms, legs. Now I am crying, really crying, with the hopeless sobs of terror and exhaustion. I can see faces twist out from the soil; eyes rolled back, mouths black holes. Women, so many women, all buried and rising from the ground. I falter, stop, and fall towards them. My limbs intertwine with theirs, my mouth fills with leaves.

A hand grabs me back up. She pulls me over the threshold of the church, and then unceremoniously dumps me on the stone flags. They are cool and smooth and beautiful to the touch. My swollen face pulses hot against the coldness of the floor. I roll over to see the woman crouch protectively on the threshold. She turns to me.

'He is coming. Go! Go to the water!' Her arm points to the stairs to the crypt. It takes the biggest effort in the world to move, but I stagger weakly towards the stairs. In the doorway I turn to her. She waves at me impatiently. My vision blurs, then clears. Her eyes flash light at me. I notice, confused, she is wearing glasses, and suddenly I realise who she is.

'*Meine Enkelin,*' she mouths to me, her face soft.

The crypt is dark and chill as I stumble over the cairn of stones to the well of the spring. I scoop up the water and spill it over my face in huge, extravagant gestures. I can hear noise in the distance, but I am beyond caring, every part of me focused on drowning the burning itch. The door is flung open. There is the ringing sound of boots on stone.

'Go away!' My voice is shaky. Overhead I can hear more noise, a commotion of banging, and can it be...? *Yes, oh yes!* It's that unmistakeable whining yelp. Lupe tumbles past Johann, down the steps, her body all scrabbling claws and frantic face as she collides with me, a bundle of love and excitement. I drop to my knees and hug her close, her body quivering with nervous energy, her desperate face licking my eyes. Her tongue on my face is glorious. The stinging heat of my eyes begins to subside. Hugging her I am safe, invulnerable. *My wolf, and my love.*

'I will get you,' he says. 'Just like I got your grandmother'

I grab a rock from the cairn and aim at his voice. It harmlessly hits the lintel of the door. He laughs. It's an ugly, low sound.

I turn my head and bury it in Lupe's fur.

There is a scream. I look up, and see Johann tumble crookedly down the steps, his arm cracking hard against the floor. He screams again. Walter stands silhouetted in the doorway, fingers still splayed out in front of him.

10

'So I've found you now, you old sinner' he said 'I've been looking for you for a long time'

For an instant time stands still, all of us frozen in a bizarre tableau: me and Lupe in a tight embrace by the spring, Johann spread-eagled on the ground, Walter, arms extended in front of him on the stairs. Johann is the first to recover.

'Du Hurensohn!' He scrambles up, panting, holding one arm. Walter runs, jumps down the steps to grab him in a tackle that sends him sprawling again, shouting in pain. Their bodies clash, wrestle, they shout and pull. Johann punches Walter in the stomach; he buckles, and then grabs at him to twist his crooked arm. The scream that rises from Johann is wild and desperate. He staggers toward me. I drop Lupe, grab a pointed rock and strike Johann hard on the head. There is a crunch and a sickening give, as the stone sinks in like a spade through sand. He falls heavily, still groaning in pain, and lands in the water. Walter and I look at each other, a long moment of agreement. Our hands reach out to push his head down, under the water. Johann is filled with a frantic strength; we feel it thrilling through our arms. He twists and turns, breaking the surface briefly with a roar that turns to gurgles as we push him back under. The tendons on his neck stand out like great ropes. Water bursts in desperate streams of bubbles from his nose and mouth, until they finally slacken and he lies still and limp beneath us.

Walter's hands cover mine, strong and warm. I see him clearly for the first time. His eyes are beautiful, blue and steady. 'I'll look after it,' he says quietly, his breath in my ear.

11

As long as I live I'll never again leave the path and run into the forest by myself.

Walter and I are married now. I'm waiting for him to come home. There is a pot of stew on the stove, the rising steam filling the kitchen with the smell of herbs, and misting great patches of the windows. I rub a hole in the condensation on the window pane to look out. I see the path curve around, and the darkness where it meets the trees. Everything is perfect, crisp and clear. Since that night, my sight is perfect, keen, sharp. I am lucky, in so many ways. I rub the slight, warm bump of my belly, and beneath my fingers, I feel the flutter of possibility. I hope it's a girl.

The story is rooted deep in my bones.

My days have fallen into a pattern. In the mornings, I walk Lupe across the forest to the church of St. Ottilien and light a wax-cold candle for my grandmother. I wrap her old red coat around me tightly as I walk back, gathering dry twigs for kindling. *Meine Oma*. I see myself as a piece of the puzzle, a link in the chain, a vessel of family memories both old and new. As I weave my way through the forest paths, I enact and re-enact her story, the stories of those before me, and those who will come after me.

This is my homage to one of the Grimm tales, 'Little Red Cap.' Like the narrator, I've spent time in the Black Forest, and was entranced by the green stillness of it. It's easy to imagine how the Brothers Grimm found so many folktales within it. The shrine of St. Ottilien is real, and rather wonderful. I stumbled across the church while walking through the forest outside Freiburg. As soon as I saw the strange statue with the eyes on the book within the church I knew it would recur in something I would write.

THE GREEN ROAD

fter the crash there's a beat of silence, then a babble of voices. I can see a green pool of light behind my eyelids.

'Are you OK?'

'Help her up!'

'Here you are, darling.' I feel a heave, a pull, and I'm standing, crushed against the firm, rounded body of a middle-aged woman. I can barely see her; the dazzle of green-yellow light is hurting my eyes. 'Thanks,' I say, faintly. I try to straighten up, but my body smarts and aches in an unfamiliar way. *I must have hurt myself when I fell,* I think automatically, lightly touching my elbows, my arms, my face. Then I stop. Something is wrong. Something is very wrong. I squint, my eyes weepy and dazzled, into the streaming green light.

I know where I am. I recognise it straight away.

I'm on the Green Road.

—

When we were children, every Sunday, regular as mass and clockwork and the fade of day into night, me, Robin, Jack and my parents would go on a drive together. The rationale for these Sunday drives was mysterious, their origins lost in the early days of our family history. In some confused way, I imagined that these drives were some kind of national rule, that all over the countryside children my age were obediently piling into cars, fighting over the window seats, twining legs over each other to forestall a need to wee, and preparing to beg for sweets at every conceivable stop. There was often no specific destination, although sometimes my dad would stop the battered old Hillman Hunter, abruptly, just when we'd succumbed to a collective, stuffy, back-seat coma, and the child-proof doors would unlock with a solid *clunk*.

'Go on,' he'd say. 'Go run around for a bit.'

We'd unpeel ourselves from the sticky seats with impressive sucking noises, and then stand outside, wobbly and uncertain as new-born foals, eyeing the nearby castle, or forest, or ruined abbey with a sceptical eye. That was my dad's cue to shake out the battered Sunday newspaper and cover his face with it, and my mum's cue to light a cigarette and exhale her smoke in a long stream out the cracked-down passenger window.

And no matter how far we wandered, or how long we strayed away for, anytime we returned there they'd be, sitting in the exact same position, in the car, in their coats, not looking at each other, him with the paper, she with her cigarette.

Every week there was the same routine; Sunday dinner of roast chicken, the quick pile into the car, drive, stop, out, him and her tucked into their coats inside, us wandering in the slow-fading afternoon outside. I remember the smell and feel of it all, the gradual warming of chilled faces and legs on the drive home, dry smoky air puffing out through the vents. If I close my eyes I can still see the sequence, smell it, hear it. And in this way, Sunday after Sunday, we covered every local landmark, every playground, every seaside, every old ruin, every point-to-point, and every village festival. And then one day, we ended up lost on the Green Road.

—

It's Sunday and we're driving to our local forest park. We're already in the outskirts of the woods, the planted section of soaring, dark-green conifers. All around us are trees, column after column, large and sturdy and pole-straight. There's a plastic bag of sandwiches in the boot, a soggy mixture of tomato, lettuce and mayonnaise wilting together into a salad slime. Inside the car, there is a potent smell of nicotine and hot seats. I can tell from the straight line of my mum's back that she is bristling with anger. She makes little sucking noises on her cigarette – that's another reason I know she is angry, she usually waits until the car stops to crack down the window and light up. She sits stiffly upright, her lips pulling at the cigarette in sharp little dabs. My dad says nothing, but his shoulders are raised and hunched, head thrust forward, as if he's trying to burst through the dilapidated frame of the Hillman Hunter.

'Where the hell are we?' His voice is loud in the quiet car. We know this isn't the time to make noise; for once we're not complaining or squabbling. He hunches even further forward and peers out. We've left the coniferous section and we're in my favourite bit, the larger, older, darker forest of tangled deciduous trees. Beside my window there's a beech tree, bowed over to the right, its tiny leaves shimmering in the breeze. My mum sighs loudly.

'What do you mean? We're only ten miles from home.'

'I know.' His voice is curt. 'I just haven't passed anywhere I recognise in the last five minutes. Not since the last turn.' He stops abruptly, and wrenches the car around. No three-point turn, just a skiddy, angry churn of wheels and we're facing around. 'I know where we're going. We just need to back up a little.'

It doesn't work.

Half an hour later, we're still bumping over smaller rutted roads. More firsts – my mum has now sworn at my dad. In front of us. And he's sworn back. I shift uncomfortably in my seat. I need to pee, but I don't want to interrupt. I'm afraid that at any moment the car is going to erupt into one of those distant, furious rows I hear late at night, the noise coming up in underwater waves through the floor. Instead I look out the window, at the slowly twisted vista of dark old trees that opens up before us. And then I see it. The Green Road.

In front of us is a perfect cathedral nave of trees; they're the darker, older trees, but here they're lined up symmetrically, their branches winding together beautifully and completely to make a perfect green awning overhead. The whole avenue is lit with a gentle green glow. My dad stops the car, and winds the window down. The first thing I notice is the silence. No birdsong, no faint insect buzz. The green road in front of us is still as death.

'I definitely don't know this stretch.' I hate hearing my dad sound so lost and puzzled. He turns to my mum. 'I don't know what to do.' She tosses her cigarette out the window and digs out an old envelope from the glove compartment. 'I've been keeping track of our turns,' she says, a pen appearing from a pocket. 'I think if we go back and keep turning left for the first four turns, it should bring us back to the plantation.' Her fingers flash as she draws a sketchy path back to safety. Beside me, Robin is restless.

'Can we play on the green road?' she calls. My parents' heads are bent together over the impromptu map. I kick Robin in the leg to say *shut up*. She draws in her breath to issue a reproachful whine, and then sees my face and stops. She stares out at the trees instead.

'No playing. We need to get back on track.' He turns over the car engine. It makes an ugly grating noise, grinds and stops.

'Oh for...' He tries it again. This time it grates harder. It sounds like the car is coughing, harsh and metallic.

'Keep trying.' My mum's voice is softer than usual. He does, and this time it just shudders and stops. A cool breeze comes in the open window; it smells like moss and rain, and goosepimples my bare arms. I rub the hard bumps of cold flesh. My dad opens the door and heaves up the bonnet. I wander out and stand behind him, silently.

'Nothing,' he says with a sigh, wiping big hands on his hanky. I look down the green road, at the inviting strip of velvet grass running down the centre, at the glowing light overhead, perfect and uniform. There is a rustle from the hedge, like an animal scurrying to hide. He frowns suddenly, turning round to look at something on the road behind him.

'What?' His eyes swivel from the road back to me.

'Will I go and get help?' I feel an itch to run down the centre of the perfect path, to see my arms and legs dappled in vivid green. He lifts his chin and pauses, listening. I trail a hand along the bush beside me. A thorn snags my sleeve, and I bend down to free it. He turns his head to me.

'Get back in the car!' His voice is rough and loud. I jump back in.

This time when he sits down, he mutters to himself before turning the key. The engine whirrs, coughs harshly, and then – miracle! – it snarls back into life. Robin and Jack cheer beside me. Another rough reverse and we're off. I tilt my head back, flat to the back of the seat behind me and watch the green road dwindle and disappear behind me. The Green Road. Even now, I remember it so clearly, shining like a dark emerald, quiet and hidden in the heart of the forest. My dad follows the tracks, driving faster and faster, then surer and surer as we pass from the green darkness onto hard, rutted tracks. My mum sits beside him silently, and to my surprise I see her hand is tucked into his. By the time we reach the main road it's velvety dark, later than it should be. I loll my head to one side and watch the stars keep pace with us as we drive. And then we're home. We quietly disembark; an unwritten rule has been broken, we haven't been out of the car. Nor did we eat those carefully-packed sandwiches. A few days later my mum will find them in the car boot, sweating and suffocated in their plastic wrapping.

A week later my dad left for good. My memories of him now are smudged, unclear, as if I'm remembering it all through smoked glass. But, sometimes, late at night, when I think of him, I see him walking away from us, down the Green Road.

~

I'm driving mindlessly; my hands moving in a little, practiced dance from indicator to wheel to wipers, and then back again, as the car moves through a blurred landscape of smeared fields. As I drive, I scan left and right, looking for a landmark, anything in this sea of mud and trees that will tell me where I am. I know I'm only an hour at the most from the city, but the countryside around me is almost unrecognisable, battered and splashed with rain. I've been driving steadily for the last hundred miles, my eyes swelling with tears, only one thought in my head, to get back. To get to my dad. I think of him as I drive, his casual arm thrown over the back of the passenger seat, his quiet pleasure at the aimlessness of our long-distant Sunday drives. The rain's grown heavier now, hard, so hard that I can hear the insistent thrumming of the drops on the car roof, strong as a steel drum. The windscreen is a river of water, coursing in great waves from the wipers. The view in front of me buckles, twists, and then disappears.

'Christ,' I say aloud, slowing down. 'This is impossible!'

And then I see it, the dim green causeway opening up before me, the sky replaced by a thick, damp canopy of leaves, the sudden enveloping of the car in a wet cocoon. I slow to a stop, flicking on the car lights. They shine out in the green darkness, revealing a mass of knotted tree-trunks. As I wind the window down, the sudden silence roars in my ears. Then it dissolves into a mass of tiny sounds; a rustling here, a trickling there, the sound of the woods drinking in the rain.

I open the window and stare out at the dim, green light of the dripping woods, and I know I'm finally back on the Green Road, after all these years. I can't quite believe it's real. It's exactly as I remember it. I peer outside. In the real world a whole generation of time has passed; I've grown up, my parents have grown old. But here? Maybe the moss lies marginally thicker on the wet forest floor, maybe the old trees have fused closer together. But that's all. Overhead, the canopy of intertwined branches is woven tight together. The rain thrums hard on it, like the skin of a drum, but only a few large drops splotch through. One lands wetly on my head. I wipe it off absently, staring at the vista before me. What am I even doing, stopping here? I should be on my way. On my way to see my dad. *Dad*...I feel like there's a rock lodged in my throat. I see him again, I picture him driving the car, back turned to me, his habitual pose. I remember the smell of his aftershave, the broadness of his shoulders, one huge man-hand splayed on the wheel.

I shake my head to clear it and rev up the engine, rolling slowly down the Green Road. I bounce on the seat as the car hits the ruts and stones that are almost invisible in the dim light, and pray for the suspension to hold. I turn the corner, and it just keeps on going – another stretch of dark green, with twists of tree-trunks and an unwavering knitted expanse of leaves. There's a flicker of movement in the distance, as of a figure, but when I squint again, it's gone. The wheels bump, the car veers, I turn a corner and, shockingly, the trees part briefly and there's sudden brightness and pelting rain. I stop the car to try and get my bearings, but I've forgotten how hard the rain is coming down. It lashes down on the windshield, a furious barrage, stinging my arms through the open window. I scrabble for the control button, but hit the wrong side and only manage to push the window down further.

I jam on the brakes, and try to jab the button again, but it's stuck. Rain bombards through the half-open window, hard and fast. The side of my face and my arm are cold and soaked. I squint ahead desperately for cover and see the Green Road continues in another massive huddle of trees twined around a building. I put my foot down on the accelerator and power forward, great gouts of red-brown water spraying in huge arcs about me. The car skids messily to a stop under the canopy, and I sit back, feeling the seat back press solidly into me. No point in trying to move until I can get the window working – right now the trees overhead are preventing the downpour reaching me, I'm protected within the damp, green tunnel of the Green Road. The air smells of loamy earth and wet animals. I instinctively look down at the phone in my hand. The signal has disappeared – natural enough for a forest track, but I need to call the hospital – and soon. I need to call my family. I need to find the way back. I think all these things, and yet I feel my hand on the doorhandle, and then my feet swing down to hit the wet ground outside.

It's strange walking here. The tiny drips and drops are the only sounds. There should be birds here, I think, confused. Squirrels. Certainly insects. But though I scan sharply around me, there's none there, no tell-tale cloud of midges, no bumbling bee-hum, not even the humdrum buzz of a fly. Just silence, except for my feet squelching wetly on the ground. I'm already up to my ankles, mud leaking over the sides of my shoes, when I stop, puzzled. Why am I walking when I have a perfectly good car sitting parked on the road? I rub my head as I walk back. It's starting to hurt. There was a wall, I think, a wall, somewhere here. Yes, there's a wall, definitely, half-hidden by vivid green ivy. I push my way through the wet ditch, branches poking me like hard fingers. It's a little huddle of deserted buildings, linked by a tumbledown wall, with one elegant curved arch opening up into a sea of wet barley. Just behind is a lone farmhouse, a muddy, low building with pieces of farm machinery, and – Oh joy! – a Mitsubishi jeep parked outside, its red paintwork faded to a pink-puce. I put my hood up and run to it. *Directions*, I think, standing outside. I look at my phone again. Still no signal. I bite my lip and hammer a fist sideways on the wet wood. Overhead the rain pours down, relentless. No answer. I try again. Then again. There is what might be a tiny flicker of movement at one of the windows, but when I turn to look, it's gone. I stand there stupidly, my hood tilted sideways, hair now plastered flat to my skull. For a split second the house, the trees, the jeep all waver before me: a burst of static ripples across my vision.

I close my eyes, and when I open them I'm back in the car again. The window is open and the rain is pelting in.

—

For a second I just sit there, perfectly still. *What the hell?* It makes no sense, no sense at all. *I must have fallen asleep*, I think wildly. *That's it. I was dreaming.* But my feet are soaked and muddy. And then I stop thinking. I jab the button for the electric window but the pane of glass won't budge. I wipe as much water as possible off the door and try again. Nothing.

Damn it, I think, *I'll just drive on. I'll get soaked. So what?* I jam the key in the engine. It whirrs sharply, and then dies with an ominous rattle. More in resignation than hope, I try again. This time there is a rougher, clunking sound underneath the whirr, but it still refuses to start. I sit, warm, heavy drops oozing out from my hairline to splash down my nose and onto my T-shirt, leaving coin-sized marks. I am, I realise belatedly, absolutely soaked through. Shifting in my seat, I hear the *shluck-schluck* of my jeans sticking to the leather. My phone is still in my pocket. I retrieve it. Still no signal. It sits in my hand, heavy and useless.

It's the last thing I want to do, but I force myself out of the car again. I need to go back to that farmhouse. I need help. The rain has slackened off now, I think. It could be my imagination but it definitely seems warmer and less hostile, falling soft and steady against the wet tangles of leaves and briars around me. I walk towards the ruined buildings, hoping to see some flicker of life in the farmhouse behind them.

Among the symphony of raindrops, I hear the unmistakeable sound of a car in the distance, coming nearer. *A car! I'm saved!* I start running, half slipping, on the muddy path, trying to reach the sound. But just then it cuts out abruptly. I skid to a halt, confused. Where is it? There's a quick rustle in the undergrowth, but when I look there's nothing there. Common sense tells me that it's a rabbit or a rat, but common sense feels very far away. I force myself to breathe the calming way my dad taught me – seven seconds, through the nose – then hold – then out, eleven seconds through the nose. It's almost working. I feel my heart slow down slightly. And then it happens again; a tremor, a waver, a ripple of static and then everything resolves itself again.

I stand perfectly still, and open my eyes, I'm in exactly the same place I was. But it's not raining anymore – nor has it been for some time. The ground is dry and hard underneath me. I stamp my foot on it, and feel the rutted earth. *What's going on?* I look behind me. My car isn't there. But when I glance back in front, I can see the glint of light on metal. *That car I heard!* I start to run forward, then I stop, dumb with horror at the strangeness of it all.

In front of me is a car, alright. But it's not my Micra. It's a Hillman Hunter. I crouch down, heart beating thickly in my ears. *What's happening?* I part the leaves with my hands and watch. It's not just a Hillman Hunter; it's *our* old Hillman Hunter. The car seems to shimmer in a wave of white static and then is still again. Like a sequence from an old-fashioned Super 8 film, I see the door open and my dad step out. He's so young I want to cry, so easy and lithe in his movements. He flips up the bonnet and hunches over the engine. Now the back door is opening, and with a final, enormous wave of disbelief, I watch my child-self climb out. I've got my hair in plaits – I can remember the tightness of them, the way they pulled at the skin of my scalp.

'Nothing,' says my dad, almost to himself. I watch myself, little-me, stand beside him, tummy stuck out, face frowning. He rubs a hand through his rumpled black hair and sighs. I think of the last time I saw him, shrunken and white in a hospital bed. My eyes well up with hot tears. I try to brush them aside, but my arm jostles the bush beside me. He frowns, and looks directly at where I'm hidden.

'What?' It's my child-self. 'Will I go and get help?'

I think of her, of little-me, walking off by herself. I can't help it. I reach out and touch her sleeve, lightly.

And then it all happens at once. A shock reverberates through my body, a powerful surge biting my hand. The Hillman Hunter starts to waver and dissolve, but not before I hear my dad shout 'Get back in the car!'

⁓

'What the—?' I suck my injured finger, and then pull it out of my mouth. It's already bruising, a swelling purple mound blooming on my fingertip. I lean back against the wall, sticking my hand under my armpit. The rain is back, electric with sound, whipping at my face.

'I need to get out!' I shout, and my voice rings hard in the silence. I need to get out of here. I slide my phone out of my pocket with my uninjured hand. Still no signal. I need to go. *Dad*, I think, but even my thoughts seem weak, distant. I am paralysed by the sudden, stuttering rush of water from the trees above. I examine my finger again. The bruise is darkening. Out of the corner of my eye, I catch a movement to my left.

I turn and look sharply, but there's only the long grass swaying under the force of the rain. *Swoosh*. There it goes again – this time I see it, like the oily wriggle of a stoat, shaking the overgrown grass in a long, sinuous movement. I can't tell you why that frightens me so badly, but it does. Then I see it from my right side – the same snaking, low movement, the parting of the grass. All I see is a shadow, and barely-glimpsed at that. I'm suddenly burning up, a great hot wash of fear surging up me, torching my cheeks. The movement flickers again, now on both sides. I'm caught between them, whatever they are. Rain and sweat pours down my forehead, stinging hot in my eyes. In my peripheral vision, I see hillocks spring up in the long grass, and then ripple in long, sweeping arcs toward me. There's a dark wave underneath the matted grass. I moan, dry and airless; the sound of it galvanises me. I turn and run, tripping, skidding, back to my car. I press the buttons over and over trying to raise the window, anything to seal myself off, pulling at the glass in a mad fear, then giving up and twisting the key around in the ignition. It rachets and growls, then there's that awful, decisive *clunk*. My breath is hoarse, I'm saying 'Please' over and over, I don't know why, I don't know what I'm begging for. I can't look out the window, I won't. I don't know what's out there. I don't want to know what's out there. My wet hands slide over the wheel, my breath coming now in great, tearing sobs. I'm looking straight ahead, but I see the grass shaking, flailing, there's a flurry of movement.

'Please' I shout and wrench the key around again. This time the engine coughs even harder, groans and – oh God, oh joy! – it bursts into life. I throw the car into reverse and skid down the road, wheels screaming in a slide of mud and spraying water. The window shudders up with a jerk and a screech. I don't care, I'm driving faster now, windscreen blurred, bouncing down the rough road. I look in the rear-view mirror – the trees are moving now, twisting back and forth, and the grass is alive, a boiling torrent of movement. I'm going so fast now, when I look back at the road, I see a tree loom up in front of me, going from far to near in a heartbeat. A mass of wet branches that opens up to engulf me. I just have time to think *Dad!* before I hit it.

~

After the crash there's a beat of silence, then a babble of voices. I can see a green pool of light behind my eyelids.

'Are you OK?'

'Help her up!'

'Here you are, darling.'

Something is wrong. Something is very wrong. I see the farmhouse Jeep parked up at an angle in the ditch. I'm leaning heavily against my car, the rain warm and insistent on my body. I touch my face, wincing as the bruised fingertip makes contact with my chin. Something. *Something's...* I stop and feel my skin again, incredulous. It's rough and pendulous to the touch. I scrabble at my neck, folds of wattle unfamiliar and awful between my fingers.

'Dear Jesus.' I grab at the side mirror of the car. When I look it in, everything stands still. The worried voices dim, the screaming *nee-naw* of an ambulance in the distance seems to grow fainter. There's only me in the mirror, but it's not a me I recognise. I stare, my heart beating thick and fast in my ears. My face has melted in stippled, heavy, fleshy folds that run from nose to mouth. My forehead's a mass of tangled creases, my puckered lips peel back in a frozen scream. Only my eyes are unchanged, stark and bright with fright.

I've been on the Green Road.

I've been on the Green Road for far too long.

I can only stand there, transfixed by my own awful image, as the ambulance siren draws nearer. The yellow-green light of the woods pours down on me, merciless as the rain.

The Green Road comes directly from a memory – or possibly a dream – from childhood, of being driven down a road completely covered with trees; the foliage was so thick I had a feeling of being underwater. I distinctly remember the feeling this gave me, a queer thrill, like I'd arrived unexpectedly into a fairytale. I thought of Sleeping Beauty's castle, overgrown with trees and hedges. But when I was writing this, I kept thinking of Tir na nÓg, the Land of the Ever Young, which appears in the Fianna cycle of myths. In the story of Oisin in the Land of Tir na nÓg, he falls in love with the fairy Niamh and leaves Ireland to live with her in a magical land where no-one grows old. Eventually he grows homesick and decides to visit Ireland, but Niamh makes him promise not to dismount from the magical white horse she gives him. He returns, but is dismayed to recognise no-one. Eventually he disobeys Niamh's order and alights from the horse, only to age three hundred years. Time in Tir na nÓg obeys no human law, and that's the concept I wanted to play with in this story.

SCARECROW,
SCARECROW

he wind is high this morning. The wet grass flips sharply against my legs as I start my automatic ritual. I count them first – one, two, three, four, five, six. I walk around them, checking, wrapping a scarf tighter here, pulling a jumper down there, stuffing in straw, tight and snug under the tattered clothes. My eyes hurt with the low, queer light of dawn, a dirty white glare that lightens the hills. I tip the scarecrow hats back, one after the other, to reveal blank faces of ratty brown hessian, with rough black marks for eyes. My body is clumsy with tiredness, my feet stumble, heavy-footed, over each other. I take out the jam-jar from my pocket, and unscrew it. The contents are a dark, gelid red. I close my eyes and dip a finger in, then trace two daubs of red on the brown sacking, to mimic where the eyes should be. The scarecrow's red glare follows me as I move on to the next. *One, two, three...* I stop after the third one, and let my arm fall to my side. What am I doing? What am I *doing?* I screw the lid back on with chilly, reddened hands and throw it convulsively into the long grass. My legs fold up like a deckchair and I sit flat on the damp grass, crying in great, draining gulps, tearing, hoarse cries that rise up into the still air of the dawn.

—

I remember Mrs. MacDonnell coming into our shop. It's first thing in the morning and I'm sleepily filling a mop-bucket when I hear three things happen in a row like ticks of a clock – the ping of the bell, the creaking backswing of the door, and her excited suck-in of breath. Her apron is dirty and tied on wrong. Mrs. MacDonnell never left home unless she was immaculate.

'Mary?' From that one word I can tell my mother's surprise at her appearance.

'Oh Jane! I have to tell – I came over straightaway – You'll never guess,' Mrs MacDonnell's lips work over each other like purple maggots.

'Hush now.' My mother holds up a hand. 'Come through, won't you. We'll have tea.' She turns around and notices me. 'Keep cleaning the floor, there, good girl' she says, distracted. I see Mrs. MacDonnell pass through the door to the kitchen, her hands patting down and untying her apron as she scuttles in. Of course I don't keep washing the floor. I lower the bucket, slop out a noisy mopful of grey water, and then slip my feet out of my heavy shoes and pad closer to the kitchen door. The old door leaks sound through its network of cracks and draughts. That's how I heard about our money troubles and the big fight that led to my father leaving. That's how I've heard my mother crying, day after day, in a dull, useless sort of way. I press an ear to the mottled, chipped paint.

'...I tell you, it's him. Oh yes!' Mrs. MacDonnell.

'Mary, now, you can't be sure'. My mother's voice, softer, more hesitant.

A large sigh. 'I must say, I thought you'd be more excited. You know it's the only way.' My mother mumbles something inaudible. I feel a sudden, sharp desire to pee. I squash my thighs together and concentrate. Behind the door, the voices drop into a murmur. I jig up and down noiselessly in my socks and try to focus on picking out a word here and there.

'I'll be off then.' I hear the squeal of chair-legs scraping back on the worn lino. I step back into my shoes and lift the mop, churning it round the edge of the floor in a thick, wet tangle of fronds. There is a low-voiced goodbye, and then the bell pings again.

My mother takes the mop gently out of my hands. 'Go on, then, I'll finish that. You need to go and do the rounds on the hill.'

'But it's *morning*! You know I go there in the evening!' I am reluctant to go. I am curious. The ping of the door still hangs in the air, ominous, interesting; even the air here holds bubbles of possibility, barely touched.

Her face is sad. 'I think you need to.' She looks around the familiar terrain of the shop – the stacked shelves, the little fridge, the counter. 'I think everything is about to change.'

In the village we all have our jobs. Village-jobs as opposed to family-jobs. You'd call them chores, I suppose. Mr. Kelly from the village hall allots them. He's the nearest thing we have to a mayor. Some of us fix fences, some check the locks on the barns, others put flowers at the church door. The old men stand at the perimeter points of the village, at the crossroads, the church-gate, the new estate. No-one really knows why this is important, but it fills their days. They suck their pipes and watch the traffic, with every sign of enjoyment. My chores are different. I look after the scarecrows on the hill. It's nice up there, you know. I spend a lot of time on the hill, especially now, in high summer, when the coconutty smell of the gorse hangs warm and thick in the air, and the grass interweaves to form a springy carpet under bare feet. I secretly think that it's the best chore of all. These are my favourite times, sitting on the hill in high summer, overlooking the village, the late evening sun in my face, the silent ring of scarecrows at my back.

I've counted all six, checked them all and they are pristine, every straw in place. Nothing needs adjusting. From here the village looks so small. I can trace its perimeters easily, from the dark hedges around the church down the dusty road that ribbons past the school, the line of old estate cottages winding past the two pubs, the post office and the shop, then further down the road to the new estate at the end. From here it looks like any other place.

Nearer to hand, it feels like nowhere else. It is the place I was born in, the place I've always lived in and the place I'll probably live in forever. As I climb down the hill, the air becomes heavier, stranger; it smells of old dust and unopened windows. There is a feeling in the air here in the village, a feeling of inevitable endings, of rain about to fall, of shops getting ready to close, of gates swinging slowly shut. The fields stretch out like a neverland of wet mud-ruts. Down the road is the eternally identical view of the street and houses. It is a village forever trapped in a listless Sunday afternoon where the main street is dead, and clouds tremble on the edge of rain. Time is drawn out, like old, stringy chewing gum. There is a dull rhythm to life here, a sense of seasons demarcated by matches, the steam threshing, the pattern and church holidays. Cars hum to life in the mornings and evenings. Apart from that there is the dead silence of overheated stale air in summertime, replaced by a cold, frozen stillness in the winter. We're different here. Ask anyone. Ask anyone from the neighbouring villages about us and they'll look at you sideways, trying to gauge how their answer might offend. If they're being tactful they'll say we're different. If pressed they'll say strange. If honest they'll give a more forceful answer – *quare strange*. I've heard them call us that before. It fits. But it hasn't always been that way.

~

I hear the children chanting as I scramble down over the slippery grass towards the village, their thin voices rising high in the still air. They are singing the scarecrow song, the one that begins with the chant – *Scarecrow, scarecrow on the hill / Watching over all until*. Their twig-legs skitter over and back, across the rope that thwacks solid against the road. I see a group clustered outside the pub, heads together, voices lowered. A pulse of unease clenches in my stomach, low and insistent. Something is different. I walk down the road. The trees along the street shade it dark green, I feel the heat of my arms turn to a welcome coolness as I walk. Everything is neatly ordered, the houses all in a row, the cars parked tidily outside, even the tombstones in the cemetery are ordered and precise. The village is polished, except, of course, for the new estate. A jumble of half-finished houses, it stands raw and awkward against the mellow stone and green lawns of the village. Seen from the hill it's all knees and elbows, half-finished walls and piles of building material. I wander past and kick at the dirty 'For Sale' sign that leans against the verge. I imagine I can hear again the muffled sound of weeping behind the shop door, my father's angry, low voice, my mother's words twisting out between sobs. 'You knew it wouldn't work. You knew!'

We all knew, in our hearts, that the estate wouldn't work. *Why* we knew is one story. But the more important one is *what* we knew.

The oldest story told in our village is the story of St. Finn. According to the stories, Finn (or Fionn) was an early disciple of St. Patrick, spreading the new doctrines of Christianity. He came here, to our great-great-many-times-great-grandfathers and grandmothers. He stood on the hill and told them about a holy, dark-skinned man who could make magic, turn water to wine, return sick men to health. And when he finished they picked up stones and threw them. Threw them until there was nothing left on the hill but a melted red flesh-blur, heaped with splashed stones. He cursed us before he died, they say. He said 'Never prosper. Never leave.' In the centuries that came after, the legend changed, adapted. *He cursed us*, they started to say. They say it still, knowledgably, as the sun goes down, and men talk of dark things. *He cursed us until we can make restitution.* That's what the children sing about, a time that the curse will be lifted. That's why we have the perimeters, the scarecrows watching us, the locked barns, the fresh flowers at the church, a maze of ceremonies, and endless, vigilant, anxious rituals of protection. *It needs to be so*, we say. *It needs to be so until the curse lifts.*

In the meantime, we are careful. Careful not to brag. Careful not to leave. There are generations of us here now; layered on each other, aligned through a series of increasingly close unions. We don't try to leave. We still go on day trips, excursions to other towns. But no prolonged absences. We don't leave. Not anymore. Not since the last lot tried, not since the subsequent rash of accidents, the big car-crash, the drowning, the disappearance of the hitch-hiker. Now we hug the village close, close as the hill that wraps around it. But the caution doesn't banish the fear. This fear touches on the fringes of living here. You feel it in the evening when the cattle stop lowing abruptly, for no reason. You feel it when a branch snaps behind you on a dark night. You feel it when a dog starts barking, insistently, louder, hysterically at an empty yard.

I scuff my shoe against the old breeze block that rests on the road verge. Time to go back, I suppose.

'You'll kick holes in those shoes.' It's a friendly voice but unfamiliar, and close behind me. I turn, startled. The stranger smiles at me, eyes creased in a sociable grin. His hair is long and the bright sun behind it creates a hazy copper halo. He is, I guess, in his late twenties, ten years or so older than me.

'What happened here?' he asks. The sweep of his arm encompasses the estate.

I squint against the sun. 'Well, the village came together to buy the land and hired a developer. He ran out of money before he finished and just left. No-one knows where he is now. But the houses were never finished.'

He suck-whistles through his teeth. 'All of it gone? All that investment?'

I shrug. 'Curse of St. Finn', I say nonchalantly.

He laughs. 'I heard that story when I was a kid. My aunt is from the village. You know Jinny Kelly?'

Mr. Kelly's wife. 'I do' I say, looking at him with frank interest. 'Her husband's the one that gives out the village jobs. I do the scarecrows.' We fall into step beside each other as we walk away from the estate down the dusty road towards the main strip of houses and shops. Dust puffs around our feet. His name is Ryan. He tells me that he is writing a book about the local legends in the area, and the St. Finn's story is one he's particularly drawn to. I tell him about the people who tried to leave. I make it dramatic, my voice low and meaningful as I describe their unfortunate histories. He is rapt, fascinated.

'So the scarecrows *protect* the village?'

I shrug, 'Maybe. That's what they say. The children sing a song about it.'

'I've haven't heard it yet. Look forward to that.' He pauses. 'So everyone still believes in the curse, right?'

'Of course. Isn't that,' – I turn and point at the estate – 'isn't that proof of it? Nothing goes right here.' He nods absent-mindedly. This is good. I walk proudly alongside him and feel vital, important. I know he is storing all this information I can give him. With an effort, I resist the urge to skip. 'And here is one of the barns. We keep them locked, you know. I can't really remember why, it's something to do with keeping the village valuables safe.' He nods, we walk on in silence.

'Well, I'm going here,' I say, stopping at the door of the shop. 'See you around.'

'That you will.' He smiles again, that warm, creased grin. I stare at him. A watery, desperate fear fills me. My legs feel disconnected to my body, and my voice, when I find it, comes from a long way away. 'Your eyes,' I finally manage to say. His eyes are wonderful, strange, one blue, one brown.

He laughs. 'In another century I would have been burned as a witch!'

I watch him go, a heavy, hopeless feeling deep in my stomach.

~

I don't see him again. I don't see him at all till later the next night.

It had been a strange, thundery, restless kind of day, the air rippling with hot, sharp gusts of wind, like an oven opening and shutting abruptly. Late in the evening it started to rain, a long, monotonous downpour that slapped the window panes with a splattering rhythm. I had a headache and went to bed early, burying my hot face in the cool underside of the pillow. Sometime later, I woke, tense. A noise? There it is again, a shout. I switch on the lamp and stumble towards the window, eyes blurred with sleep. There's a knot of men with torches outside in the rain, arguing. I open the window, and the rain hits cold and hard on my face. There is a struggle outside, some shouts, the sound of a blow. Then grunts, the noise of something dragging. Footsteps squelch by. I strain to see. They're carrying something heavy between them. As they pass by, I see them for a second, outlined in the warm spill of lamplight from my window. The familiar faces from the shop, the houses, the barns, the hills, all pass by. Between them they are carrying the heavy body. His eyes have rolled upwards, but I would recognise that long copper hair anywhere.

I shake, frozen in the window-frame. My throat works, my lips move uselessly. *Ryan*, I think in a sharp agony. In an instant, unheard, soft, my mother's hand is over my mouth, her warm body pressed close to my back.

'Hush there, quiet now,' she breathes in my ear. Her breath smells of milk.

I twist away from her. 'What's happening? What are they doing?'

'It's what always happens.' Her face is in shadow, but I feel the sadness roll off her in waves. 'It's what happens every time. They think it will lift the curse.'

'It's happened before?'

She sighs. 'Twice that I remember. More times your grandmother would remember.' I start to cry helplessly, hot tears rolling down my face. She holds me tight to her in the darkness. Outside, a voice pipes up, a child's voice singing, thin and true;

Scarecrow, scarecrow on the hill
Watching over all until

Blue and brown eyes!
Brown and blue eyes!
How many red men must I kill? – one – two – three – four

I don't follow them. I'm ashamed that I don't follow them. But I hear what happens, every bit. His cries tear the night air. At dawn the men take him away up the hill, and soon the village is silent again. All the time I don't sleep. I lie in bed, electric with horror, then give up and simply sit at the window, waiting. Later, just as the sky is starting to lighten, I see Mr. Kelly knock on the door of the shop. My mother opens it cautiously, a crack. I can see his coat is splashed with mud and something darker, stickier.

'For the scarecrows,' he says, passing my mother the jar. He nods slowly. 'You'll tell her what to do.'

I'm on the hill. I've finally stopped crying, cold and exhausted, face stiff with salt tears. The sun is starting to streak a livid yellow across the bottom of the skyline. My head hurts with the horror of it all. I drop the jar. It falls, unheeded in the long grass. There is only one thing I can do. I get up and walk towards the perimeter, by the scarecrows, and on, through the wet stalks of corn, down the rutted path. The scarecrows stare blindly after me. I want to leave. I need to leave. I'm sick of it all; the shop bell dinging, the thick silences, my mother's low crying, the pervasive unease. I walk toward the perimeter of the village.

Can I do it?

I stand at the border. Deep in my gut I feel the pull of the village, dull and insistent, the steady drag of its sour, repetitive rituals of life.

Can I do it?

I don't know.

This is the first of two stories that I've grouped together in this collection that deal with the disruption caused by the Celtic Tiger; a period of immense prosperity in Ireland from 2000-2008, culminating in the global economic crash. Like in 'Scarecrow, Scarecrow', this crash resulted in the formation of 'ghost estates', tragic, abandoned developments that manifested all over the countryside. At one stage it was estimated that over 650 such estates existed in Ireland, developments that totalled more than 300,000 empty houses. As with 'The Crow War' I was also fascinated by the insular nature of remote villages in Ireland, places with old legends and long memories.

WHAT LIES
BENEATH

t's much later, when I go to unpack my bags in the prim, pink room at the front of the *Santa Maria* B&B, that I find the diary. It's a nice, green Moleskine notebook with the name 'James Baker' penned in neat capital letters on the first page. My initial instinct is to ask the landlady about it.

'The amount of rubbish that people leave behind!' She clicks her tongue in indignation, (a little rich, I think, given the amount of residual dust in my room.) 'Sorry about that. I'll throw it away.' She puts out her hand to take it from me. I feel a certain reluctance to hand it over. It looks interesting – and, of course, it's a very nice notebook, only half used.

'No, it's fine' I say. 'I'd hate to lose a journal myself. I'll keep it in case someone comes back for it.'

She shrugs and drops her hand.

'Whatever you think. Now breakfast is strictly seven to eight-thirty and then all guests have to vacate by eleven each morning. You can come back from six in the evening'. She looks at me with narrowed eyes, as if my story of working locally was a carefully-constructed lie. 'Six, no exceptions.' I wonder, briefly, what the lure of lurking surreptitiously around the B&B would be, with its dusty vestibule filled with sad, faded plastic flowers, umbrellas, a lone metal tennis racket and an endless array of blu-tacked signs handwritten in cramped italics on yellowed, curling paper.

I return to my unpacking. It's mostly books and crumpled black clothes that will need ironing. My toiletries go into the dark little ensuite bathroom, with its low-watt bulb and tiny porthole window that – I squint – seems to be covered with some kind of tarpaulin on the outside, rendering the tiny room even darker. I hang up a photograph on an unused hook, spread my favourite embroidered Indian throw over the bed, and try to make the cold, soulless room feel like the home it has to be for a few weeks.

All in all, it's only much later that I remember the diary.

～

August 18th

I'd forgotten how weird it is to move to a different city. I'd forgotten the way the air smells different in a new place, how hard new accents are to follow and how strange streets seem just that little bit darker at night. Coming here from Cork, I miss the oddest things; the sing-song voices and the endless twisty-turny streets that duck and dip and glide over rivers. Here, outside, the streets are full of hard-voiced men in tracksuits, there's noise and traffic and bustle all day and all night. Never mind, this was what I wanted, a new job, a new start, a promotion. Nothing left for me in Cork now that Maggie and I have broken up.

I have to remind myself of this in the middle of the night, when drunk men are singing outside my ground floor window and I'm lying awake in a cold, pink room. At least it's quiet inside, I doubt if there's more than a couple of people staying here, judging by the sounds overhead.

At least I start the new job tomorrow.

~

I put down the diary and smile. *Someone like me*, I think. Another blow-in to the city, someone just as homesick as me. For some reason this makes me feel better. I pull the pink candlewick bedspread around my shoulders (*candlewick, really? Is this the seventies?*), and read on.

~

August 19ᵗʰ

Ok, so I'm home. Well, 'home' might be too grandiose a term. Back to the place where I sleep might be more appropriate. That pink room – urgh – and that grim little bathroom that I can barely face showering in... I skipped breakfast today, too nervous to eat. Just had my first full day in the new job, and my head is aching from the different faces, the many conversations, and the nervous coffee drinking. I was so excited to get the job, it's a Fortune 500 company you know! – one of those ones that just leapt out of nowhere during the boom and in spite of the economic backlash, it just keeps on growing and thriving.

The place itself seems OK, it's on the Docklands, one of the new space-age buildings that manages to be both very high-tech and very awkward to negotiate your way around. The whole façade is glass, nice on a day like today when the sun is shining, but a bit more bleak in winter, I imagine. I'm in a cubicle facing out towards the glass expanse and within striking distance of kitchen and loos – excellent.

As for my job, it's still a little undefined. I'm beside a very quiet blonde man called Harry who spends his time slowly and covertly reading a horror novel, and a dark-haired girl called Rosa who seems as bored as I am, judging by her frequent sighs. No one really talked – we were all in a kind of limbo, waiting to be summoned to different locations. We're all new and all in Sales, from what I can judge, but no-one's assigned us anything to do yet. Maybe they're evaluating us first?

It seems like James Butler and I have more in common than I think. I'm also starting a new job tomorrow. It's stupid, but I feel a prickling of nervousness, that strange tingle of weirdness that's part-homesickness, part-fancy. I put down the diary and get up from the bed. As I do so, my foot hits something – a tennis racket, hidden under the bed. I pull it out and place it on the dressing table, wondering who has left a racket behind – James Butler himself? The room is dark now, but I can hear the sounds of Dublin nightlife outside. Shouts, a laugh, and a snatch of song. There's a strong acid scent of hot vinegar rolling out in waves from the fish and chip shop down the road. My stomach makes a squirming motion, and I realise how hungry I am.

Ten minutes later, I'm walking slowly back towards the *Santa Maria*, the scalding, delicious chips puffing out hot potato between my teeth. I turn the handle of the inner door and the landlady pops out ponderously, like a mumsy jack-in-the box. 'No hot food to be brought in.' She points at one of the thumbtacked signs. 'OK,' I shrug. 'I'll finish them outside.' I stand, pointedly, just outside the dusty doors, reading the cards idly as I wolf down the rest of the chips. Most of the signs are blunt warnings: 'Do not use all hot water', 'No breakfast served past 8.30', 'No visitors to rooms past 6pm', but some are small, pathetic boasts, like my favourite 'All our rooms are ensuite!' (It's the exclamation point I particularly like). I shake my head and laugh, and then scrunch up the bag and toss it in the pavement bin. Back in the hideous pink room I strip off my clothes and fold them over a chair back. I line up my battered Converse carefully beside my black stiletto work heels. Time for a shower. My body feels cramped and cold, and I'm craving the hard, fast spatter of hot water on my muscles. I sigh and flick on the low-wattage light in the ensuite.

Shadows dance over the greasy walls; fragments of me refracted by the shower glass. I look at my hollow-eyed reflection in the spotted mirror as I pull the shower cord.

I take a deep breath and step into the spray. But as soon as I'm lathered in orange and bergamot shower gel, the water starts to cool to lukewarm, and my soapy skin is suddenly bumpy with gooseflesh.

'For God's sake!' I reach out and pull the shower cord angrily, once, twice, three times, until the water jerks out again. This time it's hot – like a shot of fiery needles. I jump back clumsily and knock my elbow hard off the glass. The shower glass vibrates, and as it does so, the light starts to flicker. The tiny room goes dark; there's just my ragged breathing and the sound of water on tiles. For a few seconds I feel a flicker of terror; I'm buried in this hot, wet darkness like an insect under glass. Then the light glimmers weakly on again, but I've had enough. I grab my towel and push the door open, towelling myself dry in the cold air of the pink room.

I sit down on the bed and let my breathing subside. I need to get up early to make a good impression. I look around my chill little room and switch on the bedside lamp, partly for its pool of yellow warmth, partly to read. *Just few entries more*, I think.

⌒

August 20th

Had a strange day today. A strange day and strange night. At work today, I started talking to the dark-haired girl, Rosa Molloy, who sits at the desk next to mine. (I had to do something, the boredom was starting to kill me – it was either that or read the phone directory.) She's from Omagh in Tyrone, and just moved down. Turns out she's staying in exactly the same B&B as me! We were exclaiming over the coincidence, when Harry quietly pointed out that he's staying there too. Apparently there's some deal with the company that all newcomers stay there while looking for accommodation. We spent a gleeful half hour comparing rooms; turns out her pad is decorated in a dark puce, so perhaps I'm luckier with the pink than I thought. We agreed the bathrooms are a marvel of modern science, like some kind of experiment in engineering discomfort. Rosa claims they were originally wardrobes, converted at minimal expense. She's funny, and pretty too.

We waited all afternoon, until a man with a beard came by, checked our names on a clipboard, confirmed our addresses and left, muttering about us being assigned tasks tomorrow as part of a new division. Harry's still placidly reading his horror novel – all this time and he's only a quarter way through. Maybe I'll bring a book tomorrow?

—

I feel my eyes slowly fall shut, and then open again. I try to read on, then wake when the book falls from my hand. It's morning, the lamp is still on, and I'm late for breakfast.

—

'Hey. Haven't seen you round here before, have I?' The man beside me at the coffee machine is smiling and well-groomed, slick black hair gliding back in neatly parallel lines from his brow.

'No,' I say, and hesitate. I've strayed from my allocated empty room upstairs, and am unsure if I am entitled to the cappuccino I now hold. 'I'm new.'

'Ah. Which division? Marketing? – go on, say it's Marketing!' His brown eyes crease in a wide smile.

'Sales. A new division of it. Up on floor five.' I smile by way of apology.

'Oh.' His face is suddenly and carefully polite, the warmth washing away, his eyes avoiding mine. 'Well that's fine. I guess I'll see you around.'

I'm left, mouth slightly open, feeling foolish. *Damn Dublin men*, I think bitterly. Obviously Sales is some kind of lower-caste operation compared to the hallowed realms of Marketing. I feel an acid prickle of tears behind my eyes and walk quickly back upstairs to the lonely room of deserted cubicles. I've no idea who my early arrival was meant to impress. There's no one else here, nor has there been all day. At least the rude Marketing man acknowledged my existence – before he cut the conversation short. No-one's paid any attention to me otherwise, not the receptionist who directed me here, with barely a bored flicker of her eyelids, nor the bearded man who came by earlier to confirm I was, in fact, here. He didn't even ask me anything but my name and address. *Just like in the diary*. I wonder if this is the same place. It must be, if they have some kind of contract with it to house new employees.

'Hi!' I say when he comes by. It comes out a little too enthusiastically.

'Hi.' He seems surprised. 'I'm Sean. Do we know each other from somewhere?'

'No.' I feel awkward. 'I think you know a... um... a friend of mine. James Baker?'

For a moment, there's a strange flicker, like a spasm, that crosses his face. 'Not sure I know who you mean,' he says smoothly.

'Oh. OK.' I know he's lying but can't imagine why. Remembering James makes me think of the diary, and wish I'd brought it. Anything to pass the time. I shrug, kick off my uncomfortable but smart shoes, and read The Guardian on my smartphone, as the clock ticks drearily by to five o'clock, when I'm free to roam about the city in my crippling stiletto heels until I can go home at six.

This is so stupid, I think when I'm back in the *Santa Maria*. *I'm here in this amazing city and I can't think of anywhere to go*. I'd been so jubilant, pointing out all there was to see to my envious friends back home in Dundalk – the galleries, the shops, the theatre. But the galleries and shops are shut and there's no way I'm going to fork out to go to the theatre on my own. So here I am, lonely as hell, stuck in the pink room that always seems vaguely cold. My crackly analogue TV only gives me the choice of either a blizzard-like jumpy version of 'Fair City' or a current affairs programme. I switch it off with a sigh and make a mental note to spend my lunchbreak tomorrow buying a jumper or a hoodie. And some books to read. For now at least I have the diary. I unwrap a bar of chocolate – one of two, tonight's nutritious dinner – and settle down with a sigh.

~

<u>August 21st</u>

Today was a lot more cheery. Got to walk to work with Rosa today (I didn't see Harry at breakfast), and we spent an amusing morning playing cards for imaginary millions (Rosa had the forethought to bring a pack of cards in). She has a gorgeous Northern accent, musical and sonorous, with a little flick upwards in intonation at the end of her sentences. I think I'm getting a little obsessed. It's probably a lot to do with missing Maggie. If I'm honest, it's probably even more to do with our internment in this godforsaken room. No sign of Harry all day. Maybe he's given up waiting to be assigned. Or maybe (and this one stings a little) maybe he's already been assigned to a higher-level job? I tried to ask the man with the beard today – Sean is his name – but he just muttered something about a re-organisation taking place, and that we'd know more later in the week.

Went home and to my surprise, Rosa decided we should go out – the good ship Santa Maria is just too awful to bear another night of. Spent an inordinate amount of time getting ready – normally it's just five minutes, but I wanted to iron my favourite Paul Smith shirt and apply just the right amount of aftershave. I even managed to elbow my way into the ensuite to have a long shower, though the damn light kept flickering on and off. Probably a faulty connection – if I wasn't in a happy haze about going out, I'd be legitimately worried about the electrics here.

Rosa's knocking. More anon.

August 22ⁿᵈ

So Rosa and I went out for something to eat in the city centre (Italian, delicious, crazy expensive), and then for a few drinks at a nearby bar, somewhere old-fashioned and (according to Rosa) frequented by Joyce. Living the cultural life at last! Actually, to be honest, it was more than a few drinks. We were fairly langered coming back, the lights were blurring around us like fireworks, I was weaving about the footpath, and we kept bumping into each other. One of those brilliant nights where everything seems hilarious – we were imagining staying in that nest of cubicles, playing cards and drinking coffee until we retire. Bumped and banged up the stairs, no doubt waking everyone with our gurgled laughter and shushing noises (I'm convinced I saw the landlady's sour face peep around her curtains as we fumbled with the front door). Flung my door open and invited Rosa in for coffee (with a massive, eye-dislocating wink that makes me shudder to remember it), but she just gave me a hug, tutted loudly and tottered off.

Awful hangover all day today. No sign of Harry again. This time, when Sean appeared, I didn't have the will to ask him anything. I just drank water, ate paracetamol, and watched the clock. Rosa spent the day with her head on her arms, fitfully sleeping and groaning. Writing this in bed – when I came in I just went straight to bed, no dinner, no shower, just these bare few notes to mark the day, that's all I was able for.

August 23rd

Harry's gone. I asked the landlady this morning, and though at first she pretended not to know who I meant, she finally, grudgingly admitted that yes, he was gone. Rosa reckons the same as me, that he's been moved up the chain, maybe to a fancier place, certainly to a fancier office. It's enough to put us both in a bad mood. Rosa was like a thundercloud. She was complaining about her room again – the colour, she claimed, is giving her nightmares, she spent last night fancying she could see shadows moving round the room. I tried pointing out that they were probably the reflection of car headlights, but she just moved her complaint on to the shower. Her light keeps flickering too. Offered to help sort it out for her (as if I could, but she's not to know that, I just felt it might be clever to move our chat upstairs to her room). She didn't pick up on it though – just pointed out we'd be late for work if I tried. I nearly asked 'What work?' Anyhow, we went in, same old, same old. Rosa in a bit of temper all day. When Sean came round – he just popped his head in this time – she almost lost it.

'What the HELL are we meant to do here?' she asked him aggressively. 'I've half a mind to go back home, I tell you!' He looked surprised, muttered something placatory and disappeared. She was still in a foul mood when we got home, turned down my offer of dinner. Late at night I heard her clattering around upstairs. Even her footsteps sounded bad-tempered.

August 24th

Some odd things have happened. This morning, having a shower, the light went out completely in the bathroom. It was just the bulb, I think, as the shower kept on going. It was pitch black. All I could hear was my own breathing and the noise of the rivulets hitting my head and shoulder. It's not like me, but I got creeped out, jumped out quickly and dried myself off in the main room.

Then later, when I was waiting outside the landlady's door to tell her about the faulty bulb, I found something perplexing. Tucked behind one of the fake plant pots, I found Harry's horror novel. There's no mistaking it, I'd seen it so often in *our shared room at work. It's called 'Zombie Holocaust Now' and had a gory red cover featuring a disembodied arm, with Gothic black script below the title declaring it to be the 'scariest vision of the apocalypse yet!' Why did Harry leave without it? He seemed devoted to it. I stowed it in my bag anyhow. Weirdly, Rosa didn't find this strange. Mind you, she didn't speak a lot on the way in, just to reiterate yesterday's threat of leaving and going back home. I really hope she doesn't. I mean, we're both fed up, but hey! – we're getting paid for doing nothing.*

In the afternoon, just when we were playing Go Fish, we heard the door open. Swift as a snake, I scooped up the cards. It was Sean. 'Hello James', he said. 'Can you follow me?'

'What about me?' asked Rosa.

He eyed her coolly. 'You can take a half day' She stood up, her face dark with anger, and threw her phone and wallet into her bag. I started to say something, but she just pushed past and out the door. I followed Sean and we spent a mystifying afternoon where I attempted a series of various problem-solving exercises. He presented me with a fresh problem every time I completed one and only stopped when his mobile warbled an old-fashioned shrilling ringtone. He excused himself to take the call, and when he came back in, told me that I'm finished for the day. I shrugged and texted Rosa to say that I'm on my way home. No reply.

When I got in, I couldn't find her anywhere. She didn't answer her phone and even when I went up and knocked on her door, she didn't make a sound. I think she was still annoyed I got picked and she didn't. I decided to leave her be and retreated to my dreary room with only the crackly TV, this diary and Harry's horror novel for company. At least the landlady has fixed the bulb in the bathroom.

August 25th

Ok, this isn't funny. Not at all. Now Rosa is gone. I'm writing this in the stupid pink room after another senseless day in that room of cubicles. She wasn't down for breakfast, so I headed in alone, hoping she'd be there before me. No one came by at all today, not even Sean. And no Rosa. No reply to my calls or texts. No sign of her here. The landlady isn't answering her door, but I'm going to go across in a minute and knock again. This is stupid! [At this point, the pen is scored deep into the paper, so deep it rips through the page below]

<u>Later</u>

OK, so the landlady finally answered. I just hammered on the door until she did. She was good and angry when she opened up, but I didn't care. 'Where is she?' I demanded. 'Rosa Molloy? Dark hair, staying here with the company? Where is she?'

'She's gone,' is all she would say, her lined face old and sour with annoyance. She tried to push the door shut then, but I braced it with my arm.

'I'm going to contact the company,' I threatened her. 'This place isn't fit for human habitation! They're going to hear all about it from me.'

She pushed my arm viciously, and I slipped, catching hold of the doorframe, but by the time I righted myself the door was almost closed. Her voice hissed out through the crack. 'They know all about it. Go and tell tales if you want!' And then the door shut and no matter how many times I pounded on it, it wouldn't open again.

~

The bells in the Pro Cathedral ring out. I sit up with a start. It's nearly two o'clock. I shrug – *If tomorrow is like today, no one will care if I'm there*, and return to the diary. I rub my chilled fingers together. My forgotten chocolate has melted slowly into the discarded bedspread, but I ignore it. I feel myself sucked into the narrative. What's happened to Rosa and Harry?

And even more disturbing – *what kind of company have I joined?*

I'm shivering, and it's not just with the cold, biting though that is. I'm longing for a hot shower to unkink my knotted muscles, but can't face going into that grim, dark bathroom. I wrap the chocolatey bedspread around me tightly and give up all hope of sleep.

~

The next day I go to my assigned room and wait. Just like James. Just like Rosa. Just like Harry. I'm starting to feel decidedly uneasy. I wait for Sean to arrive, with his clipboard.

'I asked you yesterday if you knew a James Baker?'

There it is again, that tell-tale flicker.

'He worked here.' Still nothing. I persist. 'How about a Rosa.' I search my memory. 'Rosa...Molloy?' He shakes his head.

'A Harry. Harry Something? They all worked here.'

Sean sighs. 'I'm sorry,' he says, so pointedly it's obvious he's not. 'So many people go through here. Your friends may have worked here, but I'm afraid I don't recall them.'

I'm determined. 'Can you ask HR? It's just that I'm trying to reach them.'

His face is smooth as glass, but I sense his growing irritation. 'Put in an official request.'

'I will.' I watch him walk away.

After another long day of nothingness, I go home and pick up the diary again. Maybe it'll tell me what happened to them all.

—

August 26ᵗʰ

Same crap, different day. I'm beyond upset. Went in and sat in that glass-fronted room on my own all day, wondering if I had the nerve to just admit defeat like Rosa, and go home. I pictured all the fake sympathy and the gleeful gossip behind my back, and steeled myself to stay. At least for another few days.

I was driven to read Harry's horror novel just to pass the time. It's stupid and badly-written but at least it stops me from watching the clock snail-trail its way through the day. It wasn't until five to five, as I was packing to go, that a small scrap of paper fluttered out.

'Don't go in there in the dark,' it said, in tiny, crabbed writing.

Harry was obviously even weirder than I thought.

I went home. Another empty night in a lonely room. I haven't heard any more sounds in the B&B apart from the landlady across the hall. If it wasn't for the traffic and voices outside, I'd feel like the last man on earth.

August 27ᵗʰ

Today, as an experiment, I didn't go in to work. 'Work' – I can barely call it that! Instead I wandered around the Hugh Lane gallery and looked at some weird installations of kinetic sculptures that moved when you went near them, some kind of laser-activated technology. Then I went to the Writer's Museum and looked at some letters by Joyce. That only reminded me of Rosa. Tried ringing her phone again, but no luck.

Eventually wandered back at six. Met the landlady in the hall. Her face was grim. 'Your work called,' she said. 'You never went in.' Her eyes are black with malice. 'I told them you weren't here.'

'I was sick,' I fibbed. 'I went to the doctor.' She raised her red, over-plucked eyebrows in disbelief, and then slid back behind her door. Great. So now I'm in trouble with work as well as everything else. All in all, it's been such a bad day that I'm not even surprised when the light goes in the bathroom again. Just when I'm showering. Again. This time I don't even bother to report it. What's the point?

But the incident freaked me out, I have to admit. There was a moment, just when the lights went out, where I could swear I heard something moving around...

I don't like that bathroom at all. Not one bit.

〜

I shut the diary and shiver slightly, remembering my experience in the shower. I think about the flickering light, the crazy wriggle of shadows on the wet walls.

〜

August 28th

I expected some kind of official warning when I went in, but no, nothing. The receptionist was just as dead-eyed as ever, and when I asked if there were any messages, she didn't even answer, just wrinkled her nose as if I was being unbelievably presumptuous. Went and sat down wearily in my usual place, too down even to read the horror novel or stare out the window (my usual two pastimes). Eventually Sean showed up. He didn't look angry, just relieved.

'You're back!'

'Yes,' I said. 'Just felt a bit ill yesterday. Sorry I didn't call in, I wasn't sure who to leave a message for as—' I paused, 'I haven't actually _started_ working for the firm yet.'

He smiled at me. 'Don't worry, you already have.' But he didn't ask me to do anything for the rest of the day.

When I arrived home, the landlady was out, so I showered in the dark again, but leaving the ensuite door open. It was too creepy otherwise. I was just drying off when I heard noises overhead. Rosa! I didn't even think, just threw on my jeans and ran up the stairs, and knocked on her door. 'Rosa!' But there was no sound. I stood outside feeling stupid. The noise was obviously coming from somewhere else in the house.

And then something happened that I can't stop thinking about. My phone rang out in my jeans pocket, startling me. When I answered, there was nothing, just a sound of movement, a series of crackles, like when someone dials your number accidentally.

But it was Rosa's number!

I hung up and rang back, and in the deep stillness of the house, I heard a faint ringing from downstairs. I ran down, and could hear it, getting louder and louder, until I got to the landlady's door. The sound was coming from behind it. On and on and on it rang, until I pressed the 'cancel call' button and stood (I don't mind saying this) shaking outside the door.

<u>What the hell is going on?</u> I'd go home in a heartbeat, leave this stupid B&B, this non-job, if I wasn't feeling so worried about Rosa.

<u>August 29th</u>

I spent about an hour in the morning looking up numbers for Molloys in Omagh. It's obviously a popular name, I worked through about twenty numbers before I got the right place.

'Can I speak to Rosa Molloy?'

'Ah now, sorry about that, you can't. She's moved, you see.' It's an elderly man, his voice slow and pleasant.

I guessed. 'To Dublin?'

'She has indeed. She has a fine job up there in Dublin. We were talking to her just last week.'

I swallowed. 'Not this week?'

'Not this week, no.' The slow-talking voice sharpened, became suspicious. 'And who is this calling?'

'This is James Baker. I knew her from back a few years, just bumped into her earlier in the week. She mentioned she might head back home to Omagh.'

Now the voice was distressed, confused. 'Well there's no sign of her here. Maybe you got it wrong?'

I didn't want to let his suspicions die. 'Maybe I did,' I said, injecting the right note of bewilderment into my voice. 'If she does get in touch, let her know I rang. She has my number.'

I hung up and pictured his worried face, him punching out her mobile number slowly on his house phone, his look of concern deepening as it rings out. I could see, clear as day, the door to the landlady's room, with the phone behind it, shrilling out into the dusty vestibule.

I felt sick. I went home early. I didn't even tell anyone. Or care. As I went in the front door, I passed the landlady – she scuttled by me before I could say anything. I stood and watched her hurry down the road, without looking back.

For the rest of the night I sat in my room and rang Rosa's phone, over and over again, listening to the muted ringtone across the hall. I rang it and rang it till it simply stopped dead.

The silence afterwards was almost worse.

August 30th

I didn't go to work today. I stayed here. The landlady didn't seem to care. I don't know if she's even there. I haven't heard or seen her since yesterday evening.

Something horrible happened this morning, so horrible it's taken me till now to put it down.

I was showering this morning. Despite everything I had planned to go to work. The light was still gone, so I left the door propped open with Harry's novel. Just as I was turning to adjust the nozzle, the door swung closed, and I was trapped in an airless, dark space, the water coming down soft and hot against me. I staggered back, and hit the plastic curtain behind me, grabbing at the rail for balance. As I steadied myself and caught my breath, I felt it. I felt something cold and solid prod me in the back, then slide up, lightly, over my shoulders, and then withdraw back into the darkness.

I screamed and threw the shower curtain back, pushed the door open and stood, naked and shivering in the grim pink light of my bedroom.

'What the HELL?' I yelled into the empty room, so loudly I hurt my throat. I shoved the door to the ensuite shut, trembling with rage and fear.

There's something in that ensuite. But I'm not leaving. I'm not leaving till I know what the hell is going on. Or what happened to Rosa. Or Harry, come to that. I'm going to wait for the landlady to come home, and then I'll have it out with her.

It's after midnight and I'm writing this sitting up in bed, watching the door to the bathroom, making sure it doesn't open.

August 31ˢᵗ

No sounds in the house. No landlady. No guests.

I haven't left the room all day. Now the sky is getting darker. I switch on my lamp, and as I do so, I fancy I can hear a rustle. I freeze. Nothing.

Now it's later. Darker.

It's getting restless.

I can hear it rustle about in there.

I open the door a crack and run back to the bed. I don't care. I'll wait for whatever it is to come out. And when it does I'll be waiting with that steel-framed tennis racket I took yesterday from the vestibule.

I turn it over in my hands, feeling the weight of it.

I'm not mad. I'm not mad.

—

I'll be gone in the morning, and I'll go to the police. I'll bring the diary to them. But it's still several hours till dawn and the shadows have crept halfway across the floor. The door to the ensuite is barred, I've moved the dressing table across it. Nothing should be able to get through. Just in case, I've piled my packed bags around me in a heap, their bulky solidity giving me comfort. The tennis racket, (whose frame, I realise with a dreamy kind of terror, is ridged with red lines) lies across my lap. I sit upright, clutching the shabby diary like a talisman, watching the shadows edge towards the foot of the bed.

Only a few hours till dawn. Then we're safely away, me and the diary. That diary is my only evidence. I need to keep it safe. Is it my imagination, or has the wardrobe shifted slightly?

It's definitely moved. And now the door is ajar. I squeeze the diary closer to my chest, the worn green binding tucked under my chin. I need to keep it safe. Just a few more hours.

But what if somebody comes back for it?

What if *something* comes back for it?

'What Lies Beneath' is a mix of the contemporary horror of loneliness and alienation, mixed in with the idea that the Celtic Tiger boom in Dublin – all around the financial district by the quays – was somehow occasioned by a sacrifice of sorts. The unseen beast of the story is my own invention – I liked the idea that it was unnameable and unknown.

COME YOU WHO
WANT TO COME

t's the light, she decides. *It's the light that's confusing me.* Waking up, she has no sense of what time has passed. What time is it? 4pm? 4am? The quality of light is always the same. It's an endless, white brightness, solid as a blanket. Even with no sun, the glare is there. The cottage has blackout blinds, but they're poorly fitted; the queer, blank light leaks through the edges. She checks her phone. 3.35 am. She shrugs, and gets up to brew a cup of coffee and go outside, as she always does when she wakes.

The view is as compelling as ever. Curved expanses of green grass and strips of dark, volcanic rock stretch out, uninterrupted, to the mountains in the distance. She feels herself perfectly alone in the soft air. It's a different loneliness to at home. Back there it's more pointed, full of bleak signifiers; a phone that never rings, a silent doorbell, nothing but bills on the mat. Here the solitary state is somehow magnificent. Natural. A silent, complete aloneness that rolls across the green desert. Far away, she can see the loop of the road, but nothing stirs.

She drinks her coffee and waits. Nothing happens. The immovable, blank light beats steadily down.

The only downside of the residency is the communal gathering in the evening. She sighs and gathers together her pencils. Today's been a day for dreaming under the huge sky; under the clouds that are always shifting and changing, never quiet. In the distance the dark brown mountains are still streaked lightly with white. If she squints she can see tiny puffs of steam rising beside them. She keeps picking up her pencil, only to place it down again, tipping back her head to savour the sight. No hurry. It's only the first week of the residency after all.

But now, time for dinner. It's Aarni's turn to cook. So far it's only been the two of them there, and Aarni's so taciturn it's almost like being by herself, apart from some necessary exchanges about food. But there's another woman coming this evening, so she'll have to – she winces slightly – make conversation. She wanders through the grey-white light over to the main cottage.

'Hey!' The new arrival is there, all blonde curls and toothy grin. She's beaming at her. 'So what brings you here?'

'Um. Like you. The residencies?' She looks at Aarni. He's stirring a pot at the stove, back pointedly turned.

The new woman laughs brightly. 'Oh, I know that. Hey, I'm Charlene, I'm from Austin, Texas, and I'm here to work on my novel.' She pronounces it *naarvel*.

'Well I'm Vicky. I'm a visual artist, so looking for inspiration at the moment.'

'Oh how fascinating! Surely you find this all real inspirational. I mean this countryside! It's amazing. And Aarni here tells me he's researching a book on Icelandic folklore.'

Is he? It's more than she's gotten out of Aarni in the week. She steals a glance at him, but he's adding herbs to the sauce, lips pursed.

'So what's your current plan?' Charlene's head is cocked to one side.

Vicky shrugs. 'Not sure. Coincidentally I've been reading up on some folklore too. About the Huldufólk. The Hidden People?' She looks across at Aarni, but he doesn't respond, just keeps stirring the sauce.

'No way,' breathes Charlene. 'Tell me more.'

There's nothing Vicky dislikes more than over-talking ideas when they're at a delicate, inchoate state. 'The Icelandic elves,' she says brusquely. 'They're believed to live in the rocks and mountains of the interior. I've no idea yet what I'd do; I'm just at the reading and thinking stage. Aarni's the expert. He'll be able to tell you more about them.' She glances over at him, but he's still pretending not to hear. Vicky shrugs apologetically and starts setting the table, clattering the old-fashioned cutlery from the drawer to try to forestall other questions.

The evening drags on. They eat the pasta. After an hour or so Vicky knows all she ever wants to about Charlene's novel (an alternative dystopian vision of the US following the triumph of the Confederate forces during the Civil War). She feels her smile becoming more fixed, her nods more mechanical. Aarni has pulled down a book from the shelf and is determinedly reading it. She envies him his stalwart rudeness. As soon as she decently can, she escapes, pleading insomnia. Walking back to her little cottage she feels nothing but relief. The breeze plays with her hair. It's soft, and it brings with it just a breath of moisture.

It's another long, sleepless night of pearly white light. She spends much of it sitting on the grass outside the cottage, staring at the mountains.

—

She goes for a walk the next day, across the green sloping plains. They're not even fields, there's no demarcation of boundaries. The grass just flows steadily in one long arc in front of her. *Who owns the land,* she wonders. No-one? Everyone? It reminds her a little of remote areas of Donegal. It reminds her a little of the Burren in Clare. It reminds her of nowhere else on earth.

She sees no one. In the distance, a car or two passes on the road; other than that the land is completely abandoned. *Not abandoned,* she corrects. The land feels occupied by itself, by the strange sense of wholeness it possesses. The more she walks, the odder the sensation becomes. From time to time the vista is interrupted by cracks in the ground. Before her, shelves of dark rock break the vista in little outcrops, as if the force of the land is erupting through. She thinks about the elves, about what she's read, of the ancient belief that the interior of the country was occupied by the Huldufólk and ghosts. It seems less like folklore, somehow believable, in this strange land of enormous, rolling skies and endless grass. She sits down and plucks a blade of grass. It tastes sweet and green in her mouth.

Later that day she starts to draw. It's more like doodling. She traces the long, sloping lines of mountains and grass, repeatedly; scoring the tiny fissures in the ground with a darker pencil. She feels a curious sense of relief seeing the marks on the page. There's the sense of breaking into a project, that feeling of trembling on the edge of making.

—

'So what did you do today?' It's not a real question. Charlene wants to tell them what *she* did. At length. She's been to Reykjavik and is full of stories of 'doing' the city. She earnestly recommends galleries, the Concert Hall, the view from the harbour. Aarni grunts in acknowledgement. Vicky smiles without replying. She serves the rice, and thinks of her own solitary day, full of sky and soft ground and gentle breezes.

Outside, it's another white night.

~

The next day she spends drifting about under a canopy of rapidly shifting skies. Every day it is sunny. Every day it is cloudy. Every day it rains. It's not like Irish rain, though; it's like a soft kiss. She tips her head up to receive it like a benediction. The landscape is charged with a silent power. And all around is silence – no insect buzz, no trees with leaves to let the breeze wash through. Just faintly, in the distance, the sound of water bubbling down rocks, clear and joyous. She follows the sound to an outcrop of dark rock, which parts to reveal a running stream of whitish green water, opaque as a clouded opal.

If there are elves, surely they live here.

She draws some more that day. This time she scores the paper harder to mark the cracks in the ground. The graphite tears holes in the paper, but she doesn't care.

~

That night Charlene doesn't stop talking. Any given silence only lasts a maximum of four minutes. Vicky times it discreetly. She talks about herself, mostly, and her novel. Then she discusses the midsummer light at length.

'It's invigorating,' she declares, 'I feel so lively and productive.' She beams around the table. Vicky avoids her gaze. Aarni clears his throat.

'It's a time of magic here,' he says, but so softly as to be almost inaudible. She looks at him. He nods at her. 'The elves are busy this time of the year. They come and mix with ordinary people, talk to them, trick them.' He shrugs. 'It's the solstice tomorrow. This kind of thing happens all over the world at this time.'

'What happens? Where?' Vicky is interested.

Aarni clears his throat. 'It happens usually around the rocks, where they're supposed to live. The Huldufólk do not look so different from us; they pass as human. So from time to time, on festivals like the solstice, they come and walk among ordinary people. Anyone *sensible* stays away from the places that they live on that night.' He looks directly at Vicky; his pale blue eyes are intense.

It's the longest speech he's ever made. Vicky wants to ask him more, but Charlene has already embarked on another elaborate story about her time in Reykjavik. Vicky sighs and forks up her salad.

'Have you been in to the city yet?' asks Charlene. Aarni doesn't respond, so Vicky feels impelled to.

'No. But maybe I will tomorrow.' It's only half an hour on the bus, after all. 'I have a friend who's on holiday at the moment. She's offered me her place to stay in.' *Maybe not a bad idea*, she thinks. *It might be more peaceful there at night.* The days are fine; it's the forced evening interactions that leave her tired. *Not here*, she thinks, obscurely. *Not here* is where she wants to be.

She's almost gotten used to the white-grey light. Almost. Later as she crosses over to her cottage, she stops to look around. There's no way to measure time except by using a clock; no twilight, no dramatic sunset, no hints from the natural world that it's time to stop and sleep. This night, she doesn't even get in to bed. She just sits up reading about the Huldufólk. They are most active in the winter, she learns, when they change homes. During the New Year, many people perform incantations to make sure they don't invade their space. She reads on and on, about Gryla and the Yule Lads as the clock ticks off the hours. When she goes to sit outside, in the pearly light, she sees that the lamp in Aarni's cabin is still on. She feels a sudden desire to ask him more about the Huldufólk, but the thought of his reaction stops her. She sits under the big sky and feels a queer sense of restlessness.

—

When she gets off the bus in Reykjavik, she is struck with the relative quietness of the city. It doesn't *feel* like a capital city. The buildings are dove grey and white and modestly sized, apart from a cluster of tall office buildings by the harbour. All the streets seem to slope gently down to the water. In the distance she can see the inevitable mountains, wreathed in cloud.

Halla's apartment is tiny and quiet; a studio with a bedroom kitchenette and a small bathroom that smells vaguely of eggy sulphur. The minute space fills her with an odd sense of restlessness. She puts her bag down, unpacks it, and takes out her sketchbook. Still that restlessness. She looks out the window at the coffee shop across the road; dimly-lit, half deserted. Maybe that would work better?

Inside the coffee shop, the colours are muted. The sunshine outside seems more subdued when reflected in here; there's a pleasing Nordic melancholy to the fall of light on infinitely soft tones of grey. The baristas are silent as they slowly, ever so slowly, brew coffee. There's something almost funereal about their quiet, respectful movements. The line of people waiting is patient and taciturn. There's a record player with a stack of shabby vinyl underneath. A woman's voice sings a breathy, whispered version of Radiohead's 'Creep.' The sky outside is layered with sun and cottonwool clouds.

She takes out her sketchbook. Her drawings seem remote. No matter how hard she looks at them, she feels disconnected from their source, from the enormous skies and flat grass outside her cottage. *Maybe it was a mistake to come here.* The sombre, bearded barista brings her coffee, but she already wants to leave. *Not here.*

She walks the streets, looking for something; she's not sure quite what. Around the corners there's the harbour, laid out in stripes of flat grass, sea and mountains. Clouds and sun mix in the same sky; a light smattering of rain falls gently, and then disappears. She sits on the stones by the harbour, rubbed smooth as wet sealskin, and lets her mind empty. The clouds burn away in the hot sun. Now the sea is a brilliant, steely blue, but the mountains are hidden, wreathed in smoky clouds that trail like blankets around their slopes. *Not here.*

She drifts towards the Harpa concert hall, the angled façade glinting with flashes of peacock blue. Inside the cleverness of the scheme is laid bare. Like scales of a giant fish, the panes of glass unlock a fragmented view of the harbour, the white sails, the sheets of blue sea and the tiny lighthouse in the distance.

She touches the glass gently. *Not here.*

Eleven thirty and it's still an eerie, pearly grey-white outside. The air carries with it a breath of rain; the finest mist, a suggestion of water. She imagines it tastes of salt, like a breath exhaled by the sea. The streets are full of people, laughing and talking. It's Midsummer's Eve. *I won't sleep,* she thinks. *Not here.*

She threads her way along the maze of footpaths like an automaton. There's a creeping sense of unreality to walking through the city at night, in this bright afternoon light and slight, daylight warmth of sun-soaked streets. All around her are people, but their chatter and noise doesn't penetrate her bubble of aloneness. It's as busy as a tacky Spanish resort strip, but all around are Nordic wooden houses, subdued shop fronts. As she walks she sees clubs start to bloom into life overhead. They're invisible by day, but by night the upper stories of bars and restaurants blossom in a rash of neon. Queues form outside. Walking along here is like pacing along a threshold. Every movement is impermanent; each moment leads to another, each footstep an element of chance.

Vicky pauses outside a lively bar. It's not the kind of place she seeks out, but she's drawn to the idea of a cold beer on this warm evening. Inside the bar is full of blonde heads, tall women and bearded men. A live band plays covers of various songs she half-recognises. She gets her beer and sits, unobserved, watching the conversations taking place around her. Behind the bar is a wheel of fortune that the bar staff spin from time to time. It's split into equal sections – every second one reads 'Sorry!', every other one reads 'Six Beers', 'Eight Beers' or 'Ten Beers.' Whenever someone wins, the girl behind the bar rings a bell with a sharp *ding-ding.* As she's sitting there it rings once, then twice. *Not bad odds,* she decides. Sitting here she feels as invisible as she did on the streets. There's the sensation that life is rushing all around her, crashing in waves that she senses but can't feel. Suddenly there's an uproar of cheers. The huge clock at the bar strikes midnight. *Midsummer's Eve.* The live band who are playing change tenor. They play a mournful folksong, all long vowels, indecipherable. Everyone joins in. Beside her is a table of Icelandic men. They sing along, bellowing the words, their feet stamping as they slap the table in rhythm to the beats. She looks at them, their beards, their hipster topknots, their bulky shoulders. *This is what the Vikings would have looked like*, she thinks, and a deep shiver runs through her.

The bell rings at the bar. She hears the sound of cheering. There's a commotion as the men behind her leap to their feet. She feels a hand on her shoulder and spins around, startled.

It's a man with long blonde hair and merry blue eyes. He says something to her in Icelandic. *Is he chatting me up?*

'I'm sorry,' she says politely. 'I don't speak Icelandic. I speak English.'

He laughs. She sees his teeth, white and strong against pink lips. 'It's fine,' he says in perfect, if lilting English. 'I was just excusing myself to get past you.'

Vicky bites her lip and colours. 'I'm sorry,' she says awkwardly, moving instantly out of his way. He laughs again, and disappears out of her line of sight. She picks up her phone and scans it, her cheeks still flushed with mortification at her mistake.

Then he's back at her elbow, a brimming glass of Gull beer in his hand. 'Here, English-speaking girl. This one is for you.'

'Oh!' She's surprised.

'We won the ten beers,' he explains. 'And most of us are drinking brennivín.' He draws out the word in a sing-song vowel.

'Well thank you.' She accepts the beer and takes a tentative sip. He sits down beside her.

'In payment you must talk to me now.' His eyes crinkle at her. 'What are you doing here in Reykjavik?'

She tells him about the residency, about the countryside, about her work as a painter. He nods. He is a musician, he tells her. Just then the band strikes up another melancholy air.

'What's that song?' she asks.

He stops and listens. 'Ah, that is a song that you hear most often around the other solstice. In winter. It is something you say to the Huldufólk at the door. "Come you who want to come. Go you who want to leave." It is both an invitation and a warning.'

'The Huldufólk? The Hidden People? I'm very interested in them.' She sits forward, excited.

'Ah yes. Then you have picked a good time to be here. This is the night that the Huldufólk are abroad. They are active at the changes of the year; now and in winter.'

'Do you believe in them?' she asks, curious. She's heard contradictory information about current beliefs; some sources claim a large percentage of the population still believe in elves, others rubbish the idea.

He pauses. 'I'm a modern Icelander. What do you think?'

She raises her eyebrows. 'I don't know, that's why I'm asking you.'

He looks at her steadily. His eyes are grey-green. *The exact the colour of the sea in the harbour*, she thinks.

'We are open to the idea,' he says simply. 'The legends are older than we are. It would be foolish to dismiss all our forefathers told us.'

They talk some more. She sips her beer. It's lukewarm and watery, but refreshing. He reaches out and strokes her hand. She feels uncomfortable, but it seems rude to withdraw from him.

'So where are you going now? What are your plans?' It's an obvious invitation. She hesitates. Suddenly his eyes are too bright, his mouth too full of teeth.

'Excuse me,' she says, pushing her chair out. 'I'll be back in a moment.' He smiles and raises his glass to her.

Outside the bar, she puts a hand to her throat. *I need to go home.* And she does, walking unsteadily back down the strange, day-lit streets, one after another, the harbour on her left side, until she reaches Halla's apartment. She sleeps that night, the whole morning, through till noon.

Her sleep is perfect, blank, overwhelming.

—

She gets off the bus the next day and walks down the winding white road to the cottages. There's a sense of relief, a homecoming of sorts. It is late afternoon. No-one's around. She breathes in deeply with relief and opens her sketchbook. Time to draw.

It's one of those days when the pencil flows. Her hand moves, fluid and certain, across the pages. She's completely absorbed. Under her fingers, the landscapes grow; a mass of tiny lines, scored with larger and larger cracks in the rocky ground.

Here, she thinks, and the word is simple, sure as an arrow.

A shadow falls across the page, and she's conscious of someone standing behind her. She's reluctant to lift her head, so she just ignores it, praying that it's not Charlene. She feels the palpable heat of proximity; the intensity of the moment grows so that her concentration breaks. She lays down her pencil, the soft lead worn to a nub.

'What is it? The words come out impatiently. She turns around. There's no-one there. There's just the faint breeze blowing through the grass, and the mountains, dimmed by clouds.

She thinks about it as she lies in bed that night.

―

The next day, she goes on a walk and picks up some pitted lava rocks. She holds one in her hand, marvelling at the intricate system of holes dotting its charcoal surface. Back at the cottage she starts to draw them into one of her landscape sketches. They proliferate, larger and larger in scale until they bury the plains and the mountains beneath their mass. She sits outside. Occasionally, out of the corner of her eye she catches a flash of colour, like a passing dragonfly. But it's an illusion. The stolid reality of the landscape stares back at her.

Here.

That evening she's walking over to the main building, sketchbook tucked under her arm. It's just her and Aarni – Charlene is away on another trip. She dips her spoon in the soup bowl, barely tasting it, barely aware of what she's eating. When her spoon scrapes the bottom of the empty bowl she jumps slightly.

'Are you OK?' It's so unlike Aarni to ask anything, she turns to look at him. He is watching her carefully.

'Yeah.' She brushes away his question. 'Just tired. I don't sleep well here.'

He nods and picks up her sketchbook without asking. She feels a flare of irritation. He thumbs through it slowly, pausing at the last page.

'The rocks,' he says flatly.

'Yes. Lava rocks.'

He puts down the sketchbook. 'This I don't like. It...' he pauses to find the right words. 'It disturbs me.'

—

She wakes from fitful dreams, feeling more exhausted than when she went to bed. She can't remember her dreams, just a vague sense of darkness and noise and commotion, as of bodies passing by her in the tiny cottage. It's four in the morning. She starts to draw. By the time she remembers to have breakfast, she's already sketched another image of lava rocks, tiny and pitted and minute, clustered over the page.

Even though it's her turn to cook that night, she doesn't go over to the main building.

—

The days slip by, white days, white nights, one after the other, like pearls on a necklace. Sometimes she joins the others at night, but more often she just sits there, outside the cottage, looking across the grass, towards the mountains.

It's happening more frequently now. The tiny blurs of movement. The feeling of a presence around her; always sensed, never seen.

Here.

—

'Vicky?' It's Charlene. Vicky sighs deeply and gathers up her sketchbook. She's sitting on the front doorstep.

'Hello,' she says, polite but cold.

'We haven't seen you in a few nights.' Charlene looks at her carefully. 'Vicky, are you alright?'

Surprised, she nods.

'It's just that...' Charlene stops and bites her lips. 'You look awful,' she says in a burst. 'We're worried about you. Have you looked at yourself?'

Vicky looks at her, nonplussed.

'Here.' Charlene brandishes a small compact mirror. Vicky looks at the tiny reflected image. Her eyes look enormous, the skin around them a bruised purple-black. Her skin is dry, a flaky patch on one cheek. She hasn't brushed her hair in days and – she looks a little closer – it has definitely gotten greyer. She shuts the mirror with an angry click.

'I told you. I'm not sleeping well here,' she mutters.

Charlene takes her hand. She feels a pull of revulsion in her stomach. 'Aarni and I think you should see a doctor,' she says earnestly. 'Won't you at least come over and eat some food and talk about it?'

'No.' She pulls her hand away. 'Please go away.'

And Charlene does, walking slowly back, turning from time to time as if hopeful that she'll see Vicky relent. She watches her go in and shut the door.

There is a long, cool breath beside her, just by her ear. She doesn't turn. She knows there'll be nothing there. Nothing and no-one. She looks out over the grass and the rocks. A gust of wind ripples the grass. She fancies she sees tiny sparks of colour ignite.

Slowly the wind builds, breath by breath. Now it sounds like people walking by her in a crowd, the slithery susurration of cloth on cloth. She looks out, and her vision clouds, dotted with floating specks. *I'm seeing stars*, she thinks, but these are more like tiny amorphous shapes. They cluster slowly, dot by dot, until they fill her vision.

She closes her eyes and leans back against the door post. Unbidden, the words rise up within her. She knows what she must say.

'Come you who want to come.'

Here.

And the air is suddenly thick with whispers.

This story was inspired by a writing trip to Iceland in 2017, where I was fascinated by the strong contemporary belief in the Huldufólk, or native elves. This belief exists to such an extent that new roads are planned carefully so as not to trespass on the realm of the Huldufólk. I was interested in the overlap between Irish and Icelandic beliefs in maintaining the boundaries between human and fae – after all, there is a strong strain of Irish DNA among Icelandic people – and from this the idea grew of transplanting an Irish writer to an Icelandic setting to experience this mythology.

THE GRAVEYARD
OF THE LOST

his all happened because of the man in Crageen cemetery. I'm soaked to the skin in the misty rain, pinched between the strange, nubby crags of stone that sprout from the sea-strand. It's sometime after three in the morning and the sky is starting to streak a pale gold, faint as a memory, glinting like lines of Bacofoil on the creeping surge of water that's rising by the minute. I'm crying almost without realising it, my tears running warm down my chilled face.

In spite of everything, it's so beautiful. So beautiful and terrible.

It's raining, again, hard. I've never experienced anything like it, these infinite variations of precipitation in Ireland. I pull the hood of my raincoat over my head and crouch under the dense green spread of a yew tree. My camera is tucked safely away in my waterproof bag. It's... *lashing* I think is the appropriate word for it. I tuck my cold hands under my armpits – *oxters*, I correct myself, using the word I learned in Northern Ireland. I close my eyes, and briefly dream myself back in San Diego: a day in La Jolla, at the beach, the startling blueness of the sky, the nodding palms and the noise of holidaymakers. The drumming of the raindrops on my head has a lulling effect. I sigh. I can almost feel the grit of hot sand beneath my feet and smell the hotdogs cooking.

'Are you all right there, son?'

I start and open my eyes. There's an old man leaning over me, hands on his knees, his lined face concerned. His flat cap is sodden and dark with rain.

'Oh, yes sir, I'm fine.' Flustered, I scramble up.

He leans back against a grave-marker. 'Ah, now, of course you are.' He smiles easily at me. 'What would you be doing here, then, a man like yourself from America?'

'I'm an archaeology student,' I confess. 'Taking the final year of my graduate school studies in Ireland. And I'm looking at Irish cemeteries.'

'You came all the way from America to see them?'

'Yes, I'm studying burial rites in Ireland, and I was told not to miss this place. I'm just waiting for the rain to pass to photograph it.' As we've been talking, the sun has begun to gleam fitfully through the grey skies, and the rain has slackened off.

'You're in the right place, so. I've seen many's the professor out here, looking at the graves.'

'They're beautiful.' And they are. Now that the sun is peeping through, the flecks of mica on the wet granite of the grave-markers glistens, and the floral tributes are beaded with iridescent drops. It's an old cemetery, the most recent plot dates back to the 1980s; the earliest is marked only by some lichened bumps of rock that may be fifteenth century, or even earlier. It's a strange sight to come on, down a bumpy little road with a strip of green running down the middle. But what makes it truly extraordinary are – I stoop down and touch one of them – the cluster of objects that decorate the graves. On plot after plot you see them, toys and tiny shoes for children, a wild jumble of crockery and books and tools and flowers for the adults, each pile gaudy and incoherent and unique.

The old man nods. 'It's a local thing,' he says. 'We like to mark the life, you know, not the death. You see that one over there?' He points to a large, imposing grave-marker. 'That belongs to Jimmy Oliver. He was a plasterer, so his workmates cemented his trowel into the headstone. And instead of pebbles, it has pebble-dashing.' I'm photographing where he's pointing, while listening intently.

'That lady over there, God rest her, she was a great person, always giving. Baked cakes for half the parish. Look at the angel.' I look closer, and see that the weeping angel statue on her grave has a rolling pin tucked firmly (if incongruously) under one arm.

I suck in a breath of pure delight. 'Thank you for this, so much. May I use this information in my thesis?'

He smiles at me and a web of ancient wrinkles dances. His teeth are strong and tobacco-coloured. 'Sure of course you can,' he says easily. 'Fire away.'

I am still photographing the stones as I talk, *click*, focus, *click*. 'This is the most wonderful cemetery I've seen in all my travels,' I say truthfully, almost to myself.

He looks at me shrewdly. 'But you've never seen the Cemetery of the Lost.' It is a statement, not a question.

~

That was the start of it all. That's why I'm here now you see. I followed that fatal ribbon of clues and guesswork that led me from that cemetery on a wet West of Ireland hillside to here. The end of the story. The end of everything. It all happened because of the man in Crageen cemetery.

—

Later that night, I'm going through all my notes and books back in the borrowed trailer (they call it a mobile home here). It's a sturdy, ugly little building with tiny bed-sized bedrooms, but also a surprisingly large and comfortable seating area. That's where I've spread out my notes. I'm confused. Nowhere can I find a reference to this 'Graveyard of the Lost'. From what he told me, I figure it's somewhere in Kerry, and on the seashore, but apart from that I'm adrift. The old guy has complicated everything. Yesterday I had the final chapter of my thesis lined up neatly, a confident little series of observations linking the burial practices of Crageen with the Bronze Age idea of grave goods, concluding that this was the perfect illustration of the persistence of the past in present cemetery rites. So straightforward. But now I'm intrigued. I flip through a pretty coffee-table book on castles of Ireland as I remember our conversation in Crageen.

—

'Ah, it's not around here, it's further south, down the coast where the big beaches start. On one of them,' – he holds up a hand – 'I won't tell you which one, there's a castle. It was famous as the home of the family that married into the sea people. The son of the castle married a mermaid, you see, she fell in love with him, and she lived and died and was buried on land. Land right in front of the castle. The story goes that her father, the King of the Sea People, was so heartbroken that he pulled the graveyard out to him, out as far as where the sea goes at low tide, so his daughter could be near to him again in death.' The old man pauses for breath. I'm standing, entranced, the rain and the camera both forgotten. He wipes the rain-mist off his face slowly with the back of his hand and continues. 'But that wasn't the last burial out there. There was a thing, if there was someone who was excommunicated from the church, or a baby that was born that shouldn't be, that was where they were buried. The mad and the bad were put in the ground there, after midnight, when the tide was out. Come morning, all the traces would be covered over again with the sea.'

'Where is it?' I need to know.

'Ach,' he says and his pale-blue eyes are faraway, thinking. 'It's not a place you'd want to go to.' He straightens up and bobs his head in an act of dismissal.

I catch at the sleeve of his tweed jacket. 'Please. I'd like to know.'

His face is serious. 'Forget it, son. Now, I didn't come here for a chat. If you'll excuse me.' He turns away and walks to the other side of the cemetery. I know I am dismissed. I walk up the grey rutted track to where my rented Jeep is parked, glinting wetly in the weak sunlight. When I drive by he is still there, head bowed in the lightly misting rain, standing by one of the gravestones.

~

As I'm thinking about it, the sun has gone down and the trailer is getting chilly. The book in front of me is almost impossible to read in the dim light, the black and white illustrations blurring into the printed words. I reach over and flick on the light, and then I see it: Drominagh Castle, overlooking the strand at Drominagh, Kerry, a castle with an ornamental coat of arms that includes – I squint closer – *a mermaid!* For a second I have that purely out-of-body experience that comes with an unexpected research revelation, then immediately I'm checking the route-planner on my phone.

~

Journal Entry. August 12.

Arrived in Drominagh last night. The castle is amazing, just a shell really, but the outer walls are intact, even the apertures of the original windows and doors. There's a weather-beaten family crest above the doorway, including the mostly eroded figure of the mermaid. The view from it is incredible, over the whole shoreline and way out to sea. The town itself is tiny, crammed with trailer parks, three pubs and a couple of shops. Staying in a B&B near the shore – the landlady, Betty, doesn't know anything about the castle, which is a pity. 'I've never even been up to it' she said, as if that was to be admired. For Pete's sake, the damn thing is about five hundred yards away from her door. (Sometimes I just don't get Irish people.)

I went down to the seashore last night for a few hours, trying to figure out where the old cemetery could be, on the basis that it should be in a direct line from the castle out to sea. It was a cloudy, windy night, though, so I couldn't see anything, I could just hear the roar of the waves hitting rocks. That must have given me the weird dreams – when I came back I kept waking up, fancying I could hear the sea, even though the window was closed.

Journal Entry. August 13.

Went down to the strand in the afternoon. Found two old sailors sitting together chatting beside an upturned boat. Were very friendly, asking me where I was from ('California! What the hell are you doing here?'), and gave me the information I needed about the tidal pulls. Apparently, the tide is completely out at around two thirty to three in the morning, then it starts coming back in from three thirty or so. It was all going well until I told them about my quest to find the cemetery. Almost instantly, one of them looked at his watch and mumbled about having to get home. The other said he'd go with him. So I'm left on the strand, scribbling down the information they'd told me. Went home early, had tea with Betty (she's very pleasant – likes my American stories, and she even supplied me with cookies, but they were digestives, those weird, Irish, salty kind), and then set my alarm for 1.45am. Walked out as far as I could manage, in a straight line from the castle, with a reef of rock to my left, but the waves were still audible, crashing further out. I imagined I could feel the earth shift slightly beneath my feet. My nerve failed me, and I turned back, but not before I played my torch out to sea and saw some small rocks scattered on the shoreline, the waves lacing them with white froth. Just then a rivulet of water gushed by my foot, and I realised the tide was about to turn. I ran then, all the way back, and when I slept, I had exhausted, constant dreams about the sand slipping beneath me, the hiss and roar of the waves on rock, and a deep rumbling beneath my feet.

Journal Entry. August 14th.

Woke up exhausted after yesterday. Only the thought of a cooked breakfast got me out of bed. Afterwards, I headed back to the shore again, determined to find those old guys from the day before. I'm convinced they know about the cemetery, and can tell me more. Finally ran them to ground in one of the three pubs in the afternoon. Instead of asking if I could join them, I simply ordered three pints of Guinness and sat down with them. I knew their hospitable Irish souls would honour the implicit pact made by the drinks. After a couple of pints (my head was starting to spin, I'm no drinker) they finally relented, and after parading the appropriate cautions – 'You wouldn't want to go out there, son. Only a fool would go there at night. There's nothing good buried out there' – they confirm my suspicions. Where I walked last night is the proper route out, they reference the rocky reef to the left of the path. It just seems I didn't go out far enough. They tell me that the place is full of unbaptised babies and what they term 'bad characters'. They even hint that it might be a place where bodies were disposed of secretly. I can see how accretions of myth and superstition have built up, but the archaeologist in me can't believe the site has never been investigated. I tell them of my plans to head out that night. They exchange alarmed glances.

'Not tonight' says one of them, Dermot. 'It's starting to blow up now. It'll be bad out there tonight, too bad to walk out.'

The other guy (Matt?) agrees. 'The moon'll be clouded over, no visibility. And the sea will be angry.' Sure enough, when I leave the pub, there's an ugly, grey sea roiling about the shoreline, and a sharp wind blowing in from the sea. I sway home (partly due to wind, partly due to Guinness) and get a much-needed early night. I dream I'm back on La Jolla beach, my feet on the warm sand, the translucent green-blue water washing over them. I pick up a conch shell and hold it to my ear. The sound of the waves grows, louder and louder till I drop it, startled, on the sand. Then the sand erupts in front of me in a wave, and I wake up with a shout. My bed is rocking, as if something has pushed it, and my window has blown open, banging against the sill. When I close it, I can hear the fierce roar of the waves outside. I'm cold and a bit shaken. I move about restlessly, write this down, and finally, as the sky turns a reddish-yellow, I fall back asleep.

~

It's the fifteenth of August. I wake up and stretch, long and luxuriantly in the sunlit bedroom. I feel surprisingly good, considering how little I've slept. There's lots of noise outside, car horns blaring, voices, music. Apparently the fifteenth of August is a church holiday, and it's tradition for all the locals to come to the seaside.

'And do what?' I ask, curious. There's no funfair, or seafood restaurants, or anything here that I would associate with leisure time in a holiday village.

She shrugs. 'Walk on the seashore, eat ice-cream, play with their kids. Just the usual stuff.' Sure enough, when I go out for a walk to the newsagent, the strand is thronged with deckchairs and parked cars, and children rage up and down the promenade, crusted with sand and salt and sunscreen.

When evening falls, the cars start to leave, one by one. Their headlights swivel and beam upwards, up the coast road and away. Children pull at their parents, whining to go, tired and querulous after a day spent running in the sun. With each carload that leaves, the strand becomes progressively quieter. I go back to rest in my B&B, but I'm too excited to sleep.

It's two in the morning. I can't wait any longer so I get up to go outside. There's still a dull buzz on the strand – one of the pubs is still open, spilling out golden circles of light and the raucous sound of a live band. There are small groups of teenagers drinking cider, and some older men and women standing and talking and laughing, glowing cigarette ends bobbing up and down in the gloom. The strand itself is empty, stretching damp and dark all the way out the horizon. I walk out, my feet leaving a set of neat depressions on the wet sand. I walk on and on and on towards the dark horizon. The night is calm, but a faint breeze plucks at my raincoat, and I can smell the cold, seaweed stink of the water and rocks ahead. There's a full moon overhead, round and yellow, that lights up the strand with a strange uneven glow. Even when I switch off the torch, I can pick out the way ahead. I'm almost there now. I'm so far out, I can't resist turning to see Drominagh stretched out behind me, the faint lights of the village scattered like a line of glitter, low down and far away. Through some acoustical trick I can hear the echoes of sounds from the beach, a thin static crackle of voices and music. I'm still looking at the lights, walking backwards, when I find the first one.

'Ow!' My ankle hurts where I've skinned it. I shine the torch on the protrusion, and then instantly forget the pain. It's a stone. And more than a stone, it's definitely a grave-marker. I can see notches carved on the top, too regular and too deep to be caused by any sea erosion. I rub my hands over the wet stone, feeling a tracery of lines beneath my fingers. I shine the torch on something that might be a Celtic carving, but it looks more tentacular, with what look like decorative eyes dotted around it. Excitedly, I shine the torch left and right. There they are, tussocks of stone, all different sizes, a *bona fide* sea-cemetery. None have names, but most have rough carvings of fish shapes or wave patterns. One, the largest one, has an approximation of the mermaid crest I photographed over the doorway of Drominagh Castle. I'm almost sick with a cold excitement that clenches my stomach. There's a group of stones clustered together, at a distance from the others, each one with a blank panel in front. With my hood up, my breath is quick and warm and fast in my ears. The wind has risen slightly, but I don't really notice the chill. I lay the torch down carefully on the strand and start to photograph the stones, at first together in group shots, and then singly. I'm getting accustomed to the faraway *whoosh-whoosh* of the waves in the distance; it's become a lulling sound, a counterpoint to my breathing. The moon is sinking, and the pale gold of the pre-dawn is streaking the sky. *Just five more minutes.* I stand between the cluster of plain stones and peer at the blank panels in front, each one bigger than my head – *Is there a carving there I can't see? Has it eroded?*

And then I feel it. I feel it rather than hear it, a distinctive, low rumbling beneath my feet. My first instinctive thought is *Earthquake!* Then I remember where I am and draw in a deep, ragged breath of relief. The waves sound stronger, nearer. The ground shifts and groans again. I grab on to one of the stones to steady myself, and it moves, slides forward with a grating sound, so I'm caught securely between two rocks. I scream and drop the torch, struggling to get free. The stones grate and move again, with a terrible, grinding sound. I can see the torch loll and roll between the rocks, its pale gleam picking out sand and stone. I'm pinched between the stones, helpless, struggling. Then the sand slides greasily under my feet and I'm... *in the air?* The rocks around me open, and I'm flat on a ledge, high up and surrounded by the long rocks that bend and close around me, an action both terrible and horribly familiar.

'It's a *hand!*' I scream. 'It's a *giant hand!*' The wind whips my words away. The blank-panelled tips – *the fingernails!* – close around me. I'm mad with fear, hitting and kicking, feeling myself lowered, until I hit the strand with a crash, still pinned beneath the rocks. Above me looms something too large and too strange and too terrible to describe. There is a roar like a thousand quarries being scraped, and behind it, I see a green, crested wave, climbing tall and terrifying, moving swiftly inland. There is another awful, grinding, grating cry that reverberates across the sand.

And then, from the village, from the strand, there is an echoing dull roar from the crowd. It rises thin and sharp on the breeze, a roar of acknowledgement for a ritual almost forgotten.

There is only time for one long, mournful thought, of blue skies and sun, of family far away, of the scribbled, unfinished pages of my notebook.

And then the wave hits.

This story came from a visit to Ballyheighue Castle in Kerry in 2015. It was part of a project I set out to do; to photograph a range of sites in the south-west of Ireland that were connected in some way with strange legends. According to local lore, the Cantillion family who owned the castle fell in love with the mermaid Durfulla, daughter of the sea king. He married her and they had children. When she died she was buried in the family graveyard on the strand below the castle. Enraged, her father rose from the depths of the sea and dragged the graveyard down with him. However, later, he regretted his actions, and decided he wanted his daughter's progeny to be buried with their ancestors. So the story goes that from then on, whenever a Cantillion died, their coffin was laid on the strand, and the sea king's minions would take it away and bury it in the ancestral graveyard at the bottom of the sea. Like with 'What Lies Beneath' I was drawn to the Lovecraftian, grandiose notion of primal, large-scale horror in the conclusion.

1. SEA. YOU.

t's always cold here in the sea. A deep, dark, salty cold that chills my flesh like meat in a freezer. The icy shock of water on my torso cuts cleanly, right down to the bone. Sometimes I picture a glowing ball of fire, circling slowing from my core outwards. It makes no difference. The cold still burns. The trick is to ignore it and keep moving. The intense cold hurts for a few agonizing minutes – my chest constricts, my organs contract, my skin is hard and rigid with gooseflesh – and then, finally, the glorious numbness sets in, that deep, sea-anaesthetic. I churn my cold-clumsy limbs about, generating a slow warmth that crawls over my body, inch by reluctant inch

But it's worth it. It's always worth it. When I'm in here the larger world dissolves; the only things that exist, sure and true, are my strong arms slicing through water, the sting of the salt, and the cold underbelly of the sea. The mainland looks like a simulacrum, a faraway, unreal bubble of pier and hotels and brightly coloured amusement rides. There are no problems out here in the water, no concerns except for the pull and suck of the current and the hidden rocks close to the shoreline. I swim. I don't think. I just swim and swim until my arms fall heavy in the water, cold and rigid with tired knots of muscle. Then I'll stop and let myself float, weightless and tired, on the current. I let myself drift closer to the rocks, but carefully. I drape my arms around the crags, my legs trailing in the sea like kelp, like a mermaid's tail. And then I drop my face in the water and whisper till a stream of bubbles boils from my mouth.

What do I whisper? It's an old secret, between me and the sea.

When I was a child, there was a chart in my classroom. I was sitting in one of those tiny chairs, with plastic bolts on the back, so I can't have been any more than eight or nine. There was a chart on the wall that I couldn't stop looking at. It showed a cross-section cartoon of a smiling man, enjoying a bathe, strolling out to sea with a jaunty stride. But what he didn't know (but I did) was that a few yards in front of him, the ground fell away into a sharp underwater cliff. It showed his dreadful fate in a cross section that sliced through the shoreline. While we were meant to be reading, or learning our long list of spellings, I'd sit there, considering his awful fate. Sometimes I even dreamt about it, and woke, screaming, feeling him falling into that deep sea-void. I dreamed that the sea was taking him away, dragging him down from the bright surface, from the sun, from his everyday life, into a deep, dark, underwater country full of murky shadows and strange, shifting shapes. My mother was contemptuous.

'It's only a dream. You're a big girl now.'

I was so nervous then, so afraid of everything, with no knowledge yet of what I *should* fear.

Now swimming is everything. It's as close as I come to flying these days. That wonderful gliding soar through the water is worth it all; the difficult journey to the beach, the cold wind, and the deep muscle aches afterwards. When I'm in the sea, I'm weightless, graceful. For a short period of time, I'm free. Free to swim, free to fight, free to struggle just like anyone else against the ancient enemies of tide and cold and current. I'm filled with a fierce joy as I hug the rocks afterwards, feeling the deep, dull ache in my arms and shoulders. Swimming is where I feel at home.

It's the only place I feel at home.

When I'm actually *at* home, I'm a fish out of water. I sit slumped in the prison of my house, winding a dull path from bedroom to bathroom to kitchen and living room. I stare out the window, my book in front of me, unread. Beside me the TV squawks, an endless stream of orange hosts selling properties, asking quiz questions, interviewing other orange people. I only leave it on so he thinks I'm being entertained. If he didn't believe that he'd be at home all day, breathing just that bit too loudly, being that bit too attentive, pressing so close to me that I want to scream.

He is so kind. Too kind. He's everywhere, all the time. Even when I can't see him, I feel his anxious gaze on me. I swim to get away from it. I face out to sea. I try not to see him on the shore, waiting for me to return.

Some days I swim out a little too far, just to see what might happen.

It's nearly twenty years since I first swam here, when I took my first, timid steps into the crashing waves that sluiced up and down the shoreline. Back in that long, sunny Neverland of summer holidays, I'd stand, cold in the surging wind that came in gusts from the sea, shivering, hugging my goose-fleshed arms tight to me. My swimming back then was as timid as I was; I was unadventurous in my ventures, hugging the shoreline. But still I loved them, those lonely little voyages out into the sea. I loved it all – walking the strand beforehand, collecting shells and carefully washing them in rock pools to clear the grit and dirt off. I loved the exhilaration afterwards, the combative, glowing feeling of a fresh fight with the waves. I still love it. It's different now, but there's still the same complex cocktail of emotions when I'm in the water, loving it and fighting it, all at once.

~

Today the sea is especially rough. The sky is charcoal. The water is dull grey, the waves whipped up into stiff, white little peaks that crash hard against the shore. He doesn't want me to go out in it.

'It's too bad out there,' he says uneasily. I pretend not to hear.

'Seriously,' he persists. 'I'd be too worried.'

'Please.' It hurts me to beg, but I need his help.

'Do I have any choice?' He says it sadly, and I know I've won.

~

It's a difficult swim. I know it will be; there's no one else out there, not even a surfer on the beach. The waves roll, dirty and hard, and the water is brackish and brown, full of sucked-up sand. The moment I leave the shore, I can feel the bad-tempered surge of the sea, huge and uncaring. I breathe deeply and thrash into it, my strong arms slicing through the surging water. I swim against the waves, head plunged below the water, moving forward steadily. It's hard work. The waves pull and twist me so my shoulder drags across a rock. It hurts stunningly for a second, and then the water numbs it. A thin line of blood trickles into the sea. *I'm bait*, I think, but I'm not afraid. The dangers are all inland.

I cling to the rocks with my soft plasticine limbs. Salt is crusted on my lips. I bob my head under the waves and whisper to them, as I always do. '*Take me away.*'

Someday they'll answer. But not now. My words are swallowed up into a stream of tiny bubbles.

When I resurface he's still standing there, a speck of black against the broad swathe of darkened sand.

'I see you,' he calls, thin and distant.

Water thunders in my ears as I dive underneath, back in that rushing swirl. I ignore him and twist to one side, my arms thrusting me forward. When I surface and shake water from my eyes, he's still there, tiny and patient. The sun glints on the chrome of my chair, parked beside him.

'I see you,' he calls.

But I still don't answer.

This is a story inspired by The Seal Woman and Her Skin – the story of the selkie who sheds her skin and is trapped within her husband's home until she finds it again. This short and simple story was inspired by ideas of entrapment and freedom found in this migratory legend where the home is a place of imprisonment and the sea represents freedom.

THEY BROKE HIS BONES
WITH STICKS AND STONES

t's always cold in her father's house. She remembers the cold from her childhood; not the bracing cold of snowy landscapes and fresh air, but a cold that seeps up from below the ground; dank, damp, smelling of wet stone and old earth. *Cold inside*, she thinks. Even during the Christmas holidays, the heating is meagre, turned on and off precisely once a day. The door opens, and she feels another breeze of chill air come into the living room.

'Don't you want to come with me out to town?' She feels herself set her teeth together in a flash of annoyance.

'No thank you,' she says nicely, moving her mouth in a smile. 'We'll be fine here.'

Her father looks at her doubtfully. 'But what about him?' He cocks his chin at his grandson, sitting curled up on the sofa, reading, face soft and absorbed.

'He's fine too.'

'It's not much fun for him there.' Her father always thinks he knows best. No, he *knows* he knows best. That's worse.

She feels her temper rise, red and slow. 'He likes to sit and read. Let him be.'

'Well if that's what you want...' His blue eyes are bright with scorn. 'Not much of a life for a boy his age. But if you want me to *let him be.*' The last words are pure vinegar.

She nods tightly, not trusting herself to speak. Her smile feels frozen; her cheek muscles rigid from grinning. It's only when she hears the car cough to life and rev out of the driveway that she can relax.

It's peaceful now in the house. She makes a cup of tea, looking out the kitchen window. The clock ticks over the stove, a reassuring metronome tick. Outside the muddy fields stretch out to the horizon, demarcated with strips of dark green bushes. The rain falls softly in a sheet of pale, opalescent mist. The light is fading into a dark grey now, the advent of an early winter evening. It's beautiful, she supposes, but she can't see it. The landscape for her is irrevocably scarred with memories; long, dreary days spent indoors, wishing for the rain to stop, wishing for someone to call, wishing for escape. Her entire teenage years were spent desperate for release from the countryside. It's the dullness of it she hates, the long Sunday-afternoon dreariness of nothing happening too slowly. She sips her tea and remembers it; the dullness, the wetness, the mud and the despair.

St. Stephen's Day today. The traditional day of doing nothing. She stretches luxuriantly at the thought. *The house to ourselves for hours.* She thinks about Christmas Day yesterday, the coldness of the celebration, the forced conversations, the long, wretched silences. If it wasn't for Eoin she'd never come back, but she loves him with a quiet intensity she never knew was possible. She wants to give him everything, even his disinterested grandfather.

Eoin wanders in, glasses tilted on his nose, book in his hand, one finger marking his page. The sight of him in his red and black striped jumper twists her heart.

'Can I get something to eat, Mum?'

'Of course. Sandwich?'

He smiles at her, his lovely, open smile. 'Turkey please.' She strokes his hair. He's thirteen now, nearly past the age where she can demonstrate her affection, so she treasures these tiny gestures jealously. For the millionth time she wonders how his grandfather can still bear him a grudge. Eoin's oblivious, of course, he just notices the presents; he takes their hugs at face value. But she sees her father look at him, eyes narrowed; she knows he still thinks about her dropping out of university, her lost career. She thinks of her father, of his white rage at her pregnancy, his stony lack of forgiveness. She looks at Eoin, still patting his head. *We'll never be like that.*

'Mu-um.' He wriggles away from her. 'Don't mess my hair.' With a little jolt she realises he's styled it with her dad's Brylcreem. It looks ridiculous, but he's clearly trying to appear more grown-up. She releases him with a little push to his back.

'Go on back in beside the fire. I'll bring in your sandwich.'

─

She's just putting the plate down beside him when the doorbell rings. She pauses, irresolute. On the one hand, whoever's calling isn't calling for her. On the other hand, her car is clearly in the driveway. Not answering the door is a mortal sin of hospitality, and her father will hear all about it. Her upbringing wins out.

'Back in a second.' She pats Eoin's arm.

She opens the door and catches her breath. The Wranboys. She hasn't seen the Wranboys since she was a child. They stand before her in the gloom, their plain masks stark and white under the porchlight. They're wearing dirty hessian coalsacks, belted at the waist, their hair is tousled, their hands filthy. One of them has tattered feathers wound up in his curly hair. She stares at them, hot disgust rising in her throat. They have a wren with them. A tiny, dead wren; a forlorn ball on the floor of a small cage.

They don't say anything at first. One of them rattles a tin at her. It clangs with the chime of small change. Then they clear their throat and their voices jumble together in the chant she remembers.

The wran, the wran, the king of the birds
On Stephen's Day was caught in the furze.
We broke his bones with sticks and stones,
Give us some money to bury the wran.

She feels her vision cloud with fury at these boys she doesn't know. She doesn't know them, but she's known many like them. They're dirty and savage and coarse. She hates them. She hates their filth and cruelty. She hates the way they pronounce 'wren' as 'wran' for no better reason than that their fathers and their grandfathers did. They represent everything she that made her leave home in the first place. With a pang of sadness, she looks at the tiny body of the bird in the cage, a pitiful ball of wet feathers.

'No,' she says coldly.

'Whaddya mean, missus?' It's the tallest one. His voice is aggressive.

'I said no.' She feels a flood of adrenalin surge through her. 'How dare you come here and parade that poor, dead bird. You should be ashamed of yourselves.'

They mutter. She steps back and starts to close the door.

'Fuck you.'

'What? Which one of you said that? Which one of you *cowards* said that?'

The masks look back at her, white and impenetrable.

She gives them a long, hard stare of contempt, and then shuts the door with a deliberately hard thud.

Back in the kitchen she picks up the gin bottle and sloshes a shaky measure into a glass tumbler. Her father will notice it, but she doesn't care. She's still trembling with anger. There's no tonic in the fridge, so she adds some orange from a dusty old bottle of Club Orange. It's dark outside now; the late afternoon has slid straight into evening gloom. The fields have disappeared into an amorphous dark grey mass.

The fucking Wranboys. Even as a child she hated them; their masks, their weird, homemade costumes. She'd cry over the dead wren, and her father would jeer at her. It was so stupid, so meaningless. She knew there were legends about the wren betraying St. Stephen to his persecutors, who stoned him to death. She remembers a medieval painting in the National Gallery of a stoic St. Stephen, a large rock on his head, blood trickling down his ornate gold robes. Even further back, there was the story of Cliona, the goddess who lured young men into the sea, then escaped in the form of a wren. Mind you, the doltish Wranboys wouldn't know that. They just enjoyed hunting the birds and scavenging for money.

There's a hot wash of bile at the back of her throat. She takes a large swallow of gin and flat soda to try and wash away the copper taste. It's only then she realises the back door is ajar, cold air leaking in. For a moment she just looks at it, then something stirs in her; a kind of unease.

'Eoin,' she calls.

There's nothing but silence. She feels her heart blunder in her chest.

'Eoin!' Still nothing. *He's reading, he won't answer.* But she runs through the hallway, into the sitting room. His book is open, splayed on the chair. She clatters up the stairs.

'Eoin!'

She opens door after door. He's not in the house.

She's outside now, calling uselessly into the dark laneway. The sound of her own scared voice terrifies her. She starts to run over the crunching gravel. Her feet pound to the rhythm of her heartbeat. He's here somewhere, he has to be.

'Eoin!'

The lane is hideous with shadows. The overhanging bushes droop down, blocking the last of the fading light.

We broke his bones with sticks and stones.

The chant rings through her head. She sees their white, implacable masks. She imagines the worst, their brutish revenge. She sees Eoin, legs tucked up under him, reading and smiling to himself. Fear rises in her like nausea. The cold bites through her jumper but she barely notices. Round the corner of the lane now. She stops and listens, but can't hear a sound. The lane is dark and empty. Somewhere in the distance a cow lows, a deep, melancholy sound.

She pushes open the tall gates and stand on the lumpy tarmac of the country road. In the distance she sees another house, the wash of porchlight gleaming. It's the only likely place they've gone to.

We broke his bones with sticks and stones,
Give us some money to bury the wran.

The words churn in her head. Her breath catches in a rough sob. *Why didn't I give them money? Why did I have to take it out on them?* She shudders and runs, eyes fixed on the light in the distance. Her feet hit a rock; she stumbles, almost falls, steadies herself and keeps on running. She can hear her breath tearing noisily from her lungs.

And then she sees them. They're standing in front of the house. She sees the door open; hears their chant rise in the still evening air. And then she's on them.

'Where is he?' Her voice is wild, frantic. The masks turn and look at her. She makes a grab at the tall one, pulls the white mask away. Underneath he's just a boy, blinking and confused. His blonde hair stands on end. She drops the mask on the ground. 'Where is he? Where's Eoin?'

The man at the door looks at her, confused. 'Amanda?' She ignores him.

'Where's Eoin?' She stares at the blonde boy, resisting the urge to slap his stupid face. She hears a familiar laugh. Then she sees it. An arm in a red and black striped jumper holding the wren's cage.

It's Eoin.

Her heart turns over in anger and relief.

'What do you think you're doing?' She slaps his arm, hard, so that the cages bounces on the concrete path. The door flies open and the wren tumbles out, tiny and frozen and dead. 'And take off that stupid mask.'

He flinches but doesn't make a sound. 'He wanted to come with us missus,' says the blonde boy, his face closed and sullen.

Eoin reaches up and pulls off the white mask. 'There, lads.' He passes it to the boy beside him, ignoring her.

'Your ma's a weapon.' She ignores them. She doesn't care what they say; the backwash of adrenalin is still washing through her like a wave.

Eoin turns to her. He's not wearing his glasses; he looks older, angrier. She sees her father's eyes shining blue and cold from his face.

She'd always thought they could escape this; the country, the slow, silent resentment, the festering anger. For years she's run from this. She's built a wall between her reality and that of her childhood. The steady neon lights of the city dispelled the gloom of her memories. But now, standing here, shivering on the side of the mucky road, she realises it's all been in vain. His eyes look back into hers, scared and angry. She feels it all; the start of the rupture, the inevitability of genetic transmission. They're trapped, replaying the old roles; the oppressive parent, the sullen child.

The countryside she hates has folded them back into itself.

She's found him. She's lost him.

In Ireland, Boxing Day is known as St. Stephen's Day, and there's a very old tradition that on that day the Wrenboys go around houses to demand money. They originally paraded around with a dead wren, but this practice has died out. Now the custom only survives in very rural areas, like the wedding tradition of the Strawboys. This is a quiet little story – I wanted to set it up so the reader is drawn along with the terrible imaginings of the mother, and the ending, although a relief of sorts, actually cements one of her darkest fears.

THE WORLD'S MORE
FULL OF WEEPING

fter what happened, they closed it down. One day it was full of women walking with their children, gently guiding them around the decorated trees, the next day there was a high fence around it. 'CLOSED TILL FURTHER NOTICE' the sign said in big red letters. And so the days went by. The paint peeled in the wind and rain. The red letters faded to a warm pink.

Now the boards themselves slope away, revealing complicated fissures and cracks; a hint of a way back in. No-one talks about it anymore, or if they do, it's in whispers, away from us. They don't think we remember. But I do.

We spent every day that summer playing down by the river. It was – and still is – a pretty place. But back then it was more – it was beautiful. The river swept by, smooth and muscular as a fish, boiling with white froth whenever the sky turned grey and the winds started up. There was an abandoned ruined castle on the far side of the river, and on the near side a little concrete bird hide on the slope down to the bank. Every morning we'd go there to play, and our first stop was the fairy village. Earlier that year we'd gone down with our class to help set it up. The men from the local estate had mowed the grass down into a tight little buzz-cut that smelled green and fresh. All that was left was a clump of trees and a neat little hillock.

'You can adorn it how you want,' our teacher, Miss Brook, told us. It wasn't true, of course. We'd spent days beforehand with her, laboriously drawing fairies and houses and working out elaborate decorative schemes for the village. We'd all gotten a door each to christen with our names, and we painted them carefully; all neat letters, bright colours and sticky glitter. It was exciting to see the doors all lined up neatly at the base of the trees. The tiny doorways shone like spots of colour against the rough grey bark.

'Now go on, decorate around them.' We stood for a few moments, unsure where to start. Our bags were full of different things: pretty stones, dolls, bits of toys. We looked to Miss Brook for guidance.

'Here. Watch me.' She dipped her hand into her satchel and brought out a little feathery dreamcatcher, which she tied onto a branch. 'Use the branches. Or make arrangements on the ground.' She smiled at us, her springy curls glowing in the sun. Miss Brook loved fairies. She told us stories about them in the afternoons, just before the bell rung for end of class. The tales were always about magic little beings that granted wishes and brought good luck.

That summer we were all fairy-obsessed. The village grew from bare beginnings into a tiny colony. Each day we'd check on it, and each day brought a new addition to the little clearing. Annmarie went to the beach and brought back shells which she carefully arranged in complicated swirling lines around her tiny red door. Jane's tree was decorated with plastic butterflies which she'd carefully painted at home. Her mother came down with her to attach them up high in the branches. Shelagh and her little brother built a tiny Lego village around hers, with tiny Lego people standing outside their houses, each one with an arm lifted in a miniscule wave. Lynda's fairy house was the prettiest of all. She'd collected all her mother's old, discarded costume jewellery, and her tree twinkled and sparkled in the summer sun, mock-pearls winking in the light, the sun-dazzle of diamante flashing signals from the branches.

And the long summer went on, hot day after endless hot day. We continued to decorate the village. Clusters of stones and pebbles delineated our different territories. The adults joined in. A tiny wishing well appeared. A local man, a sculptor, created a handsome wooden board; sanded down and smooth to touch, with letters poker-stained into the surface. We stood in front of it, spelling it out to each other.

'Come away, O human child! To the waters and the wild
With a faery, hand in hand,
For the world's more full of weeping than you can understand.'

I recognised the poem from Miss Brook's class. As I read it I could smell the dusty warmth of the classroom, a scent made up equally of chalk and felt and plastic chairs. I saw her fizz of curls bowed over a book, reading the poem aloud in the sleepy hush of the afternoon.

'Come away.' I repeated aloud. I traced the letters with my finger, absorbed.

'Come away where?' Lynda ran up behind me, laughing, with her blonde hair falling over her shoulders.

'Nowhere.' I grabbed her hand. 'Let's go collect some pretty stones.'

~

I spent more time there than anywhere. A safe place to play, the parents told each other. Fences all around, a contained space. All the parents loved it. All, that is, except mine. That was the summer my mother was sick, you see. While the summer hummed outside, all bees and running water and green light, she was inside in her room. I didn't like going in to her room. It felt tight and huddled and smothery; her curtains stayed drawn, the air smelled warm and spent. She stayed under the bedclothes, a hump of flesh; her eyes staring at me as if she'd forgotten who I was.

'She's just tired,' my father said. I wasn't so sure. She'd come back from the hospital like that, as if they'd lifted something out of her, some crucial cog that she needed to keep working. Now she lay in bed, the delicate, precise mechanisms of her run down, faltering, stopped. When he was home, my father hovered anxiously outside her door; his hands always full with trays and hot drinks and medicine. I ran wild. I ate random things at random times. My hair grew tangled, my hands were cracked with dirt, little spider-webs of grime spreading across my palms. No-one at home noticed.

Lynda's mother tried to tame me. She lent me some of Lynda's pretty smocked dresses. She even tried to brush out my tangled hair once or twice, but it hurt like nettle-stings and I pulled away impatiently. After a while she gave up.

~

We played lots of games that summer. Our dolls were dressed as fairies and we added wings to their backs and swooped them around the village. We made them swim in the little stream that flowed down to the river. There was a fairy school that we played at for a bit, but that was too boring. Some of us made wishes at the wishing well. But there was one game we kept returning to. It centred around the little hill that the men from the estate had built up, leftover dirt from their digging. As summer went on the dirt formed solid into a glossy, grassy bump, taller than us. One of the dads added a wooden set of painted blue eyes to it. He set them deep in the hillock, so it looked like a surprised giant, surfacing into a strange world.

We gave him a name. Pook, we called him. We started adding things around him. Paper windmills. Little lanterns. Wilted bunches of flowers. We played around the mound and told each other stories about him. He was a fairy king in some of them, but mostly he was an enemy.

'Pook will get you,' we told each other, daring each other to climb the hill. Only the bravest would do it, and when we got to the top, we'd jump off, shrieking. Just to scare him away in case he *did* come for us.

He got out at night, Annmarie said. He got out and walked around, looking for us. At night, when the shadows drew in and the sound of the river grew wilder, it seemed more likely.

The adults didn't like this story as much. Especially not when Shelagh's brother Mike fell off the hill after trying to dig out one of the blue wooden eyes. He twisted his ankle badly and spent the rest of the summer hobbling around with a metal crutch. *He tried to harm Pook*, we said, shaking our heads wisely. *That's what happens if you do.*

When we went there one morning, one of the parents had painted a sign and stuck it on the hillock. 'Don't climb on my head,' it read. We pretended Pook had written it, and though we knew we were joking, we didn't climb there anymore.

But we still played there. More toys appeared there: trucks, farm animals, pieces of string with baubles attached. No-one said it, but it felt safer that way, to keep adding to the store of treasures around the tiny doors.

～

I went there today.

You can see it now if you squint through a crack in the fence. It's another world in there. The grass is dark green, waist-high. It's grown up over the painted toadstools and the fairy doors. The dreamcatchers are tangled up in leaves, the tin ornaments are rusted a dull brown. Pook is missing an eye. *Did Mike go back and dig it out this time?* I wondered. The board with the poem on it has fallen down. I can just see one edge of it sticking up.

'Come away' it says.

⚐

That summer the days slipped by, bright and blue-skied, like beads on a string. Every morning smelled like a fresh promise, of coconutty gorse and the heavy, secret scent of honeysuckle. And as the summer went by, the village began to change. Just a little, at first.

One morning we arrived to find Shelagh's Lego tableau demolished. Someone had taken the roofs off the houses, and meticulously pulled out the windows and doors. Outside the tiny ruins lay the carefully dissected bodies of the Lego people, their yellow faces frozen in rictus expressions of shock. *Other kids*, we said, but the dismemberment was so precise that it felt...purposeful. Not an act of destruction, more like a planned attack. The next thing to change were Annmarie's shells. We stood in silence looking down at them. They were laid out neatly to read 'GO AWAY.' Lynda's mum was with us, I remember.

'Someone's playing a silly joke,' she said loudly, shuffling the shells with the toe of her pink Converse sneaker. The letters tangled and fell apart. We started playing again, but it was oddly subdued. I went home early that evening.

The next day I got there first. My Barbie, abandoned the day before, was hanging from a branch. A twist of blue baling twine was knotted tight around her neck. She swung gently in the breeze, her large eyes wide with reproach. I took her down and didn't say anything. But from then on the place didn't feel quite the same. The trees seemed a shade darker, the air a fraction colder. And the rustle of leaves in the air sounded a little – just a little – like whispers.

Getting down to the village first became an obsession. I would get there just as the light was lifting off the river, when the pinkish streaks in the sky were fading into blue. I'd make a private wish at the wishing well, and then wander around, noting any tiny changes. I wasn't the only one. Sometimes I'd see grown-ups there, with dogs, or joggers in their running gear. It was a magical place, one that demanded attention. Most often I would see a man there. I noticed him because he always wore a heavy tweed coat despite the warmth of the mornings. Like me, he would trace his way around the trees, stopping briefly beside each one, as if he were making the Stations of the Cross. I thought – I couldn't be sure, but I thought it – that he was checking the fairy doors.

It was sometime around then that I got the idea to re-decorate my door. I took my little door home to paint it; I covered the bright red paint with a dark charcoal and went looking for the old box of Halloween decorations.

'What are you doing?' It was my father, his kind face knotted in a permanent expression of worry.

'Doing my door for the village,' I said proudly. I started to sift out little ornaments from the box, delighted with his attention. He stooped with a grunt to unload the dishwasher.

'Just don't make a mess.'

'I won't. Can I go upstairs to show Mum?' I'd started asking since the last time, when the sight of me had made her shudder with heavy, noiseless sobs. He straightened up and looked at me. My hands were streaked grey with paint.

'Better not. Just play quietly, OK?' I shrugged and nodded, shaping the brush in my mouth. It tasted bitter, almost salty, gritty with particles.

I was so proud of my fairy tree. I put everything in place carefully and waited. It was something different, something to make everyone notice. In the faint, pink light of dawn, the tiny tombstones stood lopsided at the base of the tree. The dark grey door was open at an angle, one skeleton hand clasped around it. Each grave marker had the name of a dead fairy lettered on it – mostly flower names like Lily, Rose and Bluebell. The largest was one for Pook. I nodded at it in satisfaction, and then wandered over to the wishing well to close my eyes and wish my usual wish. *Make Mum better.*

'Did you do this?' It was the man in the tweed coat. I hadn't seen him arrive. He crouched down beside me. The tweed coat smelled of damp and grass, a heavy, slightly unpleasant smell. Glasses flashed opaque over his eyes.

'Yes.'

'It's beautiful.' He examined it closely, peering at each tombstone. His hair fell over his forehead as he stooped. For a moment we stayed in silence as he traced a finger over the lettering, until a goose flew low beside us, skimming down on the river with a series of low honks. Then he stood up, buttoned his coat, and was gone.

When the others arrived, they loved my arrangement. 'Let's play fairy funerals!' said Shelagh excitedly. And we did, weaving tiny daisy chains into wreaths, as Annmarie's Barbie was carried into the clearing by our other dolls, all wearing clothes made of black bin-liners. It was the most popular game of the day, and we all joined in – all except Lynda, who had brought down more sparkling ornaments to decorate her shining tree. Instead of playing she watched us over her shoulder.

'Your tree looks so pretty,' I said. It was true. The gold costume jewellery now filled all the lower branches so it flashed in the sun like a Christmas tree.

'Yeah,' she said, fitting the last ornament in place, a broken bangle. 'My mum says it's the nicest one.' There was a touch of defiance in her voice. I stood there for a moment, uncertain, and then turned back to my game.

~

The next day was the day that everything changed.

I stood in front of my tree that morning. I could see what had happened, but I couldn't take it in. The tiny graveyard was scattered, the tombstones upended with the lettered sides mashed into the ground. Someone had stamped on them to make sure they were broken. I could even see the outline of footprints. The skeleton hand I'd carefully glued to the door was gone, and the door itself lay face-down at the foot of the tree.

I know who did this.

'What happened?' It was the man again. This time he wore a scarf twisted around his neck. I turned to answer, but to my horror, felt my mouth turn down with overpowering misery. A smothering sob rose hard in my chest. It was ruined. It was all ruined.

'Now then.' His voice was gentle. 'Tell me what happened.'

He took off his glasses and smiled at me.

—

The next day, Lynda disappeared. She left her house early that morning, before breakfast, to go and play, but she never came back. The police and all the parents searched for her, up and down the riverbank, shouting her name. We all had to stay home for days. She was gone. For weeks afterwards I'd see her mother, her hair tangled as mine, wandering around the roads, her pretty face red and swollen, her hands clasping and unclasping by her sides as she walked. The last place Lynda had been seen was in the fairy village, by a jogger passing by. He was held and questioned, but there was nothing else he could tell them except that he'd seen a little girl with blonde hair among the trees.

After that we didn't want to go there anymore. Someone boarded up the little copse. We didn't even take the decorations away. Sometimes when I walked by, I would imagine them, rotting and swaying in the breeze.

I thought of Lynda all the time. I changed my wish. My mother wasn't getting any better anyway. She just lay inside, growing light as thistledown, her sharp bones poking through her face. No, I wished instead for Lynda to come back, though deep down I knew it wouldn't work. I couldn't wish on the little wishing well anymore, you see; it was hidden away, growing mossy and abandoned behind the fence.

—

I still think about Lynda. Wherever she went to, I still feel her here. Still ten, still beautiful. When I close my eyes I see the sun blaze down on her golden hair as she sits surrounded by the sparkling glass and metal of her tree.

I sit and remember.

—

When he took off his glasses, I could see his eyes were blue.

'Did one of the others do this?'

I nodded, still unable to speak.

'Which one?' His face was drawn into fierce lines. His mouth was a pale slash

on his stubbled face. I pointed dumbly at Lynda's tree. The rising sun caught the iridescent beads of a broken rosary, flashing tiny arcs of light on the tree trunk.

He nodded once, and then looked at me again. His eyes were a startling blue, like the sky, like the cobalt blue colour in my paintbox. I looked at him, mesmerised. I'd only seen one other pair of eyes as blue as that.

'Are you Pook?'

He didn't reply, just straightened up, gathered his coat around him and walked away.

There was no Pook, I know that now. He was just a man. But that doesn't make it any easier to live with.

I'm sitting beside the gap in the fence, looking out at the river. Midges cloud the brown water; rising fierce and massed from the dark green weeds. A boat, moored, drifts lengthways, admiring itself in the crinkled reflections of the river. Seabirds dip past, tip-tilted to one side.

Someone's scored the bird hide with savage letters in black paint. 'It's never over.'

It never is.

The idea of these colourful, fun fairy villages runs counter to this tradition of fairy homes being places to respect. The World's More Full Of Weeping was born out of a certain unease occasioned by these places. I walked my dog beside the river Shannon every day, where I passed one of these little villages, created by a committee of residents as an attraction for local children. I've been watching and photographing it now for over a year, noting the strange, incremental additions of everything from carved rabbits to miniature caravans to car tyres piled and painted to represent the Minions from Despicable Me. And something about it feels...not quite right. If Na Sidhe are as vengeful as legends have them, would they be insulted by these colourful, childlike reimaginings? What if they were to wreak a terrible revenge?

And so, slowly, bit by bit, this story grew from these walks and thoughts...

THE WITCH THAT
WAS HURT

long time ago, I read an old migratory legend about a shape-shifting witch. There are many variations of this legend; it's told in Ireland, Scotland, Germany, and throughout Northern Europe. It tells of a woman, sometimes old, sometimes young, who possesses power and uses it to harm others with small, domestic charms.

In all the versions, however, the ending is the same. The witch is hurt.

—

The blistered paint on the front door of *The Other Side* is pale and peeling. If you cup your hands either side of your head and press your face against the criss-cross pattern of the metal grille you can still make out the window display – tarot cards, black candles and hexagram jewellery, all crusted over with thick dust like whitened sea-salt. Keep looking into the darkened interior. You can see the shapes inside the shop, indistinct as ghosts; the card racks, the posters on the wall, even the dark huddle of the till. Behind them is the doorway to the upstairs. And behind that again are shadows, inky and opaque.

—

I'm polishing the window of the shop, red curls twisted up under an old-fashioned headscarf knotted on top of my head, when one of the hipster baristas from *The Penny Farthing* next door hisses at me.

'Hey! You! Yes, you, the new girl.' I look at him blankly, J-cloth and Windolene in hand.

'Come over to us on your coffee break?' I hesitate. My meagre wages are split neatly between rent, art materials and the cheapest supermarket shop I can do. He shrugs and mouths 'FREE COFFEE' in an exaggerated way. I give him the thumbs up. 'TEN MINUTES,' I mouth back, distorting my mouth horribly to mimic him. He smiles at me, and it's a nice smile, even if it is framed by a silly handlebar moustache, and then retracts his head back inside his window.

I wander into the shop happily, thinking greedily about a free cappuccino. Tanith is standing at the till, absentmindedly letting coins roll out of her hand into the different drawers. Her lips move automatically. *Some kind of money incantation?* I hardly even notice these oddities anymore. I am carefully restacking the angel cards in neat lines on the shelves when two elderly women come in, and hover hopefully beside Tanith.

'Do you have any mass cards, love?' one of them asks her. Without looking around, her face pulls into a sideways grimace.

'No,' she says shortly. 'It's not that kind of shop.' They leave in a silence that erupts into a shocked buzz as soon as they open the door. Tanith sighs audibly.

'Is it OK if I take my lunchbreak in ten?' I ask her, to forestall another rant about the closed-mindedness of the local people. She nods grudgingly.

'But be back on time. I have a meeting upstairs.' Tanith terms herself a psychic (or, more grandiosely, on her website as 'Ireland's Foremost Psychic'). She scowls into the till, her heavy eyeliner, cloud of hennaed hair and whitened face giving her the appearance of a cross, pale goblin. I tell her it's no problem – I *almost* add that I'm just going next door – but luckily remember Tanith's dislike of the baristas and don't.

＊

I bring my theosophy books from the art college library to the coffee shop with me. I've seen Tanith eyeing them, and I don't want her fingers on them, sticky with those perfumed clove drops she continually crunches. I'm in that happy, absorbed stage of research, where I'm moving continually from clue to clue, sifting delicately through a muddle of texts and trying to follow the invisible lines that lead to the clear heart of inspiration. I place the books carefully on the table and as I wait for the moustached boy to bring my coffee, I start to leaf through one at random, the memoirs of one Reverend Ninian Merrill.

'A most astonishing event took place last night. Before I narrate the sequence, I must explain that this was an experiment conducted in my own home. It did not involve spectators, or payment, or any other base vulgarity. I sat before my desk, having cleansed my mind of all superfluous thought, and waited, pen in hand. Yet again, it happened, I felt an Invisible Agency direct my hand – it wrote, in clearly formed letters – 'SISTER' –

My coffee has appeared. I close the book. He stands over me, waiting.

'OK then,' I say, finally, delicately removing my cappuccino froth with my spoon, like the top of an egg. 'Why the sudden desire to see me?'

The barista (his name is Nicholas, I discover, no abbreviations) wipes his hand slowly on his old-fashioned white and red butcher-stripe apron and sits down with me.

'Well, of course we – my brother James and me – wanted to welcome you to the neighbourhood,' he says easily, waving his hand over at the other man who's making a set of complex coffees with competent flicks of the wrist. James has an impressive dark quiff and pointed sideburns. He also has a limited repertoire of small talk.

'It's her,' he says shortly. Then, when I look blank, he adds 'Your one, the medium. *Tanith*.' He almost spits the last word. I still look confused, but he dispenses his coffees and leans heavily on the counter, beside my table. 'She's out to get us,' he says flatly. When I look at Nicholas for clarification, he just nods.

'You know she fell out with us last week about the tarot night?' I do. Tanith, furious, had talked about it for days. The boys ran a never-ending series of special 'nights' in their vintage café with its mismatched chairs and crockery, its vintage typewriters and dusty hardback books. In the last month there had been no less than *ten* special events. Yes, ten. I counted them in my head; two screenings of subtitled films, one book club meeting, one quilting night, a Drink'n'Draw evening, a quiz on B-movies, a knit-off, a coffee-sampling session, a creative writing group and – this was what Tanith had so strenuously objected to – an evening of tarot-card reading. 'She was really angry,' continues Nicholas. 'I mean, REALLY angry. She came in here and shouted.'

'Upset the customers,' says James. He watches me closely. 'Since then, well, stuff keeps happening.'

'Small stuff,' adds Nicholas. 'Stuff you almost wouldn't notice. The lights seem dimmer, the place gets dark just after midday. There's a damp patch on the wall that wasn't there before. In the mornings when we open there's a bad smell that comes and goes. The milk's gone off every second day.'

I swallow the last of my cappuccino. 'I'm sorry,' I say, as politely as I can. 'But this doesn't sound feasible. How on earth can Tanith have something to do with' – I gesture round the café – 'any of this stuff?' The boys look mutinous. I can tell Nicholas is already regretting his offer of free coffee.

'We saw her laughing at us,' says James flatly. 'That day the damp appeared, and the milk turned, and I got the first whiff of the smell. She was standing outside and laughing at us.'

'Just keep your ears open,' coaxes Nicholas. 'If there's anything she's doing, let us know.' I nod and leave, pausing at the doorstep. Underneath the strong flavours of coffee and fruit teas, I can smell it faintly, an unpleasant undertone of drains and dampness.

—

Tanith is wrestling herself into her sheepskin coat when I get back.

'Took you long enough.' Her voice always sounds slightly petulant, even when it isn't. 'Where were you?'

I lift the flap of my old satchel to show her my sketchbook. 'Drawing,' I say apologetically. 'Lost track of time.' It's the correct explanation. Her face softens. She likes the fact that she employs an artist; in fact, I'd say my course of study had everything to do with my getting the job (that and the amount of fluent spiritualism I was able to speak after reading a couple of books on my project subject). It amuses Tanith to introduce me to her customers as 'our resident artist, Holly', the obvious inference being that she is my patron. I even interviewed her at the beginning of the project, asking her about her own belief in spiritualism. She loved the experience, but was a terrible interviewee, putting on a deep voice and moving her burgundy hair over and back across her shoulder. She's not that interested in my *actual* work, in fact she doesn't realise it has more to do with film shorts and installations, and that my sketchbook is in fact a compilation of lists of edits needed for my newest pieces. With a last few instructions to me she's gone upstairs in a flurry of burgundy hair and purple sheepskin. A few minutes later, a man and two women appear. They're about the same age as Tanith (late forties? fifties?) and look like Goths gone to seed; they're all wearing varying amounts of black leather, the man has visible tattoos and one of the women has a nose-ring. Tanith often has a range of visitors to her domain upstairs, where she reads tarot cards and a rather cheap-looking crystal ball (I had to polish it during one slow day in the shop). Upstairs is also, I suspect, where she acts as a medium. I shrug. I remind myself that it makes no odds to me what Tanith gets up to. She can be grumpy and fussy, but the job is easy, I get to read during shifts, and next week I'm buying a Zoom recorder with my wages. I'd put up with a lot worse for that. I pick up my book and start reading again.

—

'– 'SISTER' it wrote again in plain script, so different from my own copperplate handwriting. The Invisible Agency then became still. I was at the point of ceasing my experiment, when I felt my hand make another involuntary movement. I saw the pen move and create a rough shape, and then refine it until it took on the semblance of an eye. This Eye – which I see before me now as clearly as I do the furniture in my lodging room – was formed like the ancient Egyptian symbol of The Eye of Horus, that revered symbol of protection. However, I recognised it as the favoured drawing of my younger sister, a sight familiar to me from her old scraps of paper. I am not ashamed to say that I laid my head on my arms and wept...'

I'm lost in the book, pausing to contemplate the overwhelming sadness of the Reverend Ninian when I hear a bell sound – a sharp metallic *ting* that cuts through the stale shop air. It's the woman from the boutique in our little cul-de-sac. There are only four buildings in total on the tiny street: this shop, the hipster coffee shop *The Penny Farthing*, a dog grooming parlour with neon-bright signage proclaiming *Pimp My Pooch* and the rather grand boutique at the far end of the street, *The Pearl Earring*. The woman who owns *The Pearl Earring* (I think her name is Mrs. White, she's far too majestic to have an actual first name) sweeps into the shop with a regal air, brandishing an envelope.

'This arrived for *her*,' she announces. ('Her' means Tanith.) 'That postman can't seem to read.' She looks about her disdainfully, nose crinkling at the ever-present scent of musty patchouli. 'It really is terribly tatty in here, dear. Can't you make more of an effort? Even with the window? My lay-dees,'– she draws out the word like chewing gum – 'think it's a little...strange to have a shop like this near mine.' She looks down at the counter, where Tanith's hand-drawn sign advertises her palm-reading skills, and her nostrils flare out in another finely-calibrated millimetre of contempt. I half-smile apologetically, and raise my palms in a *not-my-shop* gesture.

'Yes, well,' she says, almost to herself, dropping the letter fastidiously on the counter, and then tip-tapping her way out carefully on spiky shoes, almost as if she's trying to prevent her feet touching the (admittedly dusty) floor. I roll my eyes and pick up the envelope. To my secret glee, it's addressed to 'Fiona McKenna, The Other Side.' That's Tanith's *real* name, a fact I only cottoned on to days ago after innocently piling up what I termed 'the Fiona letters' to return to sender, only to have Tanith snatch them away from me. I return to half-reading my book, unsettled by the encounter, trying to ignore the voices and the occasional stamping from upstairs.

~

I'm wandering in to work the next day – a little too early – when I stop to say hello to the jolly girls in *Pimp My Pooch*. One of them – Anne – is vigorously brushing a Siberian husky, feathery tufts of hair floating in the air like dandelion clocks. The other girl, Joanne, is standing in her doorway, drinking tea.

'How's the art going?' That's the way she always greets me. I think she's secretly amazed that someone who's the same age as her could be still in school, and studying something as esoteric as multimedia and performance.

'It's grand,' I say peaceably, accepting a chocolate digestive from her brandished packet of biscuits. 'I'm working on a project, a film to try to recreate a club from 1875 called the Miracle Club. They did psychic experiments.' Her face is a blank. 'Kind of like the stuff Tanith does.'

'Speak of the devil.' Joanne points down the street with her chin. I see Tanith stumping up the road, wearing a black lace and velvet dress that drags slightly on the ground behind her, smoking one of her acrid ginseng cigarettes. She pauses when she sees me, and looks in the door of the grooming parlour. The husky, who has been standing placidly inside, letting Anne remove huge white clumps of hair from his back and sides, sees her and stiffens, hair rising in a crested Mohican on top of his head. His lips curl back over black gums as he throws back his furry head and howls, again and again. Joanne and Anne try to soothe him, but even as I stand at our door, waiting for Tanith to unlock it, I can hear him ululating and howling.

'Those bloody dogs,' says Tanith under her breath as she wrestles with the stiff door lock. The shop smells more fusty than usual. She sniffs as she disappears upstairs. Returning, she hands me a heavy armful of velvet curtains. 'Can you take these through the back later, and put them in the washing machine?' she asks, but it's really a command. 'I have someone important coming later.' I take them from her, and there's a whisper of that dank, unpleasant smell, the same smell that I caught yesterday in *The Penny Farthing*.

I'm having coffee with Nicholas again, I've fallen into the habit of doing so a few times a week. It's warm in the coffee shop, and nine times out of ten I get a free coffee, or at least a free refill. That dank smell is still there – just sometimes – as James said, it comes and goes. I notice a damp patch that wasn't there before, behind the counter. It's about the size of my arm, and runs downward in a diagonal line. Distracted, I turn back to Nicholas. While I've tuned out, he's been asking me about my work. (He's an ex-philosophy student, so interested in esoteric practices. Between ourselves, I also think he may be interested in female art-school students with springy red hair.) I get my notebook out and sketch out my plans.

'So it's a film, yeah? And I'm simulating levitation – that's what the original Miracle Club of theosophy students tried to do.

'Oh, I studied the theosophists,' interrupts Nicholas. 'They wanted to change the world, didn't they – to create a new world order of quality and togetherness, and to reconcile spiritualism with science and theology?'

'Correct. But before they were the Theosophical Society they were the Miracle Club. That's the bit I'm most interested in. When they were still investigating spiritualism, but through personal experiments. Not using mediums. So I'm trying to imagine and film their trials with actors, using old diaries and accounts of what they did. Like levitation and out of body experiences.' I suck my pen, then pop it out of my mouth and start to sketch – coarse, hazy outlines of a figure suspended in air. 'It's hard, though, I'm experimenting with cheating and cutting the film, but it looks too jerky...' I trail off, thinking. Nicholas turns around my notebook to examine my rough drawings.

James turns and shouts over – 'C'mon you. These coffees won't walk to the tables.'

Nicholas sighs. 'Brothers!' He cocks his head towards me. 'You got any?' I stuff my notebook and pens in my bag.

'No,' I say briefly. 'Got to go to work.'

—

No two days in *The Other Side* are ever the same. We have the oddest clientele. Some people just wander in, while others are on a mission, looking for everything from Buddhist mantras to angels to lost relatives. Many of them are, as you might expect, hennaed ladies with Indian fringed skirts and lots of clanking jewellery, sometimes there's the odd monastic-looking man. And then there's Tanith's 'special visitors'. They're generally a little seedier looking, a little more battered by life, a little more in need of whatever odd service she's offering upstairs in the shop. I study her covertly as she lines up the dreamcatchers in the window. *What's brought her here*, I wonder. From the bits and pieces she's let slip I know she doesn't see her family anymore. She's also told me about her own university days – she studied folklore and anthropology, as well as being in a punk girl band. She got quite animated telling me about that one, and insisted on making me several mugs of grassy-tasting herbal tea while she talked on and on, waving her arms about. She's a strange one, and no mistake. I've tried asking her some questions about her business as a psychic – I really don't want her to be one of those awful people who prey on the grieving, but she's strangely reticent about her work. 'That's between me and them,' she says, tapping her nose, and making the silver bracelets on her wrist jingle together. Sometimes, she's really rather sweet. When she's in a good mood she lets me go early, especially on a Friday – 'You'll want to tear it up,' she says knowingly. I nod, complicit in her imagined version of me, although what I really dream of is a quiet flat with my housemates gone out, the TV to myself, and a chance to play about in peace with the films on my laptop. There's often a scone in the morning waiting for me by the till, without comment. She even brought me in vegetarian chili once, in a plastic box that leaked inside my bag, giving it a pungent, oily smell that lasted for weeks.

Yet sometimes, without warning, she's angry. Poisonous. Some days she comes in and her eyes are red and puffy. Those days she's snappish, mean as a snake, and I spend as much time as possible being a moving target. I move about, fixing things, dusting, rearranging, anything to keep active and silent. I let her huddle on the chair at the till like a great, brooding crow, and chip at her black nail polish till it lies in tiny, flecked piles by the 'Special Offers' box. Only when she goes for lunch will I dare to sweep the chips away. On those days I know to keep quiet and stay out of her way.

All in all, it's unfortunate that it's one of those days that Nicholas picks to try and make peace with Tanith.

'Morning,' he says, popping his head in. He's holding two coffees and his normally happy face is tentative. I chew my lip and try to shake my head discreetly behind Tanith's back. She looks up.

'Oh it's the nineteenth-century wrestler,' she says disdainfully. I bite back a laugh. Tanith's a bitch, alright, but she's cruelly observant one; poor Nicholas in his Breton top and red braces looks uncannily like a Victorian performer. She's equally dismissive of the coffee he puts down on the counter with a mumbled phrase about being better neighbours.

'Sugar and foam,' she says unpleasantly, turning away.

'SORRY,' I mouth at Nicholas, twisting the sweeping brush about in my hands. Tanith gets up abruptly and stumps down the front steps, muttering to herself, her shoulders hunched, her footsteps heavy. Instantly the dogs from *Pimp My Pooch* set up a mournful ululation, a sequence of yips and howls that only peter out when her footsteps die away. Nicholas is too cast-down to linger.

I drink both coffees, but I don't feel good about it.

—

I'm sitting on the wall outside *The Pearl Earring*, fighting down a surge of tears. I'm not even working today, but when I walked back from college, dazed with rejection, my legs just turned automatically down the sequence of streets that led to work. My throat is swollen with swallowed sobs, my lips pressed together as I try to stop crying.

My crit in college was a disaster. The tutors looked silently at my short film, which seemed to crawl by, each agonised second more pretentious and poorly-executed than the last. The lighting looked muddy, not moody, and the jerky levitation was unbearably ham-fisted. Finally it ended, and I switched it off, face hot and hands shaking as I folded down the laptop. Their response was worse than I'd feared. 'So what's different about *your* reimagining?' asked my tutor, Sarah. Her face was carefully neutral, arms folded across her large bosom. Silence. She tried to rephrase it: 'I mean, how is it different to, or improvising on, the original ideas of the Club?' I don't have an answer, and the silence stretches like the skin of a balloon before the agonised moment of bursting. My tongue felt too big for my mouth. They were kind, which was the worst bit. My other tutor, Jerry, looked at my rough work and said he liked the interview with Tanith – 'She's an interesting character. That might give you a fresh insight?' He was so kind I felt my eyes swell with unshed tears. But I managed to save them up till I got here.

Joanne sees me sitting on the wall and coaxes the story out of me, over the yips and yowls of small dogs being groomed. She tries, she really does – she even forces a strong cup of tea on me – but to my shame, she keeps trying to uncover what she terms 'the *real* reason you're upset.' In Joanne's world, only children cry over homework.

'Why are the dogs howling so much?' I ask, glad of the distraction. Joanne makes a noise of exasperation.

'Honestly? I don't know. They just don't stop these last few days. It's not only when they're being groomed. It's all the bloody time.' She frowns and pulls on her e-cigarette with an audible sucking sound. 'Customers are getting pissed off. *We're* getting pissed off, never mind them. As for that old bag next door in the frock shop...' I look around, and sure enough, there is the figure of Mrs. White, rigid with indignation at her lower-caste neighbours, pretending to rearrange the immaculate window display. The dogs' howls rise to a keening caterwaul. I hear a familiar heavy step beside me; I look down and see Tanith's beloved Doc Marten boots.

'What's up?' She looks at me closely.

'Her college.' Joanne gives her an 'if-you-can-believe-that' shrug and walks inside, yelling 'Quieten down!' at the dogs. They pause, then start up again, in a lower, more mournful key.

'Come on in to the shop.' I follow Tanith meekly. When we get in, I expect to hear the consolatory click of the kettle, but instead she moves to the back of the shop, and lifts the beaded curtain that cloaks the spiral staircase.

'Come on up.' I don't hesitate. I've wanted to know what the upstairs looks like since I first started working here. It doesn't disappoint. It's grandly dirty, windows thick with dust and cobwebs, even the rugs issue little puffs of dust in the sunlit air as she walks on them. The walls are painted a dark purple, and there's a black, circular table with chairs set around it. There's a black velvet tablecloth, worn in patches; it's strewn with packs of cards, scarves and even the crystal ball. Tanith sits down and draws one of the packs to her. She slides the cards out and begins to shuffle them with expert flicks of her hands.

'You're at a crossroads.' Her eyes are shrewd, judging me. 'I'm going to read for you.' She passes me the deck. The cards feel cold, even clammy to the touch. 'Now cut them – that means divide them in two.' I obey and then reshuffle them and pass them back to her. She fans them out into a complicated pattern. For a few moments she is lost in silence, and then looks up.

'In your present I can see change,' she says slowly. 'Change that will hurt, but you will go through with it anyhow. Your past is dark. Confusing.' Her face tilts to one side, her expression questioning. 'I think there is some great pain there.' I clench my teeth and say nothing. 'Your future. Well, that's a little undefined. There are several paths you can go down...' Her voice trails away, dissatisfied. She pulls the crystal ball in front of her. 'Maybe this will be clearer.' She peers into it as I sit there awkwardly, unsure of where to look. The silence continues. The sun is slowly fading to a muted orange glow outside, and the shadows crawl across the floorboards. When she finally speaks, I start in my chair.

'Holly. I see you here. It's a little dark, though, and there's someone with you.' She straightens up and looks at me, and to my surprise, there's something in her eyes… *compassion?* 'I'm right. It's been hard for you. You've had a long, hard struggle to be here. Your family didn't want you to leave.' I say nothing. I've watched enough TV programmes on cold reading to know not to. But despite myself, I feel my eyes, already tender from crying, start to prickle up again. 'There's a long shadow behind you, and it's up to you if it will stretch ahead of you too. There's a health issue coming up in a few years, but it will be fine.' Her voice drones on, telling me inconsequential, humdrum facts. I nod. The sun has now gone down completely, and the room is getting colder. Suddenly she stops. I look up.

'Holly.' Her voice sounds different. She stares at me, and then closes her eyes. Her posture stiffens, she sways in her seat and then abruptly shouts *'Polly put the kettle on!'* I jump up from my chair. Her eyes stay closed. Shadows snake around her with oily flicks and curls.

'Polly put the kettle on!' The voice is thin and shrill, almost childlike. *'Polly put the kettle on! Polly put the kettle on! Polly put the kettle on!'*

She's still shouting it as I run down the stairs, then stumble into the darkened shop and out the door. I bang on the coffee-shop door but the boys are gone, so I start to run again, down the alley, out onto the main street. It's not until I find myself in a throng of beery, happy people outside a pub that I slow down and relax.

—

The next morning the café is still closed. I stand outside, reluctant to go straight to work. I didn't sleep well last night, and whenever I think of Tanith, eyes closed, moving in her chair and repeating that stupid phrase over and over, I experience a weak, watery feeling of terror. Uneasily, I shift from side to side, waiting. It's nearly nine, and the boys generally open up at eight thirty. Mrs. White walks by, arms full of scarves.

'Why is the coffee shop closed?' I ask her. She tries to pretend she hasn't heard me, but she's obviously dying to complain about something, so she stops.

'They've gone,' she sniffs. 'Folded up. Customer complaints, apparently.' I feel a small pang. I'll miss Nicholas and his smiling friendliness. Even taciturn James. Mrs. White's gazes sweeps down the tiny street. 'And the police were in yesterday to *that pet shop*.' Her voice is glacial, the words in spiky italics. 'That constant barking – well, I phoned them. Those girls can't control the dogs.' I glance sympathetically over at *Pimp My Pooch*, but the doors are still closed, even though it's after nine. She sees me looking and makes a tutting sound. 'I don't wonder no-one wants to bring in their dogs. At least my ladies will have some peace today, it seems.' I think she is happy, but she's clearly not. She tells me she is looking for a better class of place to move to. (She spits this last sentence out like a mouthful of TicTacs.)

'And then there was one,' I say, almost to myself, as I turn and walk to *The Other Side*.

Tanith and I don't discuss the previous night. I'm afraid she will be in another gloomy mood, but she's looking quite cheerful as she sips her tea. I've been up most of the night thinking. I've already decided how to appease her and help myself, all in one move. 'Tanith,' I say, 'how would you like to be interviewed for my new project?' She turns her face towards me, and she's smiling. 'How about after lunch?'

—

The fine art degree show is packed out. It's all happy, overdressed mothers, and proud but bored fathers. Small children run around shrieking, being told not to touch things. I say hello to other people's parents. I don't see my own there, nor do I expect to. My mother doesn't leave the house, and my father stays with her, in solidarity. It's OK. I'm happy. Jerry my tutor pats me on the arm.

'Good work. Brave. Interesting.' I smile at him.

'Better than the last crit?' My voice is teasing, showing him that I know how much I've improved. He smiles.

'Sometimes a bad dress rehearsal is exactly what the soul needs,' he says easily. 'This works very well. You didn't pull any punches.' He moves on then, another student, another compliment, another family to greet. I'm content. I know my work is good. The little, critical voice inside me is silent for once. I turn and look at it. It's a two-screen installation, with one monitor running a loop film showing the levitation film. But I've changed it. Now it's a vintage stop-motion animation with a jolly plinking score that makes the participants look ridiculous. They bob up and down, faces like anxious blobs as they spin in the air and return to their seats. One the second monitor is the interview with Tanith. There's a pair of headphones beside it. I put them on and listen, smiling. I've hacked the interview to bits. Editing is too soft a word. I've made Tanith sound even more ridiculous than she is. Every silly, pretentious claim she's made to possess powers has been left in, and I've even mixed in a hint of the upbeat pink-plonk music to poke fun at her mournful voice.

It's then that I see her. Tanith. For a moment, I'm too horrified to take off the headphones. She looks strangely archaic in the whitewashed setting of the studio walls. The brightly dressed families part in front of her, her white makeup and dark layers of velvet and lace marking her out as different. She looks – *shy*? My chest fills with a hot, painful air. She stops in front of my panel. The plaque in front of it reads 'Bewitching Others. For my sister.' I see a dark swell of remembrance on her face as she touches the mounted plaque beside my work, almost tenderly. Her eyes meet mine and she smiles. I put down the headphones and wait.

You know when you try to remember something? Try it now. Really try. See how flat and exaggerated it seems. Everyone moves stiffly. The light is all wrong. Things happen in slow motion. The action reverses, forwards, goes back again to replay. It's like that whenever I try to remember that nightmarish, slow-motion inevitability of Tanith picking up the headphones. She's still smiling. In a horrid montage I remember the small kindnesses; the early evening breaks, the mugs of horrible herbal tea, the pride in my work. I think of her dark days, the clouds of depression that hung, almost tangibly, over her.

Through a fog of the same, slowed-down horror, I see a single tear trickle down her face. A track of black mascara cuts through her white make-up.

—

A long time ago, I read an old migratory legend about a shape-shifting witch. There are many variations of this legend, it's told in Ireland, Scotland, Germany and throughout Northern Europe. It tells of a woman, sometimes old, sometimes young, who possesses power and uses it to harm others.

In all the versions, however, the ending is the same. The witch is hurt.

One of the oldest legends in Ireland is that of The Witch That Was Hurt. In Ireland it signifies a hare that is shot in the paw by a woodsman. It bleeds and he follows it to a village house. Entering it he finds the hare has disappeared, to be replaced by an old lady with a bloody hand. She is of course, a shapeshifting witch, and her fate can be guessed. However, in this story, I was interested in the different meanings of the word 'hurt', from the merely physical to the mental. I also wanted to bring in ideas of the occult and the Theosophists to echo that interesting period of Celtic mysticism in Irish history which was marked by the foundation of the Hermetic Order of the Golden Dawn.

THE HUNGRY GRASS

t's the last hill that does it. I hurl the backpack onto the flattened, yellowish grass in front of the old Famine cottage, not caring if I break everything in it. My breath is coming in tearing snorts, and there is sweat everywhere – under my arms, down my back, trickling down my damp neck.

I hate you. My fists clench, white-knuckled, in front of me. *I hate you.* I pull up my T-shirt, not caring if any ramblers in this blighted landscape see me, and roughly wipe my face, feeling the heat of my cheeks through the thin, damp fabric. *I hate you.*

It is Maebh's idea, of course. Fit, athletic Maebh who can't conceive of anyone being unable to go on marathon walks. She's organised this whole hiking trip. And it's driving me crazy. Her stringy legs in expensive hiking boots stride ahead of me, her backpack shifting easily on her shoulders like it's made of candy floss. I'm behind her, always behind her. I pound on, all chunky legs and red face, my rucksack lumpish as a coalsack, sweat collecting in my eyebrows till it runs, salty and stinging, into my eyes. It's only the first day and already she's stopped calling me on.

I drink out of the warm, plastic bottle of water. The stale liquid gushes down my scorched throat. The faded grass feels warm under my thighs. I touch the velvety blades and remember the old stories of the Hungry Grass. According to my mother, the Hungry Grass was the local name for those flat patches of green-yellow grass. The patches were named for the terrible nineteenth century Famine where starving people, bellies full of grass, lay down and died by the roadside. I lean back against a warm rock as a flurry of birds flit by the ruined cottage. I close my eyes and see them pass, dim shapes fluttering against in the pink shade of my eyelids. I don't know if it's the rest, the water, the heat, or the cawing of the crows, but I feel something shift deep inside me; suddenly, impossibly, my mood has started to lift. I stretch out on the flat rock and think about Maebh and our long, tangled relationship. We've loved and fought each other since childhood. Until that last summer before university. Then, shockingly, it was ten years later and we'd lost touch. I'm not surprised she wanted to meet up, I'd often thought about it too. But I still can't believe she chose these fields for us to meet again in.

I close my eyes and draw in deep breaths, just like my therapist taught me, three deep breaths to drive away the bad thoughts. *One.* A pheasant bursts straight out of the grass beside me into a heavy, stumbling flight. *Two.* I feel a breeze shift and flow around me. *Three.* I close my eyes and inhale the smell of hot grass and moss. I keep my eyes closed. The sun goes in, and the pink glow of my eyelids darkens to a dull red.

~

I open my eyes. It's cold and damp and I'm shivering hard, my muscles spasming in the chill air. I can't see anything but a white swirling fog, soft and treacherous. I scramble up, my feet slipping against the slick grass. I feel around cautiously but my tracksuit top and rucksack are gone. *They must be somewhere*, I think rationally, and start to pat around the wet grass. Nothing. My thin vest is drenched. I can't stop shivering. I need to get out of this pocket of mist and find Maebh. I walk forward into the whiteness. There's nothing but soft, wet cloud pushing against me, and no matter how far I go – carefully, carefully – hands stretched in front of me, I can't find its perimeters. The damp grass squeaks beneath my boots, dark and slippery. I'm filled with a bright, hard panic, solid as a rock in my chest. I need to find my way out.

'Maebh!' I call, hopelessly. 'Maebh!'

There's no reply. I continue to walk, hands still raised, feet hesitant. I expect at any moment to hit another rock, to stumble against a tree. But I don't. My feet skid onwards, as I slip slowly down the grassy hollow.

'Rebecca?' It's soft as a breath in my ear. My heart hammers hard in my chest.

'Re-be-cca?' There it is again. This time it's drawn out, almost sing-song.

'Maebh?' I say weakly. But I know it's not. It's a deep voice, a man's voice. I'm alive with a pure white terror.

'Who is it?' I yell, my heart crashing in my throat. 'Who is it?'

I blunder about, terrified. I know who it is. My feet skid, stutter on rock, stop, and I pitch forward on my hands and knees. The limestone cuts my palms, and the rock bites through the right knee of my jeans. I feel the material split, and pain blossoms red-hot in my knee.

'Re-be-cca?' The soft voice is still there. Still sing-song. It sounds even nearer this time.

I start to cry, lying on the ground, covering my head with my arms. My wet hands clamp over my ears.

Then I hear a shout.

'Rebecca!' It's a different voice – a woman's voice – Maebh's voice!

I choke down my sobs and yell as loud as I can. 'Here. Over here!'

'What the hell?' She looms over me, angry, but blissfully solid and present. The mist starts to curl away, resolving itself into thin white strands, suddenly flimsy and innocent. 'I've been looking for you for hours. Where have you been?'

'I – I don't know.'

'Well you've completely ruined the hike'. Her voice is cold and livid. Suddenly I am angry.

'What the hell possessed you to come here? Here of all places? You know what happened here!' The words pour from me like a torrent, my heart shaking within me to a tremendous, pendulum beat. 'What made you think coming back would be a good idea?'

Maebh twists her face up in confusion. With a shock I realise she's trying to remember.

'What are you talking about Rebecca?' It's the honest puzzlement in her face that destroys me. I'm engulfed by a hot sick panic; I close my eyes, feeling the blood pounding in my face. When I open them, Maebh is looking at me curiously.

'Don't you – don't you?' My voice falters, stops. The very idea she's forgotten gives me a sick, vertiginous feeling.

'Don't I *what*?' Now she's getting angry again. She starts to gather up the contents of my spilled bag, throwing the bottle, tracksuit top, wallet all back in, a sequence of hard, vicious thuds.

'Don't you *remember*?' My voice is choked. I can see it so clearly, the bright, yellow sunshine on the grass, the hill, the rocks, me falling over, and Maebh running on, leaving me behind. Even now, when I close my eyes, I can hear the rough tear of his breath as he whispered my name, and feel his hard hands as they grabbed me.

But as Maebh shakes her head dismissively, and bends to pull me up, I know that she has forgotten; that is, if she ever really remembered. That bright summer was the last time we were truly friends. Since then Maebh has continued to run ahead, laughing, ever onward, while I've stayed behind, circling the fields, left behind in the Hungry Grass.

The Hungry Grass is a Great Famine legend. In Ireland, from 1845-47, there was a potato famine that, because of massive over-dependence on one crop, ended with two million people either dying or emigrating. There are very few folkloric stories about the Famine, possibly because it is such a stark and terrible story, but 'The Hungry Grass' is one of these. It claims that flattened yellow-green patches of ground in the countryside are places where people during the Famine lay down and died. It is also linked with the Irish legend of the Stray Sod – walking on these patches will make you lose your way; although you may know where you are, you won't be able to find your way out.

In this story I wanted to bring that notion together with the idea of repressed and dangerous memories that act to keep people imprisoned in their own thoughts.

THE BLACK DOG

The day I pull my hair so hard that I cry, I know it can't go on. Or to be more precise, that *I* can't go on. Everything has become muddled and chaotic, infused with anxiety. I operate in a panicky zone of uncertainty. I can only work alone; anything involving other people is problematic. I work on evading anyone who annoys me because I might – no, *I will* – become unreasonably angry. I am enveloped in a suffocating, selfish fug of dread. The possibility of intimate conversation terrifies me. The simple question – *how are you?* – could provoke any manner of honest and terrible responses. My fear of dogs, always present, intensifies. The sight of a tense, bristling dog makes me sweat and shake. Even my body is breaking down. My energy dips and wanes each day. I crave sugar and salt, chocolate and meat. My skin itches. My leg has developed patches of eczema, like rust on metal, lichen on stone. I scratch them mindlessly till blood leaks under my fingernails to form a perfect burgundy crescent line separating the white from the pink part of the nails. My chest beats fast, staccato, *one-two, one-two*, like a tight red drum in my chest. I sleep with earplugs in to dim the sounds that might make me panic. I read to dull the thoughts in my head. In moments of lucidity, I am terrified. I sit in traffic, thinking – *Is this it? Is this ever going to end?* and, most terrifying of all, *Is it still me?* Because, you know, it doesn't *feel* like me anymore. It feels like a bad version, a blurred photocopy, a self of newsprint smudged with tears.

I'm no longer in the driving seat you see.

—

The Black Dog. He names it for me, the kind doctor. His eyes squint at me in sympathy. 'Poor you,' he says, gently. 'It's a brute, that dog.'

I've listed my ailments, those strange, pressing urges, the blank undertow of sadness that smothers me, night after night. I've told him of the fear that disrupts my rest with teeth-clenching anxiety and, conversely, the long, heavy, blank sleeps that sometimes overpower me, so I wake dry-mouthed and heavy-eyed.

Finally he straightens up. He cocks his head to one side and says quietly, 'Poor old you.' It is such an un-doctorly statement, I forget to cry.

'Well, I don't think this is PMS. What you describe – the listlessness, the panic, the overwhelming feeling of sadness – these all tally with the definition of depression.' That's when he names it. *The Black Dog*. I feel a terrible sorrow mixed with a dawning relief at his diagnosis. His face is calm and kind.

'Is there a history of depression in the family?' he asks.

—

Is there a history of depression in the family?

Yes. Yes, there is. I can see that now. Like an ancient poison it has infected us, generation after generation. I see it now, exposed for what it is in the clinical environment of the doctor's office. I see it in my mother's despairing rages, my grandmother's glassy stare and the strange, asynchronous workings of her mouth. And now I see it in my own mirror, in the ugly lines at the corner of my mouth. I see it in my flat, panicked eyes. It's a dreadful, quiet homecoming, a recognition of what has always lain beneath. *Is it still me?*

It's been inside, quiet, dark, waiting. As a child, when I bit my hand in rage or pulled my dolls to pieces...was that it? Like a detective I examine myself for clues. That night I hit my head off the wall to stop thinking. That was definitely it.

Maybe in time I'll be proud of this. I'll see it as part of my family heritage, as genetically distinctive as the dimple in the cleft of my chin, my long fingers, or the slight upward tilt of my nose that I see replicated, endlessly familiar, on strange faces at family funerals. For now, the tears trace lines on my face, a map of erosion, the long, slow slide of hot salt over sore skin.

—

I start taking the pills. They are tiny, like little dots of white on my palm. I find it implausible that they can stem such a huge and weighty tide of emotion. But I try. I remember to breathe deeply when I can. As the days go by, the tautness in my chest loosens, little by little. I can now drive my car without visualising all the possible accidents that will happen; the flickering images of blood and twisted metal begin to pale and recede. I sleep past the white-night hour of three in the morning. I say hello. I ask how people are. Once I caught myself laughing, unguarded.

Some things don't get better though. As the general anxiety fades my fear of dogs intensifies. There are so many dogs. They are everywhere. Little dogs bark at me from gardens, short, throaty, angry yaps. When I go by they hurl themselves against gates, in a blurred frenzy of pink gums and sharp white teeth. It's the big ones that terrify me most. I see them throw their large bodies against their leashes, their powerful chests working with ribby muscles as they strain and pull. I stop walking around the city to avoid them. These animals are only domesticated on the outside. I can see them for what they are. In their rolling eyes, their curled snarls, I see their true nature; they are jackals, wolves, carnivores.

The heavy wall of anger and despair is lifting, slowly but surely. Now, like a recovering car-crash victim, I feel the pain in my limbs. I can't stop eating. Everything tastes pungent and delicious. I don't fall asleep anymore, I crash into sleep, and it's heavy and blank, a flat, implacable wall.

It's then that the dreams start.

The dreams are always the same. I'm walking down a road, a flat, unmemorable, country road. It's summer. I can smell the dry heat, the cut, shrivelled grass. I hear the hum of insect-buzz, and feel their tiny wings bat against my face. I'm walking parallel to a deep ditch, backed by a large dark-green hedge. Suddenly I realise I'm seeing with a curious double vision, one that remains fixed on the dusty road, and the other which has risen to give me a bird's-eye view. Behind the hedge I see him, a huge black dog, crouching, his hackles raised and his powerful body coiled and tense like a bowstring. I know he is waiting for me, but I can't stop my feet leading me inevitably towards the hedge he lies behind. I wake just as he is about to spring, my mouth parched and open, hot, damp patches livid on my chest and the back of my neck.

That's bad enough. But just last night, the dream changed. I was walking down the road, when I realised my viewpoint had changed. I could still see from the bird's-eye view, but when I looked downwards, my old trainers had disappeared. In their place were two glossy black paws, stretched out to show long, cruel nails. The wave of horror woke me abruptly, sweating, panting, lungs bursting with effort. *Is it still me?*

—

'So now you dream you *are* a dog?' The doctor is making interested notes. He shakes his head. 'The good news now,' he says. 'I'm very happy that your symptoms have dissipated, and that your blood-pressure is down. You're feeling better in all respects but this very particular anxiety.'

He puts his pad down. 'I'd recommend cognitive behavioural therapy to you. It's a good way to address these kinds of fears, which seem to come from nowhere.' He pauses, head cocked on one side 'But I'm curious. Are you sure you've never been bitten by a dog? Scared of one as a child? Heard a story about one that frightened you?'

I think. Something in that last sentence sounds familiar. I close my eyes and raise a hand to stop him. There is silence. I hear the clock tick on the white-painted wall, slowly, calmly measuring the seconds, the minutes, the hours...

'Yes,' I say finally. 'Yes. I heard one.'

—

I'm five years old. My grandmother is making a new dress for me in the kitchen, her clever fingers pulling and tugging the material under the whirring needle of the sewing machine. I am tiptoe-stretched, head following the flashing movement of the needle. Quietly I reach out one chubby hand towards it – 'Stop!' shouts my grandmother, suddenly, pushing my hand away. I'm opening my mouth to cry, when she pulls me onto her lap. I rest my head against her soft, warm neck. 'Hush now,' she says, and her voice is quiet, murmuring. 'Hush or the Black Dog will hear you.'

—

The Black Dog of Cratloe. How could I forget about him? According to my grandmother, the Black Dog ran beside the road beyond Limerick. If he ran alongside you, that was good, and you'd have a safe journey. If he jumped out at you, Fate would follow you, like the dog itself, until you met your bloody end. My grandmother claimed to know a man who had died a week after a cycle home. The dog had run at him repeatedly during the stretch of road by the estuary, he told her, run at him over and over again, so he had to keep cycling and shouting, faster and louder, until it finally vanished at the foot of the Cratloe hills. 'It did him no good,' my grandmother says, nipping off the thread with her sharp teeth. 'Sure wasn't he dead a week later, fallen off the bicycle. God rest him.'

~

I get to my feet and leave the surgery, rejecting all offers of referral. There is nothing wrong with me anymore. My fear is real. It is out there in the woods, hiding by the road, waiting for me.

~

That night I dream again. I'm back on the road. This time it's dark. Beyond the hedge is the silver salmon-flash of moonlight on water. The air smells different, moister and loamier than before. I stretch myself out. Every muscle in my body lengthens and tautens as I flex slowly behind the hedge. Then I hear it, faint in the distance, the whirr of bicycle wheels. I tense. Nearly there. The whirr grows louder, and I am running quick, sure, low to the ground, the grassy earth under me damp and firm. He sees me. His mouth opens in a perfect round O of shock. I keep running, darting out and back from the hedge. It is intoxicating, the dew-fresh smell, the speed, the frightened, phlegmy catch of his breath as he pedals faster and faster. The chase goes on, I run in and out, just missing his front wheel, until the bike swerves, and with a ripping sound of rubber on tarmac, it stutters and crashes to the ground. I grab his collar in my mouth and start to drag him away. He is crying now, in hot, blurting breaths, face contorted, but the faint light shows me who it is.

The doctor.

~

When I wake up, heart blundering in my chest, everything has changed. There's blood in my mouth, but I can't find a cut. There's blood under my nails, but there's no scratches on my legs. I feel a glass-shatter of pure, high terror in the soft pouch of my stomach. *Is it still me?*

What do you do when what you fear most becomes invisible?
When it hides *inside*?

I sit down with my mother and my grandmother. Their eyes tell me they know what I am going to say. My grandmother is already nodding.

'I have it too,' I say simply. 'The Black Dog.' My mother's face is gentler than I have ever seen it. She brushes a hand over my hair, with a gossamer-light touch.

'We know.'

Wordlessly, I extend my hands to her and my grandmother. *Is it still me?* Their eyes are warm, reassuring. We grip each other, palms warm, fingers taut. Together, our weakness is our strength. I feel the power coursing between us, from generation to generation, from Black Dog to Black Dog.

'The Black Dog' is a story that weaves together strands of a local legend, that of 'The Black Dog of Cratloe' with the wider apparition of the Black Dog in folklore. It also intermingles these legends with shades of pathography, genetic illness, and lycanthropy.

The Black Dog is a popular trope in global folklore. Its most popular manifestation is probably in English folklore, with variants of the Black Dog legend in most counties in England. The Black Dog may be a direct descendant of Cerberus in Greek mythology; most stories tell of it as a pre-shadowing of death. It also makes several appearances in Irish folklore. T.J. Westropp, in his A Folklore Survey of County Clare, documents the story which directly inspired this one, that of the 'Black Dog of Cratloe'. He writes:

Many believed that they had seen the apparition, which used often to accompany the D'Esterre's coach and the mail car...I was present at its first telling, before they heard from our old servant, Mrs. Julia MacHugh, of the local belief... A large, dark, shadowy dog seemed to run upon the moonlit water, first to one side and then to the other of the carriage, and was more than once lashed at by the driver. It disappeared near where the road ascends from the low marshy 'corcasses' along the foot of the Cratloe hills. Julia MacHugh, a woman of wide local knowledge, at once 'explained' the apparition and said that the omen was good if the dog ran alongside, but bad if he leaped at the carriage or horses.

Westropp's account is one of several recorded in the south-west – another, more local one heard anecdotally is that of the Black Dog of Thomondgate, in Limerick city, where I live. All of these accounts have several features in common; the Black Dog is larger than life, with glowing eyes, and his presence is a malignant one, often a portent or a warning.

When I write, I'm particularly attracted to ambiguous images that call to mind a range of meanings. In 'The Black Dog', I wanted to pay tribute to the folkloric story, but I was also interested in the wider meaning of the black dog in contemporary culture, as a euphemism for depression. Diarist Samuel Johnson first used the term in the 1780's as a metaphor to describe his own struggles with a depressive disorder, and Winston Churchill popularised the term to describe his own encounters with the illness. This image is a striking one; the idea of a dog who follows, who won't go away. Writing about a mental disorder also introduces the idea of the unreliable narrator – to my mind, a story always works particularly well if there are several different explanations for how the narrative unfolds.

THE CILLINI

've lived in Killeen all my life, and I know well not to mess with the Other Folk. People look at you if you say it like that, out loud, but I know it, as my mother did, as my grandmother did, all right back down the family line, like dominoes on a table. We've always been careful people. The Other Sort have lived in their places, we've lived in ours, and over the years we've taken great pains to avoid them. When my grandfather built this house he consulted a local man, Johnny Byrne, who drew a map on the back of a dirty envelope to show him the fairy paths. I stood at Johnny's elbow as he laboriously pressed the pencil on the paper to dot the location of neighbouring houses.

'That should be grand, then,' he pronounced finally, nodding at my grandfather. 'And sure if you cross these paths, just say a quick 'by your leave' and they'll let you be.'

My grandfather carefully folded the old envelope and pressed money into Johnny's hand, who muttered and shrugged, but finally tucked it into his pocket. I was fascinated.

'Who is he talking about?'

'Not a thing you need to know about,' said my grandfather severely. 'Now go inside and be a good girl.'

Over the years we always kept to the old rituals. Before we got the bath put in, we'd throw the water from the tub out behind the house. That was my job, as only child. Dirty footwater would attract them, my mother said, so even though the tub was heavy, and the lukewarm, soapy water slopped and spilled over onto my shoes, I did it. We'd put out a saucer of milk for them, though I often saw the cats lurk around the corner to pounce on it once the back door was shut. We never left the door ajar, nor invited them in. We stayed away from the forts and the cillini, the patch of tiny graves, those hillocks of earth after which the village was named. On Hallowe'en, when other children went trick or treating, we stayed in. There were only a few farm houses around, strange places with large, rough dogs, spaced apart too far down rutted, unlit lanes. So I told myself, but I knew the real reason. I knew that on Hallowe'en the Other Folk escorted the souls of all who had died that year to the Gates of Paradise. I didn't want to meet them in a funeral procession, with the uncanny wind blowing, and their music, sharp and piping, hanging in the still night air.

We were careful. We kept the old ways. Everything was as it should be until Angela came home.

Angela was my best friend when we were growing up. We sat side-by-side at scarred wooden desks in school; we played complicated anthropological games with our dolls who lived in houses made from splayed encyclopaedias that smelled of dust and expensive American paper. Later on, we would sit on her bed after school and talk long and earnestly about boys, as the light pooled darker and darker on her pink bedspread. When she left for university I cried for a day, peeling vegetables for dinner that night, my face stiff and sore with salt. We said we'd stay in touch, she wrote some letters full of city life and bars and books, letters I never answered. How could I? What would I write about? 'My father is still sick, so I'm minding the house so my Mam can work. The apples are coming early. Old Mrs Hoey down the road died.' It would be as pointless as writing to her in Swahili. Sometimes I thought of her and imagined her new life. I pictured her dressed like girls in magazines, smoking a cigarette, louche, sparky.

Then one day she's back in the village. She looks nothing like I'd imagined her. She comes knocking on the door, with her hair grown long and knotted, wearing a swingy tie-dyed dress and clanking beads. When she hugs me tightly to her I can feel a rounded, hard bump between us. She is pregnant. I feel myself shrink in shock. She is brown and freckled and bold and laughing, and her name is now Angel.

'Much more suitable, don't you think?' She flicks a careless hand at the dirty rucksack she's dumped in the doorway. 'I read angel cards, and of course I'm carrying this little angel too'. I lower my eyes, annoyed at myself for being embarrassed. Over at the range, my mother gives a scandalised snort. I can see her back tighten and stiffen as she pointedly looks away from us.

'Where are you staying?' I ask hastily. She frowns, trying to remember. 'Over the road, beside the blue barn, in that lovely little cottage that's idle.

I rang ahead to the shop.' I nod. The grocery shop is also the local estate
agent. 'Oh, the old Sheehan place?'

There is a crash in the background. My mother stands, the brown
casserole dish on the ground in front of her, cracked in two.

'The Sheehan place?' She's given up pretending not to eavesdrop. In
fact, she doesn't even seem to notice her good casserole dish on the floor.
She is staring at Angela, her face creased in fear. 'Don't go there, child!
Sure no-one's ever prospered there.' My teeth tug at my bottom lip. She
looks old and crazy. Still she persists. 'People say it was built on an old
fort. No good can come of that. Sure didn't the old Sheehan fellow
disappear for years and come back with his wits wandering?'

Angela, (or Angel, as I will have to call her now) just laughs, delighted.
'Fairies!' she shouts. 'Fantastic! I can't think why I've been away so long.
This place is so authentic.' I watch her go with a wave, leaving behind a
smell of honeysuckle and patchouli.

'The bould strap,' mutters my mother. I don't answer. I feel small,
parochial, and authentically dowdy beside the laughing, golden girl
walking away from me.

—

For a while, everyone talks about Angel. She hangs feathery dream-
catchers in the trees around the cottage. Wind-chimes tinkle in her
windows. Her door is always open; she likes to sit outside on her garden
bench, calling out cheerfully to everyone who passes. Sometimes I see her
cross-legged on the seat, one of the young village girls beside her, dealing
out large, coloured cards like a croupier. I find myself walking down the
road to her more and more. She loves her new house. 'It's full of good
spirits,' she insists. 'Sometimes at night I hear laughter.'

I twist my mouth, unconvinced. 'The Other Folk only laugh when
they're planning something.' It's something my grandfather used to say.

'Oh, Grania,' she says fondly. 'You need to open your mind. You carry
round so much heaviness with you. Close your eyes and visualise
breathing in golden light.' I smile in spite of myself. Everyone likes Angel.
Except my mother, that is. My mother never mentions her by name but
her sniffing gets louder every time I come back from her house.

Sometimes I try to tidy the cottage. It is spectacularly messy; full of collapsing piles of books, heaps of Indian cheesecloth, wax puddled from old candles, incense sticks, herbs and a vast array of tea-bags. It is also outstandingly dirty. I worry about her child. Angel just sits and strokes her bump, getting bigger and more placid by the day. I bring over rubber gloves and bleach, and start cleaning as she sits idly, turning over cards in her spread. Angel cards seem to be all about telling nice fortunes, as far as I can see. She often asks to give me a reading, but I'm never tempted. I scrub and scrub, and finally feel satisfied that the kitchen and bathroom are clean. The next day I go over, and her cat has coughed up a hairball in the hallway, and shredded one of her dream-catchers. In the kitchen I find Angel asleep in the armchair, spaghetti trailing down her dress, a wineglass on its side, contents pooling slowly over the kitchen floor. I stop trying to tidy up.

⌐

It's August, a humid, itchy, damp night. I turn and turn in the bed, throwing out my limbs in stiff, angry shapes. Da has been ill and cross all day, I'm tired from bringing in glasses of water and listening to his complaints. Then I hear it. A scream. A loud, undiluted scream. *Angel*, I think, although I don't and can't know. I'm up, stumbling, running out the door and down the street. I know what has happened when I see the light spilling out of her house, a crowd gathered round. I slow down, my heart bumping hard in my chest, my hands to my mouth like an elderly lady. And it's her. She's lying on the floor tiles, her face a contused purple, crying hard. Her body suddenly starfishes out and then back into a tight, cramped ball. I see a dark red stain spread beneath her and I feel such a wave of sadness I can't speak. I crouch down and hold her hand, until the ambulance comes. I keep tight hold of it all the way to the hospital.

⌐

The Angel who comes back is a changed woman. She looks more like the old Angela. She wears the drabbest of her long, swinging dresses and ties her hair back in a tight, unforgiving pony-tail. Her face is pale, and she moves slowly, as if in pain. I sit with her, helpless, my need to help her like a hot ache inside me. She sits on her bench, dully, and people avoid her eyes. I make tea, bring over food. Once I bring her angel cards out to her, but she turns her face away. Later I find them scattered on the grass like cardboard flowers.

Then she starts walking. At first I'm relieved. Her face is brighter; her colour is almost back to normal. Then she goes away for longer and longer. She walks all evening. Once she stays away all night. I'm worried. Who can I tell? My mother still pretends Angel doesn't exist. My father is only concerned with medicine, pain, comfort; his world extends only to his few square meters of bedroom. Angel becomes stranger. She's still walking. She starts to forget things. She goes to the shop barefoot and leaves her groceries behind. She cries in her front garden. Mrs Healy from the butcher's saw her wander out of her house 'in her UNDERWEAR' she mouths silently to me across the counter. Angel has gone strange, like turned milk. Fey.

So I follow her. What other choice do I have? She walks around the village and up the hill to where the big fort is. I see the dark circle of trees close around her and feel a flicker of fear. I've never gone into the fort myself; I've always been warned away from it. Then I notice, she has stopped beside it, and is kneeling on the ground at the cillini.

At first she doesn't see me; she's humming, and pulling up weeds around the tiny mounds of earth, the small stones. I call to her lightly. 'Angel'. She turns to me and smiles, a small, bright smile. I kneel down beside her.

'What are you doing here?' My voice is soft. I put a hand on her arm. She wriggles away from my touch.

'Visiting the babies.'

I pause. She smiles again. Her eyes seem bright blue in the twilight. 'The poor babies,' she says quietly. 'I could never believe they went to Purgatory. Do you know that before Purgatory was invented, they believed that unbaptised babies went to hell. Imagine?' Her voice is still low, but it has begun to quicken. 'I think about him every day, you know. Every day. This is the only place I can come to where I feel at peace.'

There are tears in my eyes. She draws a quavering breath. 'All these babies. Buried at the fort. People wanted to forget them, you know, they wanted to hide them in a forbidden place, where no-one would find them.' She is crying loudly now, long, trembling sobs. 'But I can hear them! They tell me he's alive. He's not in Purgatory.' I hug her head to my chest. I feel her thin hands grab at my arms.

And in the distance, I hear a silvery, low laugh.

~

Of course I tell her not to go back. Of course she does. She's getting stranger. Her hair, always unkempt, is now almost green with matted leaves and pieces of grass. She doesn't sit on her bench anymore, but moves restlessly, like a hummingbird, around her small garden, waiting for evening to start her walk. I am standing outside her gate one afternoon, with a bag of milk and bread and fruit, simple things to persuade her to eat, when my mother stops by. She looks at me, and then at Angel who's moving around, distracted, pulling leaves off bushes. 'Don't.' she says softly. 'Leave her be. She's away with the fairies, God love her.' I am startled by the uncharacteristic kindness of her tone. She shakes her head briskly. 'I'll start a novena for her. But she's in a bad way.' I nod. I know.

She goes out at Hallowe'en. I try and reason with her, but she's not listening.

'You need to stay in! See a doctor! Eat something!' I plead. Her eyes are blue and uncaring, like flat stones. When I put an arm out to stop her, her hands scrabble at me, her fingers are bent and hard like bone claws. She pushes me off and leaves. I let her go, angry, and start sweeping her floor, jerking the brush in hard, irritated strokes. When I have swept all the floors, I stop. I need to go after her, I realise. She is in no fit state to wander about. I have no idea when she last ate, or slept.

It is a while before I find her. The October night is velvet-dark, the sky a smooth navy, the grass a dense black. She is back among the cillini again. I can just make out her stooping figure among the graves. She is singing an unfamiliar song, her head bobbing about. I draw an exasperated breath. It is cold, and I have forgotten my cardigan. I rub the hard gooseflesh on my arms and wait for her to finish her rituals.

Then everything happens at once. The moon gleams from behind a cloud, lighting the hill with a pearly glow. There is the sudden loud, metal clap of a bell that sounds again and again. It is the old village church bell, I realise, ringing in midnight. I stretch my arm out towards Angel, when the earth seems to move under my feet. I fall heavily and hit the ground awkwardly, one leg bent beneath me. A flash of pain sears my ankle, I try and get up and fall again. And then I see her. Angel is staggering. She is being pulled left and right. The ground swarms with tiny figures that drag her down and climb up her; there are more and more of them, they swarm over her. I see her mouth open once; then she is gone, overcome, taken.

—

I could have stopped her going, but I didn't. I needn't have followed her, but I did. I couldn't do anything, so I didn't try. Or so I tell myself, but that doesn't mean I don't dream about it, late at night, when it's dark. I see her fall beneath their dark little bodies, and hear that soft, silver laughter, just before I wake.

In Irish folklore there is a belief that the fairies were gradually driven into hiding in the fairy-forts, those islands of trees and bushes that festoon the Irish countryside. These are actually ring-forts, remnants of much earlier settlements. These forts also incorporate burial mounds –tumuli and cairns – leading to a conflation of na Sidhe with ghosts and the undead, thereby adding a further uncanny layer to the forts. Much of this site-specific folklore still survives today.

The forts have been used and reused over the centuries as places where things are left and hidden. Most significantly, in terms of 'The Cillini', they were also used as a place to bury unbaptised babies. The presence of these graves is marked by tiny humps of ground, called killeens, or in Irish, na cillini.

THE MAY DOLL

he roar and hiss of the waters breaking on the rocks reverberates in her head; ancient and relentless. Elizabeth shivers and wraps her cardigan tightly around her. It's spring, she thinks in disbelief. The open fire burning in the pub doesn't seem to cast out any heat; it just fills the narrow space with a peaty smoke that makes her eyes smart. She checks her watch, which tells her that it's just after five thirty in the evening. Already the sky is midnight-dark. Looking out the window she sees a dark wash of blackness, only broken up by a streetlight at the pier. The light glints on the white froth of the waves. It's a stormy night out there. She thinks of the small ferry, bobbing up and down on the dark sea and shivers again. Her tea sits on the table in front of her, undrunk; the rim of the mug tobacco-stained with the results of repeated, half-hearted washing in the pub sink. All around her rises the subdued chatter of voices; alien, indecipherable. They're speaking in Irish, of course. It might as well be Mandarin. She lets the unfamiliar words wash over her as she sits apart.

I'm lonely. The words rise, unbidden, from deep in her chest. She's spent all day wanting to escape the dull, cold house, and the incessant crying of the baby, but now she's here, contrarily, all she wants is to be home again. She checks her phone. Ten past six. A bubble of anger and resentment starts to rise. She forces herself to think calmly. Matthew's late. To be more accurate, the boat from the mainland is late. Despite herself she looks again at her phone; a useless, pretty toy with a screen full of redundant apps. Of course there's no signal here. There's barely any signal anywhere on na Maighdeanacha, this godforsaken island, except in the odd unexpected place. Impatient, she taps the dirty table-top, ringed with the imprint of a hundred sticky glasses.

The pub smells of old beer, peat and stained seats. Cigarette smoke plumes and twists in the gloom. Two of the old men at the bar counter are smoking reflectively in clear defiance of the ban. Sean the barman ignores them. The local police, the gardai, go home after their working day, after that the laws of the mainland lapse into old customs. Everything is different here. Everything is strange. She stops tapping her fingernails on the table, and lets her breath out in a deep *whoosh* of air. *Where is the damn boat?*

The door opens and though she knows it isn't him – not yet – she looks up. One of the old men nods at her. She smiles back, desperate and grateful, until she realises he's hailing the girl who's just come in. Embarrassed, she picks up the mug and takes a deep drink of tea. It's lukewarm and bitterly strong. Tears prick at her nose, seeping hot and sore behind her eyes. This bloody island. She plays with the beermats, nervous fingers stacking them in an erratic pile. The girl sits down at the bar, voices around her swirling in a flurry of greetings. Elizabeth looks at her, envying her the careless ease with which she unwinds her woollen scarf, exposing a laughing face and a great flood of black hair. She smiles at the barman and taps the counter twice. Unasked, he fills and slides a glass of what looks like whiskey over to her. She catches it with one hand, flings it back, and stands up. Someone claps.

The girl leans against the counter and opens her mouth, holding up one finger for silence. Elizabeth waits, curious. And then the girl starts to sing. It's like nothing she's heard before. The girl's voice is sweet, rising pure and high through the babble of conversation. It's a simple, mesmerising melody with a recurrent phrase.

Samhradh, samhradh, bainne na ngamhna,
Thugamar féin an samhradh linn.
Samhradh buí na nóinín glégeal,
Thugamar féin an samhradh linn.

Bábóg na Bealtaine, maighdean an tSamhraidh,
Suas gach cnoc is síos gach gleann,
Cailíní maiseacha bán-gheala glégeal,
Thugamar féin an samhradh linn.

It's beautiful. The lines dance through her head; looping, melodic. For the first time in hours, she feels herself relax. Outside she can hear the whoop and screech of seagulls, the sound of a lone car engine toiling up the hill, and – she tilts her head to hear it better – finally, the deep, throbbing roar of an engine drawing up.

Then the door opens again. She hears him before she sees him, his loud, barking laugh. He's with one of the oldest of the fishermen, a man called Michael; they're chatting away happily. She feels her anxious breath expel with relief.

'Liz!' He smiles at her, starting to struggle out of his zippered raincoat, heavy and slick with rain. He wrestles the sodden coat off and sits down with a sigh. His hair is flat and stuck to his forehead.

'How was your day?' she asks, but he's already turned away from her.

'Listen!' he says delightedly.

She looks at him, distracted. 'Oh, the song?'

'It's the May song. I've never heard it sung here before.' His face is aglow with the fervour of a researcher. She catches herself about to roll her eyes and stops with some effort. Matthew's an anthropologist, that's why they're here. Anything to do with old customs and traditions has him transfixed.

'It's a very old song. They used to sing it in the fields to make sure that the crops came.

'What's it called?'

'*Thugamar Féin an Samhradh Linn*.' He pronounces it effortlessly. 'It translates as 'We Bring the Summer With Us.'

'What's the song about?'

He listens intently. 'I'm paraphrasing, but it calls on the May Doll, the maiden of summer, who, with beautiful girls, brings the summer in. Most of the verses talk about where they've brought the summer from – from the hills, the woods, the hills, the glens...'

'The maiden? Isn't that the English for na Maighdeanacha?' The words sound clumsy in her mouth. Not for the first time Elizabeth wishes she spoke Irish.

Matthew nods absently. 'Yes, that's right. Now the really interesting thing about it is that the song and the customs associated with it have almost completely died out, but here's proof that on na Maighdeanacha it's never gone away. Interesting.'

She's lost him now; she can see the dreamy look in his eyes. 'Liz, I'm just going to go over...' He's moving before he finishes his sentence.

She watches him talking to the pretty, dark-haired girl, sees her face flash with interest as Matthew bends towards her, earnestly gesticulating. A small spark of hopelessness that's almost, but not quite, jealousy flares in her chest. Elizabeth stares blankly at her reflection in her cold cup of tea. *This again.* She wishes, and not for the first time that evening, that she'd brought a book to read.

—

Later that night, she asks him about it. She's just trying to make conversation, half-listening out for Rosie, asleep upstairs, but he launches enthusiastically into an explanation.

'So in Ireland, millennia ago, there evolved a custom to do with May Dolls; a custom that persisted into the twentieth century. People would weave straw dolls and parade through the fields with them. It's an old fertility ritual that goes back to the time of matriarchal gods. This is one of the very few places where the song and traditions of it persist. I think it's to do with the erosion of the island.'

'Erosion?'

'Yes, you know this island is only one of twin islands that were originally joined.'

She nods; she's seen the other island in the distance. It's uninhabited now except for grazing livestock; it looks more like a green rock in the ocean.

'Well, according to Muireann, they still carry on the May Doll practice on that island. It's like a preventative ritual, she thinks, protecting it against further erosion of the farmland.'

'Is that the girl who sang in the pub?' She strains her ears. Was that a whimper upstairs?

He waves a hand. 'Yes, she's the local teacher here. She's a real mine of information about it.' He pauses excitedly. 'She's even asked me if I wanted to come to a village meeting about it.'

'That's nice,' she says absently. Upstairs the whimper has bloomed, become a cawing sound. He's still talking as she runs upstairs.

—

Later that night, as she climbs into bed, she puts a tentative arm around his back.

'Don't,' he says. 'I have to get up early for the boat in the morning.'

'Right.' She withdraws to her own side of the bed. Lying beside him in the darkness, the distance between their bodies feels like a living, solid entity.

꙰

The next day is exactly the same as all the days before it. Matthew gets up at dawn; she lies there in the annoying wasteland between sleeping and waking for an hour or so before getting up. Rosie cries, her tiny mouth swollen as the sharp little teeth stab through her gums. She tries singing to her, rocking to her, but all through the day, the thin seagull sound continues.

She strokes Rosie's swollen face and tries to feel sympathy for her congested crying. Elizabeth closes her eyes and remembers the birth; Rosie's tiny body a small yowling miracle in her arms. She recalls the time they brought her home; their reverent silence as they stood around her cot, watching her sleep, tiny fists pushed against her face. She stares at the stained wall of the kitchen and feels the tears prickle the back of her eyelids.

That evening Elizabeth cooks dinner without enthusiasm. As she paddles the wooden spoon about in the stir-fried vegetables she feels a wave of simple hopelessness.

I don't know how much longer I can do this.

Her only break comes when she's cooked, when the teenage Saidhb next door comes in, as she always does, and silently sits with Rosie, letting Elizabeth go and meet Matthew.

꙰

She sits in the pub again, waiting for the boat. It never keeps to the scheduled times. Its arrival depends on a maze of factors; the size and velocity of the waves, the under tug of the current. She sips at her blackcurrant and water; luckily this time she's remembered not to order the stewed tea. The dark bar is smoky and quiet, just a few men there with heads bent in conversation at the bar.

Meeting Matthew off the boat felt like a romantic thing to do at first. It felt like she was marking his return each evening, celebrating it. Now it feels like another chore. The only thing she likes about it is the freedom from Rosie's querulous crying. She feels guilty even thinking this – she loves Rosie, of course she does – but it's harder than she ever thought it would be, living on this strange island. She's never felt more English, more alien. She sees it in the face of the locals, their bafflement at her crisp vowels and their sidelong, quiet looks at her as she wheels the pram over jagged footpaths.

'Liz!' Matthew looks surprised to see her. She gets to her feet awkwardly, picking up her coat.

'How was your trip back?' she asks, but he's already talking over her.

'I told you, I'm going to the village meeting tonight. They're planning the May Doll procession.' Elizabeth feels a flush of disappointment; the thought of walking back to the lonely house makes her feel like crying. She looks down, unwilling to show him how much he's hurt her, and when she looks up again, dark-haired Muireann is by his side, smiling at her.

'We're so happy he's joined us to help us plan the day on the island,' she says softly. 'He knows so much about the old rituals.' She cocks her head and looks at him like Elizabeth has seen his postgraduate students do; with a mix of confidence and admiration. Muireann says something to him in Irish, he laughs and replies. And like that, they're united. Them against her. Elizabeth looks at Muireann's hair, black as ink, her shining smile, and feels herself shrivel and dwindle in comparison. She doesn't say anything, just puts on her coat and leaves. When she pauses at the door, Matthew is standing at the bar, relaxed, an arm on the counter.

~

The next night she doesn't bother to go and meet him. He doesn't say anything, just comes home an hour later. When he goes up to bed she presses her face against his waxed jacket, hanging in the hall. It smells of smoke and salt.

~

Each night that week it's the same. Matthew's out till late, only returning to reheat his dinner and eat it before disappearing upstairs. For the first few nights he tries to talk to her about the procession, about the way the locals organise it, about the dolls they make. He even brings one home, a crude thing, made of twisted hay. It has primitive slashes for its mouth and eyes; from it rises the odour of rain-spoiled stalks. She refuses to look at it, doesn't listen to him, taking a spiteful pleasure in interrupting him with news about Rosie, her teething, her feeds.

They gradually stop talking. She withdraws further and further into herself. She can almost feel her hurt and sadness like a blanket around her.

Every day it rains. And every night he's gone.

Some days she doesn't even bother to get up until Rosie's crying gets too loud to bear. She just lies there and thinks.

With every day that passes you feel the distance between you grow. It's like the slow withering of the trees in autumn; a drifting, gradual thing. It's the intimacy of speech that goes first. It becomes purely functional; a series of questions, absent answers, silences. Then the touching recedes. The instinctive, sleepy embraces. The handholding. The little hugs. The intimacy of brushing crumbs from each other. Then it's the desire to be around each other that fades. Every gesture, every breath just irritates. You don't want to be in the same room.

Elizabeth cries and cries until her body is exhausted with the wracking sobs. But still the waves keep coming, over and over again, dreary washes of tears that leave her face salty and stiff like half-cooked meat.

One night she's sitting upstairs, by the cot, trying to soothe the fractious baby. She feels a surge of anger at the incessant noise.

'Shut up!' she shouts. There's a silence as shocking at the screams, then Rosie opens her tiny pink maw to cry again. Elizabeth puts her hands over her face. *What am I doing? This is down to Matthew. Not me.*

'It's not your fault,' she says, lips pressed tight against Rosie's silky, padded skin. 'It's not your fault.'

You try and remember exactly what being in love feels like, but all you can conjure is a set of snapshots, of two-dimensional kisses and laughing faces in holiday settings, each one more fake and absurd than the last.

Then suddenly you wake up and it's winter. It's cold and lonely and the baby won't stop wailing, and you leak hot tears into the pillow and wish for it all to stop. Just stop. Be over.

And still Rosie cries on, steadily. The noise is needle-sharp.

~

That night Elizabeth goes to the pub to wait for him. She's had enough. She needs to let him know. The pub is fuller than usual. The smoke makes her eyes water. From her seat near the door she sees Muireann come in, her hair for once bound up in a neat bun on her head. She looks less striking that way. Elizabeth is meanly happy, until she sees how many people start to gather around her, listening to her talk. *Bitch*, she thinks, dislike rising in her throat like reflux. Matthew's late. She looks out the window at the setting sun, the play of orange on water. And she waits. She waits and waits, sifting restlessly on her hard wooden seat, her fingers shredding beer mats.

'Hey,' he says when he comes in. She can tell he's startled to see her. Almost unbidden, his eyes slide across to where Muireann stands at the bar. 'I have another meeting tonight. Didn't I tell you?'

She draws a deep breath. 'You've had meetings every night.'

He dips his head, not meeting her eyes. 'I know,' he says quietly. 'But they really need me.'

'We really need you. Me and Rosie. You never spend time with us anymore,' she says. Although she's practiced this at home, mouthing the sentences in front of the old, stippled mirror in the hallway, she feels the words waver in her mouth. *Don't cry*, she thinks fiercely. He looks at her then, properly, for the first time in weeks.

'I'm sorry,' he says. 'But I have to stay.'

At the bar, Muireann has begun to sing. Her voice rises, soft and sweet and strong above the babble of voices.

Thugamar féin an samhradh linn

She closes the pub door with a vicious thud, cutting off the song.

~

Like a metronome, she gets up every day, wheels Rosie out for a walk, goes home, cooks dinner. In between she stares out the window, over the ever-changing grey ocean, and the green jutting lump of the other island moored in it. And so February passes into April, and the days continue to tick by, each one more endless and dreary than the last.

It's only six o'clock, but she hears the front door opening. Matthew stands in the doorway, flushed and smiling.

'Liz. Get your glad rags on. We're going for dinner in the restaurant in the village.' She looks at him, her mouth opening in surprise.

'We can't. What about Rosie?' For a second he pauses, and then he opens the door to reveal a smiling Muireann. 'Look who's offered to babysit. There's no problem now.'

'Oh.' It's all Elizabeth can say. She looks at Matthew, at his stupid, beaming face, his pride at fixing the situation, and she suddenly wants to hit him. Hard. But what's the alternative? She stays at home and he and Muireann go out? She can just picture the girl sitting opposite him at the restaurant table, the soft lamplight shining on her tar-black hair.

'Alright then,' she says shortly. 'I'll just need to get ready. Can you show her where Rosie's things are?'

To her surprise, she enjoys the night. It's been so long since Matthew even spoke more than a few sentences to her. And tonight he's almost back to his old self. Of course he still wants to talk about the May Doll procession, but he's actually talking *to* her instead of *at* her. She smells the warm, herby scent of the lasagne on her plate and closes her eyes briefly in pleasure.

'It's going to be great tomorrow,' he says. His face is alive with enthusiasm. 'it's been such fun working on this. I've given a few lectures to the committee about the old fertility cults in Ireland and elsewhere. I've told them about the traditions around them, and they're all so interested in what I have to say.' *Unlike me*, thinks Elizabeth, and for the first time in a long time she feels a tingle of guilt at the thought.

'Tell me more,' she coaxes. He smiles across the table at her, a wide, happy smile. 'Well, like a lot of rituals, this one of the procession goes back much further than its present incarnation.' He's in full lecturer mode now, she notes, but with amusement.

She sits and sips on her rich red wine, enjoying the lasagne, enjoying eating something she hasn't cooked herself, enjoying – and it feels to strange to think this – talking to her husband. Dimly she can hear Matthew talking about animal and human sacrifice, and the mimicking of these in the form of dolls, but she's not really listening. Instead she's realising what this is. After all her worrying, this May Doll stuff is nothing more than his other obsessions. The time he spent two weeks in Wexford researching the Strawboys. Or the time he got so embedded in the Aran Islands he forgot completely about their wedding anniversary party back home. It's just him. Matthew. It's what he does. A weird, dizzy relief engulfs her. She smiles. She can afford to.

He's talking about erosion again. 'That's a big deal here, isn't it?' she asks cautiously. 'I've heard you mention it before.'

'Yes,' he says, and she can tell he's delighted she remembers. 'The land out there is battered by the ocean swells, so every year it recedes a little more. That's why the ritual survives here and is considered so important. It's no longer about crops, it's about protecting their farmland. It's huge to them.' He points at the window, where the mass of the island is silhouetted against the darkening sky. 'They need it to ensure their livelihood. And that's why folklore survives here. Because it's relevant.'

On the way home, she stumbles and he takes her hand in his big warm one. It feels good.

In the doorway of their house he kisses her, soft and fierce all at once. She clings to him, triumphant, as Muireann appears.

Matthew disentangles himself from her arms.

'Thanks,' he says heartily. 'I hope she was no bother to you.'

'No,' says Muireann. She smiles, catlike, showing a row of small white teeth. 'She's perfect,' she says. 'Absolutely perfect.'

—

The next morning she feels Matthew stir beside her.

'Shhh,' he says, as he kisses the back of her neck. 'Sleep on. You deserve it.' She pulls the duvet tighter around herself and smiles deep into it.

'Thanks,' she says drowsily. 'I'm off now, he says quietly. 'There's boats going over all day for the procession, but I want to be there early.'

'Mmmhmmm,' she says, but she's already halfway back to sleep.

—

When Elizabeth wakes again, the room is flooded with sunlight. She lies perfectly still for a moment, savouring it, feeling the deep happiness of their reconciliation. Maybe we'll plan a trip she thinks. *Just me and him and Rosie* – Rosie? Suddenly she's wide awake. There's no crying. That's good, she thinks, that last tooth must have come through. Then, she doesn't know why, but the silence feels wrong; too long, too heavy.

'Rosie?' She pads across the room and into the corridor. 'Rosie?'

The cot is empty.

She stands beside it, her mind a perfect blank. *Matthew must have taken her, her bottle is gone too,* she thinks. She presses a hand over her thumping heart, trying to calm herself. *I was asleep,* she reasons. *I didn't hear him say it.* She checks her phone. No signal. But panic still floods her in great, seeping waves. She pulls on clothes hastily, jeans, a jumper. No time to find socks, she just pulls on her old Converse, lacing them up with shaking hands.

The boats. She needs to get to the harbour now. And she's out the door and running fast, as fast as she can, all the way down the street, down past the pub to the wharf.

'Can you take me over to the island?' she shouts at one of the fishermen. He's wearing an orange fluorescent bib and he's handing an old lady onto his boat. She glances at her phone again. Still no signal.

He looks at her. 'I'm going over there, alright.'

Elizabeth can't wait for the old lady to finish boarding. She runs through the water. It's shockingly, bone-chillingly cold and it soaks her jeans to the knee. She scrambles onto the boat.

'Are you going now?'

'In a minute,' he says in his slow, unhurried way. He takes out his pipe and starts to pack it with tobacco.

'Please!' she says wildly. 'My husband is over there, and I think he has our daughter, but I need to be sure.' She's almost crying now, she can feel her face reddening. 'Please!'

The three old women on the boat look at her narrowly, their faces pursed and judgemental. She doesn't care. Instead she stares at the fisherman who sighs and puts his pipe back 'We'll go so,' he says, bending to the oars.

It seems to take forever to cross the narrow strait of water. In the distance she can see tiny specks of movement on the green slopes of the island, people walking about. She jigs one leg over another, oblivious to the sodden denim chafing her. *Please may he have Rosie safe and sound. I'll never fight with him again. I'll be good.* She bites her lips and makes impossible promises. Around her it's a perfect day. The waves lap around the boat, the sea reflects a clear blue sky. One of the women is saying what sounds like a prayer in Irish. The other two are talking among themselves in low voices.

Please may he have Rosie, safe and sound. It runs through her head like a mantra, a talisman.

When the boat pulls closer to shore the colourful dots start to grow larger. She sees most of the people there are wearing white.

'I'll jump out here,' she says hastily. Elizabeth isn't sure if she's meant to pay him, so she digs in her pocket and hands him a damp tenner which he looks at and then pockets with a shrug. She jumps into the glassy water, and her jeans, half-dried in the salt air, are promptly soaked again. She doesn't even notice.

'Matthew!' she calls, running over the hard shale. 'Where are you?' She pushes past the people disembarking from boats, a flurry of angry mutters in her wake. She scans the fields with a hard-beating heart. *Where are they?*

Then she hears it, a pure, high voice carried clear and bright on the sea breeze.

Bábóg na Bealtaine, maighdean an tSamhraidh,
Suas gach cnoc is síos gach gleann,
Cailíní maiseacha bán-gheala glégeal,
Thugamar féin an samhradh linn.

On the ridge of the hill she can see a line of people wearing white.

That's where Matthew must be. She runs, stumbling in her waterlogged jeans, her Converse squelching under her.

'Matthew!'

A grey goat springs up in alarm, uttering a sharp *Meeeh*! She reaches the crest of the hill and stands there panting. The song carries on, melodious and strange.

Samhradh, samhradh
Samhradh, samhradh
Is cé bhainfeadh dínn é?

It's a group of girls that stands on the hill, slowly descending in single file. They're carrying dolls, she realises, those strange misshapen dolls woven out of straw. She sees familiar faces in the crowd watching them; Sean from the pub, old Michael the fisherman, the silent Saidbh. The procession turns and she sees it's led by Muireann, her long black hair waving in the wind, face tilted upwards as she sings. Elizabeth's breath is hard and tight in her chest. *Where is he?* And then she sees him, his old oilskin jacket as he stands with his back to her.

'Oh Rosie,' she sobs, liquid with relief. At the sound of her voice Matthew turns to her, startled. His arms are empty.

The earth tilts on its axis.

'Rosie,' she says faintly. Her knees give way and she sinks to the ground. The sun shines down, flat and implacable. The grass around her is a deep vivid green. Everything is beautiful and nothing makes sense.

'What about her? Is something wrong?' His face is foolish with confusion.

'She's not at home,' she sobs, great heaving sobs. 'She's not in her cot. She's *gone*. Oh Matthew!' Her voice is wild. She grabs at his arm and heaves herself up. He tries to hold her, but she wrestles free.

They stare at each other, terrified. The singing is getting closer. A fly buzzes past Elizabeth's ear and for one strange moment she thinks, stupidly, *it's awfully early for insects*.

'Rosie!' she shouts. She sees the villagers staring back at her, their faces uncurious. The song stops abruptly, mid-gracenote, and is swallowed up into the silence of the sunny, perfect day.

Muireann walks forward in the sudden silence. As the procession surrounds them, Elizabeth sees it. In Muireann's arms is a parcel of white cloth. Her face is a pale blank.

The last year falls away, sharply as a split apple. She smells the antiseptic tang of the labour ward, she hears Rosie's kitten-mewls for the first time. Under her hands she can feel the soft floss of her duckling-fuzz head, the tiny, incredible weight of her against the crook of her arm.

There's a fresh, rusty stain on the white linen parcel. Elizabeth's breathing hitches and falters. Blood booms in her ears. Her fingers tremble. She reaches out and gently, oh so gently, touches the bundle.

For one infinite moment, as the sun shines and the insects hum, nothing has happened and happy endings are still possible.

This story is based on an ancient Irish tradition, which my grandmother told me of, the custom of carrying a straw doll around the fields on the first of May to ensure fertility for the crops. It's linked with the old Irish festival Bealtaine, one of the four great Irish festivals that mark the different phases of the year. This tale plays upon this tradition to conjure up the idea that there may be older, darker roots of the custom.

Tracy Fahey is an Irish writer of Gothic fiction. Her debut collection, *The Unheimlich Manoeuvre* (2016), was nominated in 2017 for a British Fantasy Award for Best Collection. Her short fiction has been published in more than twenty Irish, US and UK anthologies and her work has been reviewed in the *Times Literary Supplement*. In 2016 two of her short stories, 'Walking the Borderlines' and 'Under the Whitethorn' were long listed by Ellen Datlow for *The Best Horror of the Year Volume 8*. She has also written a folk horror YA novel, *The Girl In The Fort* (2017). *New Music For Old Rituals* is her second collection.

More information is available on her website: tracyfahey.com

Lightning Source UK Ltd.
Milton Keynes UK
UKHW012007261021
392884UK00001B/14